He could wake h..y unkind. Or he could easily pick her up and carry her to the guest room. Although his arms fairly itched for the opportunity to hold her, chances were good she'd wake. Best to let her sleep where she lay. No chance of waking her, with the added benefit that he could sit and watch her as long as he wanted to.

And he found that he wanted to.

Very gently he lifted her legs to the sofa. He reached for the woolen plaid folded over the back of his chair, and draped it over her sleeping form, tucking it around her shoulders. It outlined rather than hid her soft curves.

She moaned and snuggled into it.

He studied the woman on the sofa. Soft golden curls, too short to do more than barely brush her shoulders, framed a delicate face. Smile lines around her eyes hinted of a woman who looked for the good in life and also of a maturity.

Certainly she was attractive to him. From that first astonishing glimpse of her soul, to her unexpected behavior, right down to the way she looked lying on his sofa, covered with his own plaid, he was drawn to her.

His instincts, however, screamed that there was much more to this woman than met the eye.

ALSO BY MELISSA MAYHUE

Thirty Nights with a Highland Husband

Available from Pocket Books

Highland
Guardian

MELISSA MAYHUE

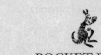

POCKET BOOKS
New York   London   Toronto   Sydney

Pocket Books
A Division of Simon & Schuster, Inc.
1230 Avenue of the Americas
New York, NY 10020

This book is a work of fiction. Names, characters, places, and incidents either are products of the author's imagination or are used fictitiously. Any resemblance to actual events or locales or persons, living or dead, is entirely coincidental.

Copyright © 2007 by Melissa Mayhue

First Pocket Books paperback edition November 2007

POCKET and colophon are registered trademarks of Simon & Schuster, Inc.

For information about special discounts for bulk purchases, please contact Simon & Schuster Special Sales at 1-800-456-6798 or business@simonandschuster.com.

Design by Min Choi
Front and back cover art by Jaime DeJesus
Interior design by Davina Mock-Maniscalco

Manufactured in the United States of America

10 9 8 7 6 5

ISBN-13: 978-1-4165-3287-3
ISBN-10:   1-4165-3287-0

Acknowledgments

There are always people who have a huge impact on my writing, helping to make a particular book come together. I send my thanks out to each and every one of them.

Always first, my thanks to my wonderful family, whose love and support make my writing possible. Frank, Marty, Bee, Chris, Nick, Chandra and Megan—I love you all!

Thank you to my wonderful critique partners, the Soapbox Divas, for all their help. Irene, Kirsten and Viola—you're the best!

Thank you to Marc Richard for technical advice and information on hand-to-hand fighting.

My thanks to all the wonderful members of Colorado Romance Writers for their support, friendship and encouragement. You've all become such a special part of my life.

Finally, a huge thank you to my fantastic editor, Megan McKeever, for her patience and all her hard work. I feel so fortunate to be working with her!

Highland
Guardian

Prologue

⁓

"The threat is over." Dallyn bowed to the assembled Fae dignitaries, long blond hair sweeping across his shoulders at the movement.

"Not over," Darnee corrected, her green eyes flashing in his direction. "Only suspended for the moment. The threat will never be over as long as a single Nuadian lives."

Dallyn acknowledged her point with a slight nod. "Granted, but we have disabled most of the Portals. A guard has been set round the Fountain of Souls."

"We must do more. The souls on the Mortal Plain are still at risk. The Nuadians can gain limited amounts of the energy they seek by releasing souls from the Mortals' bodies. Without access to the Fountain, that will be their next logical target."

"The Fae can no longer fight on the Mortal Plain. You know that." Dallyn scowled.

"True. But they can gain control of weak Mortals,

ones who will gladly carry out the destruction they desire. We must guard against that eventuality."

"What would you suggest, my child?" The woman seated at the center of the great table spoke up.

"Guardians, Earth Mother, placed at each of the remaining Portals." Darnee turned to the woman who had asked the question. "Guardians drawn from the Mortal Plain itself."

"How can Mortals possibly defend against Fae? Our kind can only be seen by Mortals when we choose." Dallyn faced her directly now.

"Not ordinary Mortals. Mortals who share Fae blood." She arched an eyebrow, scanning the assemblage. "Many of our kind have half-Mortal offspring."

A low murmur spread through the room.

"This is true, Daughter." The Earth Mother frowned. "Our people have not always demonstrated proper restraint in their dealings with the Mortal race. Many of these offspring exist and the numbers will continue to grow through the generations. Even a small amount of Fae blood would allow them to see us. But most are unacknowledged. How would you find them?"

"I will seek them out."

"I agree that they would suit well, Darnee." Dallyn shrugged. "But Mortals have such short life spans. They would barely learn their task before their time would be at an end."

"That's another advantage of their Fae blood. They'll already be longer lived. And we can easily enhance that by exposing them to the Fountain of Souls. The energy will add many centuries to their time."

Dallyn rubbed his chin thoughtfully. "I see the

merit of this plan. It could work. And many of them may carry gifts bestowed by their bloodline."

"Exactly." Darnee nodded in agreement. "Second sight, extra strength, other perceptions unusual in the Mortal Plain. All of these things will make them easier to identify and more capable of the task."

"I can see you've given this proposition a great deal of thought." The Earth Mother looked around the assembled group. "We cannot allow the Nuadians to disrupt the timelines of the souls on the Mortal Plain. We know firsthand the chaos that brings. Forcing too many of them from their chosen bodies before they are destined to leave could ultimately damage the very flow of time itself." She rose from her seat, lifting her hands to signal an end to the discontented murmur that swept the hall. "My decision is made. You two, Darnee and Dallyn, will share responsibility for choosing and training these Guardians. You will share oversight for their performance. Any questions? No? Then you will begin at once. There is no time to spare."

"Thank you, Earth Mother." The two bowed and hastily left the grand room, quietly discussing how to carry out their assignment.

One

⁓

"Bloody hell."

Ian McCullough glared at the telephone receiver he had slammed into place. Nothing was going as planned this week. He needed to be in London, following up on the latest threat. Instead here he was at Thistle Down Manor, waiting to play innkeeper to some stressed-out American while Henry lay in a hospital bed recovering from knee-replacement surgery.

How many times had he tried to discourage Henry from renting out the cottage? He'd lost count decades ago.

"This one needs to be here, Ian," Henry had told him on the way to the hospital. "I know it displeases you when I let the cottage, but rarely does it have any impact on you or yer responsibilities."

"Well it does this time. Honestly, it isna like you need the income. I've seen to that many times over. These guests of yers always need watching. You know the primary responsibility is to protect the Portal."

Henry had given him a sheepish grin. "I know, I know. But I have my own gifts, and I canna ignore them. I could feel it when I spoke to this woman. I believe her soul has been wounded. The peace of Heather Cottage, and the nearness of the Portal, will do much to help her." He'd grimaced in pain as he shifted in his seat. "If no for this damn knee, I would no have troubled you with this." He'd smiled then, his wrinkled face reflecting his inner calm. "Dinna worry. I'll be up and around in a few days. Peter and Martha will be there to help keep an eye on her as well, and you can get back to the things you need to be about."

Ian continued to glare at the telephone, his dark eyes narrowing, as if that inanimate object held full responsibility for his latest problem. Peter and Martha. They were the only hired help at Thistle Down Manor, although they were more like family than employees. Peter had taken over the position of caretaker after his father retired. When he married Martha, she came to work there as well, as housekeeper and cook. They really did shoulder most of the day-to-day care of the grounds and house. And now they wouldn't be returning until early tomorrow morning.

Their daughter had gone into labor early this morning. Her husband's call had come out of the blue, so there had been no time to prepare the cottage for their guest's arrival before they left. Now, thanks to the weather, they were staying at the hospital overnight.

Just one more thing to complicate his life.

The intensity of the storm raging outside only

added to Ian's irritation. The downpour that had begun hours ago would probably flood the valley below. That would most likely mean power failures again. From what little news he'd heard, the storm front was huge, extending north well beyond Glasgow.

Surely the American wouldn't try to navigate the narrow backroads in weather like this.

"Perhaps this storm is good news, after all," he mumbled to himself as he rummaged through the hall closet searching for the emergency supply of candles. He glanced at the clock. She was an hour past due. Chances were she had stayed in one of the larger cities once she'd run into the storm.

"Thank the Fates for that, at least." The very last thing he wanted was to deal with the vacationing American on his own. Now it appeared he wouldn't have to.

Ian smiled to himself, and, feeling somewhat relieved, he carried the candles back into the library. After building a large fire in the fireplace, he settled back into his favorite chair to read, relaxing for the first time all day.

"Good Lord!"

Sarah Douglas slammed on her brakes to avoid the cows in front of her car. It wasn't the first time in the last three hours she'd almost collided with livestock. She had known driving would be a challenge here. After the first hour or so, even traveling on the wrong side hadn't been so bad. But since leaving the A76, she'd also had to contend with wandering animals and roads that were narrower than her driveway back home. By the time she added in the rain coming down in buckets for the last few hours, her nerves were almost completely frazzled.

Driving conditions alone would have been bad enough, but that was on top of twelve hours spent either on planes or in airports waiting for planes, not to mention the most horrible flight ever from Toronto to Glasgow. The woman seated next to her was traveling with two small children, one or the other of which was crying from the moment of takeoff until they'd landed. Sarah had literally been without sleep for more than twenty hours.

She should have stopped at one of the hotels she'd passed near the airport. Or even the one she'd noticed as she'd turned off the main highway, if you could call it that, at Dumfries. But she hadn't.

"Get a grip," she muttered, and then chuckled in spite of her circumstances.

Oh, she had a grip. On the steering wheel. So tight, in fact, that her fingers were starting to cramp.

Taking a deep breath, she consciously relaxed her hands and slowly accelerated as the last of the cows cleared a path in front of her.

It shouldn't be much farther now. Panic returned briefly as she again considered that she might be lost, but, taking another deep breath, she regained control.

The directions that nice Henry McCullough had emailed her were very thorough and she'd been careful. Well, except for starting off in the wrong direction when she'd left the airport. Once she'd gotten that figured out and headed back the right way, she'd been very careful. That little scenic detour had only increased her driving time by an hour or two.

It was simply exhaustion wreaking havoc with her

emotions now. Exhaustion and the storm. And the dark. It was intensely dark. Between the late hour and the weather, she could only see those areas lit up by her headlights or brief flashes of lightning.

As if on cue, lightning sliced through the sky, striking directly ahead of Sarah's car. Illuminated in its flash was the figure of a man, staring straight at her, his face a mask of surprise. Once again she slammed on her brakes, but this time she accompanied the action with a scream, as her car began to slide slowly toward the man. He stood as if frozen for only a moment more before leaping—actually leaping—over her vehicle.

The automobile came to a gentle stop, nestled against a high rock wall. Breathing hard, Sarah peeled her fingers from the steering wheel and looked around. There was no man anywhere to be seen.

Closing her eyes, she let her head drop back to the headrest, the sound of her pounding heart filling her ears. He must have been a figment of her imagination. Real flesh-and-blood men did not leap over moving vehicles and then completely disappear.

Slowly she opened her eyes. Through the rivulets of rain running down her window, she read the plaque on the wall next to her. Thistle Down Manor. At least she wasn't lost.

The car, firmly stuck in the mud, refused to move either forward or back. Sarah turned off the ignition. The absence of noise from the engine only magnified the sound of rain beating on the metal above her head. Now what?

Choices and decisions. She could sit here all night, waiting to be rescued, or she could get out and walk.

How ironic. Wasn't that really what this whole trip was about, choices and decisions? After all those years of having no choices, of following others' decisions as was required of her, she'd finally chosen to change her life, to take charge. She'd decided for the first time in her life to embrace, rather than ignore, the intuitive feelings that had plagued her from childhood. It was one of those feelings, a driving need to do something before it was too late, that had landed her in this very spot.

Now it was time for her to act. Certainly not the most convenient time to realize that action doesn't come easily to a natural-born coward.

Peering through the gates, Sarah could faintly make out the looming form of an enormous old mansion, across a bridge and down a long drive. The little cottage she'd rented would be somewhere nearby on the estate, though she couldn't see any sign of it from where she sat.

The distance would make for a pleasant walk on any normal day. It didn't, however, look very pleasant right now. Of course, it wasn't a normal day. It was late at night in the middle of a storm. Not to mention the man she thought she'd seen earlier.

Taking one last look at the rain pouring outside the car, Sarah sighed and reached back for her shoulder bag and purse. Her choice made, she opened the door.

The rain's icy chill hit her as she emerged from the car. She'd left the headlights on to illuminate the path. The battery would be dead by morning, but that was the least of her worries right now. If that figment of her imagination showed up again, she wanted to see him coming since she doubted she would hear him over the noise of the storm.

She scanned the trees and shivered. The back of her neck prickled, as if eyes watched from those woods. The feeling grew in intensity and she started to run.

The bridge was much longer than it had looked, and not until she'd crossed over it did the panicky fear of being followed leave her. She stopped, leaning over to catch her breath. Glancing back, she saw nothing through the rain except the wavering glow of her headlights.

If this whole thing weren't so frightening, it would be funny.

Shifting the heavy bag on her shoulder, she turned toward the house and started walking up the long drive. She hoped Henry McCullough was still awake.

Ian awoke with a start. He'd been dreaming. Dreams were rare for him and, to his way of thinking, that was a good thing. He learned long ago—very, very long ago—that when he dreamed, it always meant something. The "something" was always a very accurate warning of the future and, more often than not, it warned of something bad.

He tried to recall the dream now. He'd been in the forest and there had been a woman, although he hadn't been able to see her clearly, and some type of danger. And that blasted pounding.

Pounding, he suddenly realized, that continued even now that he was awake. He stood up, feeling disoriented. The book he'd been reading fell unheeded to the floor.

Where was that noise coming from?

Moving into the hallway, he followed the sound, his senses coming fully alert.

"Hello? Mr. McCullough? Is anyone there?" Muffled words reached him, followed by more pounding.

A woman's voice.

Damn. The American had come, after all.

What was wrong with the woman? Didn't she realize how dangerous driving in one of these storms could be? Didn't she have any sense at all?

He strode to the door and threw it open, fully intending to give his visitor the tongue-lashing she deserved for her reckless behavior.

"Do you bloody well realize what time it is?" He'd begun to yell when the sight of her on his doorstep struck him speechless.

Standing there in the pouring rain, with her hair plastered to her face, she was completely drenched and shivering hard enough the movement was visible to him even in the dark.

At the sound of his voice, she drew back sharply, losing her footing in the puddle that had formed on the stoop. Only his grabbing her elbows prevented her taking a nasty spill down the steps.

"Sorry. I'm sorry." Her teeth chattered so violently he could barely understand her mumbled apology. "I . . . I didn't think about the time. The drive took so much longer than I'd planned."

She feebly tried to pull her arms from his grasp.

Rather than letting go, he tightened his grip, drawing her inside the entrance hall, where she stood, dripping, her eyes cast down as if studying the intricate patterns on the marble floor. She made no move to stop him when he slipped the strap of the heavy bag from her shoulder, and dropped it at her feet.

She glanced up then, almost furtively, and their eyes met.

Green, like the deep forest. Her eyes were an intense green that sucked him in, captured him, prevented him from looking away. They widened an instant before darting back down to resume their examination of the floor.

The contact broken, Ian gave himself a mental shake.

How unusual.

"Stay right here. I'll get something to dry you off and soon we'll have you all warmed up."

He raced upstairs and grabbed an armful of towels, stopping only to pull a blanket off the foot of his bed before returning to his guest.

She stood as he'd left her, huddled into herself, shivering as a small puddle formed at her feet.

Wrapping the blanket around her shoulders, he guided her toward the library. She'd be much better there. Thanks to the fire he'd built earlier in the evening, it was the warmest room in the place.

"Here are some towels. I'll pop into the kitchen and find something warm for you to drink. Is tea all right, or do you prefer coffee?" She was an American, after all.

"Tea would be wonderful, thank you." Only a whisper.

She took the towels and began to dry her face and hair as he left the room.

While he waited for the water to boil, he let his thoughts drift to the woman drying off in his library.

She intrigued him. A great deal. Which was most unusual in and of itself.

The old saying about eyes being windows to the soul hadn't become an old saying without very good reason. It was absolutely true. Catching a glimpse of what lived behind those windows, however, was extraordinary. Souls valued their privacy.

Looking into this woman's eyes, he'd felt an unusually strong energy pulling at him. Her windows had been wide open, her soul leaning out, demanding his attention like the French harlots he'd seen so many years ago, hanging out of the Barbary Coast bordellos.

He couldn't recall having run across anything like it in all his years. She was something entirely new.

A thrill of anticipation ran through his body. "Something entirely new" was a rare experience for Ian. After six centuries spent shuffling between the Mortal Plain and the Realm of Faerie, he often thought he'd seen it all.

During that time, he'd also learned countless valuable lessons. One of those lessons was that the rare experiences were usually the best. Certainly the most important.

Yes, he was quite intrigued by Miss . . .

"Damn."

What was her name? He couldn't remember. He couldn't even remember if Henry had ever told him her name. He'd spent so much time thinking of her as "The American," her name had been of no importance.

That was certainly changed now. Playing innkeeper to his little American tourist had unexpectedly become a much more stimulating prospect.

* * *

Bending over in front of the fire, Sarah vigorously scrubbed at her hair with the towel. She'd read all about Scotland's unpredictable climate in the bagful of travel guides she'd bought, but nothing had prepared her for the reality of it. In spite of the fire, the blanket, and the towels, she was still cold and soggy.

And enormously embarrassed.

One look at her host and she might as well have been a teenager again, completely tongue-tied and unsure of herself. That first glance had fairly taken her breath away, leaving her stammering and unable to make eye contact with anything but her own feet. It wasn't the sort of behavior she expected from a mature woman. Particularly not when she was the mature woman in question.

Handsome men had always had that effect on her, and this one was certainly a prime example. The classic line "tall, dark and handsome" could have been written especially for him. He towered over her by a good six inches. His eyes, a brown so dark they might actually be black, matched his hair. Hair a bit too long, curling around his neck, just onto the cream-colored turtleneck sweater he wore. The sweater clearly outlined a chest that belonged on a pinup calendar. He could be Mr. January, perfect start to a new year. A man like that might even get more than one month.

He was one outstanding specimen, all right. And he was also a good ten years younger than she, at the very least, which made her reaction to him all the more ridiculous. What was wrong with her, anyway?

"Serious jet lag," she muttered, scrubbing harder at her hair.

"Pardon?"

Sarah jerked upright, dropping the towel to her neck. Her host stood in the doorway holding two steaming cups.

Oh great. He'd caught her talking to herself, a bad habit that had caused her problems more than once. Heat crawled up her neck and over her face.

"I didn't realize you were back already."

His only response as he moved into the room was a smile. And what a smile. It played slowly around his lips, growing, spreading to his eyes, where it shimmered like polished jet.

The heat on her face ratcheted up a notch.

"I've taken the liberty of adding a touch of honey to yer tea." He set the cups on a low table. "Please, sit yerself down."

Sarah started forward, but stopped, looking down at herself.

"Oh, no. I'd hate to sit on your sofa in these wet clothes. Maybe it would be best if you just direct me to the cottage where I'll be staying."

His smile altered, a look of chagrin passing over his features.

"Well, that needs some explaining, you see." He picked the folded towels up from the floor and spread them on the sofa. "Here. Sit." He held up his hand to stop her when she started to protest. "Sit. Have yer tea and then we'll get you into some dry things."

After carefully arranging herself on the towels, Sarah extended her hand to accept the cup he offered her, acutely aware of his penetrating gaze. Trying desperately to think of something to say to fill the silence, she was horrified to hear herself blurt out the first thing that came to mind.

"You're not at all what I'd pictured." If she got any redder, surely flames would erupt from the top of her head.

"Not what you'd pictured? What were you expecting?" He was smiling again.

"Well, Mr. McCullough, you sounded much older when we spoke on the telephone."

"Ah, well, that explains it then. I'm no Mr. McCullough."

"What?" Had that squeak actually come from her?

He placed a restraining hand on her arm as she started to rise.

"Let me rephrase that. I am Mr. McCullough, just no the one you spoke to. That would be Henry, he's . . ." He paused for a moment, glancing away from her as he moved his hand from her arm to pick up his cup. "I'm Ian McCullough."

"Oh." That explained why he didn't look at all like the sweet old man she'd imagined Henry McCullough to be. "But you're also a McCullough. You're related?"

"Aye. We're as related as an uncle and nephew can be." He briefly flashed that brilliant smile again.

"Where is your uncle?"

"Henry? Oh, in hospital, actually. Minor knee surgery. He'll be home in a few days. In the meantime, I'm supposed to be looking after things, but I'm afraid I've mucked them up a bit." The smile reappeared. "Starting with knowing nothing about my lovely guest, no even her name."

"Oh." Her conversational skills were rapidly disappearing in his presence. The blush returned. "I'm Sarah. Sarah Douglas."

"Sarah." He repeated the name slowly. "It suits you. Now that we know one another, we've only the problem of the cottage, it seems."

Uh-oh. "My cottage?"

He nodded. "Regrettably, our caretakers were called away on emergency this morning, so the cottage isna prepared for you. With the storm, I dinna think it a huge problem. I was sure you'd stay in the city when you saw the weather. Which reminds me."

His eyebrows lifted in a manner reminiscent of a school principal about to chastise an errant student.

"This is no night to be out on the roads, lass. Did you no think about the risk you were taking by driving here in this tempest?"

His tone implied lecture, not a conversational question. It might even have been offensive if not for his lovely accent. The lightly lilting brogue made everything he said sound good. The brogue and the deep baritone.

"I guess I didn't at the time. But I certainly recognize it now." She put down her tea. "Mr. McCullough—"

"Ian," he corrected.

"Ian." She briefly made eye contact and smiled. "If the cottage isn't prepared, then . . ."

"It's no worry. We'll put you up here in the main house for tonight."

He sat back, looking very satisfied, and took a drink of his tea.

"I was under the impression that you didn't rent out rooms here." Henry had been rather emphatic about that point, assuring her there would be no other lodgers.

"We dinna. You'll join us tonight as my guest. We'll get you set up in the cottage tomorrow. Now . . . ," Ian stood and held out his hand in invitation. "Let's get you all settled. When did you eat last?"

"On the plane."

She rose to her feet, clutching the now damp blanket tightly around her. If he'd noticed she'd avoided his hand, he gave no sign of it.

"We'll remedy that right after we get you in some dry clothing." He paused, tipping his head to the side. "Come to think of it, I dinna recall seeing yer auto in the drive."

"It's not exactly in the drive. It's down at the entrance gate." She shrugged. "I sort of slid off the road and got stuck in the mud. I can go back down and get my suitcase."

As they neared the door, thunder rumbled ominously close, rattling windows.

"I'm thinking that's probably no the best idea. In fact, I'm sure we can find you something dry to slip into here. We'll collect yer things and yer vehicle in the morning when the rain's done."

He'd stopped talking so she risked a quick glance up. It appeared he was waiting for that, catching her eyes and once again extending his hand. Perhaps he had noticed her earlier evasion after all.

"Here. Come with me."

There was no chance this time to avoid his touch without seeming unusually rude and she couldn't bring herself to do that. He'd been much too nice.

Simply one hand against another. No way to prevent her unprotected skin from contact with his. No blanket or clothing to filter it through this time. She'd simply have to steel herself against the assault she knew would come with the touch, as it always did.

She'd learned to accept it. From childhood she'd suffered the trauma of absorbing other people's thoughts and emotions when she touched them, and the strange, random "feelings" that assailed her, trying to direct her actions. Almost worse had been the pain of knowing she was "different" from everyone else. She'd accepted that long ago, too.

While her preference was, as always, to escape the unavoidable result, sometimes, like now, it couldn't be helped.

She took his hand.

Eggs.

He scanned the contents of the refrigerator. He knew how to cook eggs. Not well, mind you, but he could cook them. And there was bread. He'd make toast. Surely there was canned fruit of some sort in the pantry. Martha served it with almost every meal.

Under optimal conditions no one would ever mistake him for a chef, but with the current distraction standing in his kitchen, well . . .

Best to keep it simple.

How was it a woman, any woman, could look so appealing when you dressed her in men's clothing? *And if it happens to be an attractive woman, dressed in my own clothing?* Without a doubt, anything other than simple would be beyond his abilities at this moment.

"Is there anything I can do to help?"

"You can have a seat. Yer my guest." He flashed a grin. "I'll have you a tasty meal whipped up in no time."

Ha. "Tasty" was pushing it a bit, but as Henry was fond of accusing, he'd never been an overly modest man.

"Are you warmer now?"

He'd grabbed the first things he'd come to in his drawers; the things he wore to loaf about: sweatpants, thermal undershirt, woolen overshirt and thick cotton socks.

He was positive those items had never looked so appealing on him.

"Much better, thanks." She rewarded him with a shy smile as she padded over to the table and sat down.

Before long, he was setting plates filled with scrambled eggs, toast and canned grapefruit sections on the table. To her credit, she gave it only one small dubious glance before sampling a bite.

"You don't do a lot of cooking, do you?"

So, a diplomatic woman.

"Is it as bad as that?"

"No, not at all. It's just that you appeared to be hunting for things in the kitchen while you were fixing this."

Observant, as well.

"And here I was afraid it would be the rubber eggs that gave me away."

"Actually, the burned toast was more of a tip-off than the eggs."

Even a sense of humor.

He grinned at her and was rewarded with a quiet laugh and another blush softly coloring her cheeks.

Simply charming.

"So, how did you come to choose our little cottage for yer holiday?"

"Working holiday," she corrected. "My three months will fly by, I'm afraid. And as to this location, I chose by sheer, blind luck. Once I knew I had to come to Scotland . . ."

She paused, her eyes flickering up to meet his, betraying mild alarm, as if she'd said something she hadn't intended, before she hurried on.

"I . . . uh, I sat down at the computer and searched. Heather Cottage was the first entry that came up. I know this sounds stupid, but when I clicked on the site and read about it, it just felt right." She shrugged without looking up. "So I emailed Mr. McCullough—Henry—and he called me, and here I am."

"What kind of work are you here to do?"

"I write." A furtive glance up.

"Ah, a storyteller. And what do you write?"

"Uh, women's literature. Pretty much." Another quick, furtive glance.

"Hmmmm. I dinna believe I'm familiar with that."

"Really?" As a deep crimson stain slowly crept across her face, she rose and carried her plate to the sink. "At least I can help wash up."

So, her work was something she did not want to discuss. *A most intriguing woman indeed.* Too bad he didn't have time or room for a woman in his life.

They finished the dishes with relatively little talk, her weariness a tangible thing to him. His goal was to show her to the guest room as quickly as possible.

Their walk to the stairs was interrupted by an enormous boom of thunder, accompanied by a flash of lightning so close he could feel the hairs on his arm lift. Followed immediately by every light in the house going out. He'd known it was only a matter of time.

Sarah's gasp was audible.

Standing so close to her, he fully expected she would throw her arms around him, or lean into him at the very least.

In his experience, which was extensive, frightened women always turned to the closest man for comfort and protection. Particularly when *he* was the closest man.

It wasn't conceit, simply an observation. He was well aware of the effect he had on women. He'd certainly had long enough to get used to it. After all, he'd met a goodly number of women in the past six hundred years.

But she didn't do either of those things.

In fact, as his eyes quickly adjusted, he saw that she stood as she first had in the hallway, huddled into herself, her arms wrapped about her own middle.

"Dinna be afraid. It's only the electric." He touched her shoulder and she flinched.

"I . . . I'm not afraid. Just startled."

But not completely truthful? He could sense the fear rolling off her in waves.

"Well, maybe a tiny bit afraid," she amended in a whisper.

Ah, that's better.

He guided her into the library, where the fire afforded them a modest light.

"Have a seat and I'll go find a torch for you to take upstairs."

"Torch?"

"Aye. A hand light. You put batteries into it?"

Recognition dawned on her face. "Oh, a flash-light."

"No, a torch." He grinned. "One day you Yanks will have to learn to speak proper English."

When he returned with the torch, having spent a good ten minutes hunting in the dark for fresh batteries for the thing, she was fast asleep, slumped over sideways into the corner of the sofa, her feet still on the floor.

What to do? He could wake her, a choice that seemed patently unkind. Or he could easily pick her up and carry her to the guest room. And, although his arms fairly itched for the opportunity to hold her, chances were good she'd wake, again not the result he wanted. Best to let her sleep where she lay. No chance of waking her, with the added benefit that he could sit and watch her as long as he wanted to.

And he found that he wanted to.

Very gently he lifted her legs to the sofa so she could stretch out her full, what, maybe five and a half feet at most? He reached for the woolen plaid folded over the back of his chair, and draped it over her sleeping form, tucking it around her shoulders. It outlined rather than hid her soft curves.

She moaned and snuggled into it.

Ian crossed the room and reached into a recessed cabinet to withdraw a bottle of his favorite whisky.

Full glass in hand, he sank into his chair and propped up his feet, savoring a swallow before turning his attention to study the woman on his sofa.

Even in sleep her features reflected uneasiness, a

tiny frown fixed on her brow. Soft golden curls, too short to do more than barely brush her shoulders, wildly framed a delicate face. Smile lines around her eyes hinted of a woman who looked for the good in life and also of a maturity. He'd guess her to be in her early- to mid-thirties, perhaps not a classic beauty, but a very attractive woman in her prime nevertheless.

Certainly she was attractive to him. From that first astonishing glimpse of her soul, to her unexpected behavior, right down to the way she looked lying on his sofa, covered with his own plaid, he was drawn to her.

His instincts, however, screamed that there was much more to this woman than met the eye.

He hadn't missed her flinch each time he'd touched her, or how she'd tried to avoid taking his hand. Nor had he missed her look of resignation when she finally had. Perhaps more to the point, he'd seen the surprise that had flashed through her eyes at that moment, as if she'd expected some inevitable something that hadn't come.

He took another drink of his whisky, savoring the warmth that flowed down his throat.

"Just what were you expecting, wee Sarah?" he whispered before draining the glass.

Hunting the answer to that question would, at the very least, give him some distraction while he waited for Henry to come home.

Waited to return to what really mattered, protecting Mortal men from those of his kind who would destroy them all.

Two

*H*eather Cottage was perfect.

On her walk from the main house down to the cottage this morning, she'd had very little opportunity to really soak up the surroundings, but what she had seen pleased her senses. The manor house itself was a huge, rambling mansion with ivy covering its walls. Her cottage was an adorable little house, looking like something out of a Disney cartoon, right down to the window boxes and big wooden door. The path between the two abodes was a riot of color, lined by masses of flowers.

She knew from what Henry had told her that Thistle Down Manor was an ancient, secluded estate. Her rental, Heather Cottage, was a later addition, one not leased out often. She felt fortunate that she had somehow passed whatever screening Henry used to determine who would be lucky enough to rent the cottage.

Sitting in the peaceful little sunroom off the

kitchen, Sarah felt like she was where she was supposed to be for the first time in her life. Now if she could only figure out *why* she was supposed to be here. It would be so much easier to follow up on these feelings if they would simply be a little more specific.

When Sarah had stumbled across the rental listing during her late-night internet search for a place to stay, it had, as she'd told Ian, *felt right.* He'd nodded politely as if he'd understood. No point in explaining that meant something entirely different to her than to anyone else. The whole evening had been unusual enough without pointing out her oddities to a complete stranger. Besides, he'd notice them on his own soon enough. Everyone who got close to her did.

"What am I thinking?"

She stood and shook her head. She wouldn't be getting close enough to him, or to anyone else for that matter, for anyone to notice anything. She was here for peace and quiet—to get in touch with her "feelings" and to finish the book she should have finished months ago. She was not here to meet a man. Especially not *that* man.

She chuckled as she began to unpack her bag. Seriously. Where was her head? Even if she weren't too old for him, which she was, he was way out of her league. Gorgeous men like that, gorgeous young men, went for gorgeous young women. She was neither. She had turned thirty-eight on her last birthday. Even in her twenties, no on had ever accused her of being gorgeous. Not her mother, nor her grandmother. And certainly not Brad. Her ex-husband had called her a number of things, but *gorgeous* was not one of them.

Still, Ian McCullough was a most unusual man, and not just because of his drop-dead looks.

Everyone, every single person she'd ever touched since her seventh birthday, gave off some type of current. Her sensitivity to it often made that touch almost unbearable. Sorrow, greed, anger, joy, pain— all of that and more came through in the touch. Even the good emotions could be painful when too intense.

But when she'd touched Ian last night, there had been no jolt, no frenzy of feeling, only a flow of warmth. That had never happened before.

Of course, she had been exhausted at the time.

Perhaps that accounted for it. Perhaps, if the opportunity presented itself, she'd touch him again. Only to test what would happen. Like a science experiment. To see if it had been fatigue that had interfered with the feelings.

Right now she needed to concentrate on getting settled in and getting to work. No more daydreaming. She laughed out loud at that thought. Daydreaming *was* her work.

She walked into the central room and lifted her heavy shoulder bag from the floor onto the little desk, opening it and removing her laptop. Looking around, she knew she was going to like it here. From this spot, she could see the whole of the cottage interior. Two doors opened off the tiny hallway to her right. One led to the bathroom, the other a bedroom. Her living room was open to the kitchen, separated only by a countertop and cabinets. A wooden table and two chairs filled the floor of the small kitchen area. A love seat and coffee table dominated the living area, with a fireplace on one wall and the desk and large window on the other.

From that window, the view of the early summer gardens was exactly what she needed. Absolutely inspiring.

She should start to work. That was the first thing on her list. Well, maybe a walk through those lovely gardens before she actually started work, but work was really, really close to the top of the list.

And no more thinking about Ian McCullough. He wasn't anywhere on the list.

A knock on the door of the cottage saved her from the battle she was losing to procrastination.

When she opened the door, Ian stood there, one large suitcase held effortlessly in each hand.

"Good morning, luv. I've brought yer things up from the auto. Seems the battery is run down, so Peter's working on that now. Did you know you left yer lights on?" He grinned.

Wow . . . Who would have guessed he'd look even better in the daytime? He wore a black T-shirt, tight enough to outline every muscle in the wall of chest confronting her.

"Yeah, I guess I did." She shrugged, unable to stop the sheepish expression that stole over her face. "After what happened, I couldn't quite bring myself to deal with the dark."

"Ah." He narrowed his eyes. "What happened?"

"It's a long, silly story." She shook her head. Here in the welcoming atmosphere of the cottage, she'd almost been able to forget the man she'd seen last night, the fear she'd felt as she ran from her car. She wasn't particularly anxious to relive it by sharing the tale. "Thanks for bringing my luggage. You didn't have to do that."

"It's nothing. Besides, I thought you might like to get out of those ill-fitting things."

She was still wearing his clothes. She'd been so captivated by the cottage since Martha had brought her here after breakfast, she hadn't even thought about what she was wearing. The slow burn started up her face.

He wasn't trying to hide his grin as he shouldered past her with the luggage, which he carried directly to the bedroom. Coming out, he swiped his hands together as if dusting them off.

"There. All settled. Tell you what, you get yerself dressed and then I'll show you around the gardens. The estate's large, so it's best if you know what to look for so you dinna get lost." He arched an eyebrow. "And you can tell me the long, silly story that made you leave yer lights on last night."

"Well, I really should . . ." She hesitated and glanced out the window. The beauty there called to her. And it did make sense. She should find out about the place if she planned to be here for three months. "Okay. I'll just be a couple of minutes."

After all, how could a simple walk cause any problems? It wasn't like someone could learn all your deep, dark secrets in a couple of hours.

She's naïve.

Who would have guessed? Especially in a woman her age.

Ian walked alone in the deep forest of the estate. He had spent the better part of the day with Sarah, showing her around the gardens and pointing out different trails she might enjoy should she decide to spend time outdoors. More important, he'd pointed out the trails she would want to avoid—those he wanted her to avoid—to keep from getting lost or wandering onto private land belonging to others who didn't take kindly to intruders.

He smiled to himself. The fact that she'd assumed he meant neighbors only worked to his advantage. In a way, he guessed, it did mean neighbors. Just not the Mortal ones.

During the course of the day, it had become apparent to him that she was obviously inexperienced with men, and quite unsure of herself. Not something he would have expected in an attractive woman like her. He'd been skeptical when her cheeks had pinkened as he pointed out she was still wearing his clothing, surprised as the color reappeared when he'd complimented how she looked at the start of their walk. But the deep crimson that had flowered on her face when he'd invited her to dinner was what finally convinced him.

He still wasn't exactly sure what had prompted him to issue that particular invitation.

He didn't avoid women. Far from it. He only avoided women who required commitment. He was already committed—to his work. What he did was too important, required too much of him for there to be any room left for more than a quick fling. Required that he hide too many secrets for any type of relationship. So he avoided genuine, authentic, innocent women.

Women like Sarah.

Not that Sarah wasn't hiding secrets of her own. Perhaps that, as much as her appealing innocence, was what enticed him to spend more time with her. Though it didn't really matter.

Henry would be home tomorrow and then he would be gone. Hunting those who needed hunting. Protecting those who couldn't protect themselves.

Ian felt the presence before he heard the words.

"I see Henry's let the cottage again."

"Aye, he has. I was looking for you to make sure you knew."

Not that much ever escaped this particular Fae's attention. Dallyn was his direct contact with the Realm of Faerie—the closest thing he had to a boss. And although Dallyn could be exceedingly arrogant at times, Ian trusted the Fae with his life. He could count on one hand the beings who fell into that category, and still have fingers left over.

"Looking for me? Would that be before or after dinner with the woman?"

Exceedingly arrogant.

"It's why I'm out here now." Ian shook his head, choosing to ignore the imperious expression worn by the Fae. "And why are you out here? Spying on Henry's guest?"

Dallyn attempted, unsuccessfully, to control a tiny smile threatening to break free. "Partly. There's something about this one . . ." He left the thought hanging.

"Aye, there is that." Partly, he'd said. "And the other reason you're out here?"

"Have you spoken to Daniel? Do we know if he's made any progress?"

Lord Daniel Stroud, Ian's partner, was his best

friend and his connection into the British authorities. Like Ian, Daniel was a half-blood Fae. He also happened to fall into that small number of beings Ian could count on one hand.

"No. I left word for Danny, but they said he was in London. I'd imagine he's in for a briefing. I expect to hear back by tomorrow. Either way, Henry will be home by then and I'll go down there meself."

"And abandon your lovely guest?"

"Henry's guest. Once he returns, he can keep an eye on her."

"So, you've no other interest in this woman? Nothing but 'keeping an eye on her,' as you say?"

They stared at one another for a long moment.

"In all this time, when have you ever known me to let a woman get in the way of my duties?"

Dallyn bowed his head, the smallest of movements. "My apologies, if I offended. It was not my intent. I only meant to question the amount of time you've spent with her."

"After tomorrow, this conversation will be for naught. I'll be gone and Henry will be looking after the woman."

"Yes, well. As for Henry's deciding on another guest, what was it this time? How did this one talk him into letting her stay?"

Guests were here so rarely, it was only logical Dallyn would question the presence of this one.

"You'd best chat with Henry about that."

"Soul healing again?" Dallyn closed his eyes, making a *tsk*ing noise as he did so. "Well, it's no more than I should expect . . . give a Mortal a gift and they think they have to use it."

Ian didn't comment. There was no need to defend Henry. In spite of Dallyn's attempt to appear irritated, Ian knew Henry's use of his healing gift pleased the Fae.

"What does he think it is? Another wounded soul?"

"Aye. But . . ." Ian paused, unsure of whether or not to share his unfounded suspicions.

"But . . . ?" The Faerie High General's scrutiny would wither a lesser man.

"Nothing, really. It's just that I've my doubts about that being a wounded soul. I'm wondering if the lad might have gotten it wrong this time."

There was a first time for everything.

"Really?" Dallyn pursed his lips, tapping his finger to them lightly. "Perhaps I need to have a closer look at this woman."

"I would no think that necessary." In fact, Ian found the idea of Dallyn's spying on Sarah to be more than a little irritating. "Or particularly wise."

"I fail to see a problem with it, Ian. It's not as though she'll even know I'm there. And my interest is piqued now." The Fae turned and walked away. Before he disappeared into the trees, he tossed back a final comment.

"Besides, as lovely as she is, it certainly won't be an onerous duty."

The sound of soft laughter drifted back from the direction Dallyn had gone.

Exceedingly arrogant.

Sarah had changed her outfit three times already, and Ian was due any minute. What on earth had she been thinking to agree to have dinner with that man?

"Not thinking. Not thinking at all," she muttered, reaching for a fourth outfit. That, at least, was true enough.

They had spent hours walking through some of the loveliest gardens she'd ever seen. Just when she'd almost started to relax, he'd begun by telling her that he'd be picking Henry up at the hospital tomorrow, bringing him home. That he'd be leaving shortly after, since he'd only planned to stay long enough to help out in Henry's absence. She'd wavered somewhere between relief that she wouldn't *have* to see him anymore and distress that she wouldn't *get* to see him anymore. It was then, while she was weakened, torn between those ambivalent feelings, he'd done it.

He'd caught her with her guard down.

He asked her to dinner. Offered to show her the village nightlife, although he warned her it wasn't much. Told her how he'd hate to eat by himself on his last evening here. What could she do? He'd been so nice taking time to show her around and trying to make her comfortable—even though what he'd done was make her most uncomfortable. But he couldn't be held responsible for that. That was all her.

She stood in front of the mirror, frowning. And peeled off the sweater she'd just put on. She looked around the mess in the bedroom and, sighing, picked up the dress she'd started with. A simple, sheer summer dress. Nothing elegant, nothing fancy. It would have to do. She dropped it down over her head, letting it slide into place. Then she slipped her feet into sandals and stared down at them in distaste. For going out with a man this tall, she'd really prefer to wear high heels, but she hadn't brought any. She'd simply have to be short tonight.

Wait.

She wasn't really going out. This wasn't a date. It was only dinner. Dinner with a man who didn't want to eat alone.

There was a thought that made her smile. As if a man like him couldn't find plenty of eager dinner partners, no matter how small the town might be.

More likely it was dinner with a man who had promised his uncle he'd be nice to the current renter, regardless of who she was or what she looked like. Nothing more than a man doing a favor for his uncle.

She sighed. Ah well, perhaps if she actually dated, she'd know more about what a date was or wasn't and wouldn't be stressing out right now.

No—she didn't really regret not dating. Women dated to find a husband. She'd had one of those. Briefly. Let those other women, the ones who still wanted husbands, fill the dating pool. She'd pass on that pain again, thank you very much.

She was running the comb through her hair, wishing there was something better she could do with her unruly curls, when he knocked on the door.

It might not be a date, but her stomach did the butterfly dance as she went to answer all the same.

She opened the door and stared. Was there a *GQ* issue missing a cover guy somewhere? Black silky T-shirt, black dress pants, black sport coat. *Wow!* Why had she even bothered to worry about what to wear? No one was going to notice her anyway.

"Good evening, Sarah. Are you ready?" He smiled. It was a devastating look on him.

"I just need to get my purse."

When she returned, he extended his elbow and escorted her to the front of the main house, where his car was parked.

A racy little black sports thing. Why wasn't she surprised?

She walked ahead and stood by the door, waiting until she looked up and saw his grin.

"What?"

"Did you want to drive, then?" he asked.

"No, I . . ." Wrong side. Stupid British backward cars. Stupid American tourist. "Sorry. Forgot." Stupid blush that forever plagued her life.

"No worry, luv. One day you Yanks will wake up and straighten out yer cars, learn to drive properly."

"I wouldn't hold my breath if I were you," she muttered as he helped her into the passenger side.

His smile turned into an outright laugh as he joined her in the car.

"I thought we'd have Indian cooking tonight. I hope that's good for you." He glanced over at her with an inquisitive look.

"That's fine." She'd never had Indian food before. Imagine coming all the way to Scotland to taste Indian cooking.

As it turned out, the food was delicious. As was the wine they'd had with dinner. It had been a lovely evening, filled with inconsequential, safe conversation and periodic silences.

They were headed home now, a full moon overhead as they neared the gates of the estate.

"It feels so different tonight." It slipped out. She

hadn't intended to say that out loud. Of course, she hadn't intended to have two glasses of wine either.

"Different how?" His attention stayed on the dark road in front of them.

"Different as in not threatening now."

"The storms we get here can be pretty violent and frightening at times."

It wasn't that. It hadn't been the storm that had slipped into her memory unbidden so many times during the day. It had been that man and the feeling she'd had when she'd seen him.

The road curved toward the estate drive and Ian motioned toward the gates. "Is that where you thought you saw the man?"

She nodded. "My figment. I guess exhaustion can play some pretty wicked tricks with your mind, huh?"

"True. If you'd mentioned it last evening, I could have checked for footprints when we collected yer auto this morning. Still, I suppose the storm would have removed any evidence." His voice trailed off.

"I'm sure I must have imagined it. He couldn't have been real. Real people don't jump over cars before disappearing into the woods."

His eyes narrowed in an assessing look, glancing away from the drive to her for only a moment. "I'm sure yer right. Well, here we are."

He stopped the car and got out, coming around to open her door and assist her. "Yer awfully quiet now." He smiled.

"Thinking about last night, I guess." She shivered. Though the early summer evening brought a chill with it, she knew it wasn't the temperature that caused her body's reaction.

"The evening's been much too nice to let it end on a sour note because I made you think about yer fright. I know." His face brightened. "Have you ever seen a night garden in bloom?"

"A night garden? I don't think so."

"It's delightful anytime, but on a full moon night, it's a true wonder. Wait here. I'll be right back." He took off on a trot toward the main house.

He'd only been gone a moment when the tingles raced across her neck. The feeling of being watched. Not threatening, not like last night. Just watched.

She wrapped her arms about her middle and hunched her shoulders. She felt vulnerable out here on the path, halfway between the main house and her little cottage, both of which represented safety to her right now. Then Ian was back, carrying a covered basket, long strides bringing him quickly to her side.

He reached out and grasped her hand, and she let him without thinking. His touch felt like he'd brought the safety of the house to her. Surprise rooted her to the spot.

"Come on, I have something wonderful to show you. It's over this way." He tugged on her hand, pulling her down the path after him.

The fragrance reached her long before they actually turned down the garden path. They'd come this way earlier in the day, but had bypassed this plain area. It was filled with mostly white flowering plants, and, although lacking any real color during the day, it was a thing of beauty now. Moonlight reflected off the white blooms, creating a landscape unlike anything she'd seen before. And the fragrance. Unbelievable.

"I didn't notice it smelling like this today when we

passed here. This is wonderful." She looked up at him.

"Henry's mother created this area. She was quite the gardener. She said that during the day, the heat dinna allow the scent to spread. Only at night, after it cools a bit, does it smell like this."

He led her to the center of the Night Garden and, dropping her hand, pulled a blanket out of the basket he carried. He spread it on the ground with a flourish and motioned for her to have a seat.

"This is lovely." Peaceful. She closed her eyes and turned her face up to the moon, feeling as if she could soak up the light shining down on her.

"Yes, quite lovely."

His voice sounded odd, and she opened her eyes to find him staring at her. He turned back to his basket and brought out a bottle of champagne and two glasses.

"Here. Hold these." He passed the glasses to her.

"I really shouldn't have any more, Ian. I don't normally drink more than a single glass."

"Well, luv, it's no like yer driving now, is it? Besides, it'll relax you." He expertly popped the cork and poured the sparkling liquid into the crystal.

She stared at the moonlight reflected in her glass for a moment. It was like a scene out of a movie. A really good movie. Her not-really-a-date evening had been simply wonderful. Lifting the champagne to her lips, she took one small sip and then a second before she felt it again.

Eyes. Watching.

She froze.

"What is it?" His body tensed. "What's wrong?"

A shiver ran through her. "I felt . . . it's nothing, really. Just a little chill." She wouldn't ruin this by jabbering on about the feelings.

He seemed to relax. After a moment, he shrugged out of his jacket and leaned close to wrap it around her shoulders. His face was so near she could see the moon reflected in his eyes, a great shining sphere floating in a sea of onyx.

She was held captive there as she felt her own eyes widen, locked on his. She couldn't turn away, couldn't even blink.

Then, as quickly as it began, it was over, whatever it was. It had lasted only a moment, but it left her drained, her muscles quivering, as if she'd exercised hard.

He sat back, an inscrutable look on his face. "Finish yer drink, Sarah."

When she'd emptied her glass, he stood and smiled down at her, extending his hand.

"How thoughtless of me. Look at you, trembling there. I should have known it'd be too cold for you out here dressed as you are. Come on. I'll take you back to yer cottage now."

He helped her to her feet and walked her to her door, where he did a formal little bow that made her feel like royalty from a far-gone era. Then, taking her hand, he lightly kissed the back of it before turning and walking away.

She watched him briefly before moving inside and closing the door behind her. Clutching the hand he'd kissed tightly to her breast, she closed her eyes and leaned back against the wooden frame. She tilted her head so her nose was close to her shoulder and the jacket she still wore. Ian's jacket. A deep breath and his fragrance filled her senses.

She'd waited for the rush of emotion from his touch, but, again, there was only warmth. She might have suspected at long last the unexplainable feelings had abandoned her if not for the other awareness. The one she could explore now if she only had the courage.

This was as good a time as any to start. It was what she'd promised herself she'd do when she came to this place—to embrace all that she had attempted to ignore for so long. Taking another deep breath, she reached out with her being and opened herself to the sensations all around her, the vibrations in the air, allowing them to wash over her.

Whatever it was, it was still out there. She hadn't been the only one watching Ian walk away.

Ian was annoyed. More than annoyed. Angry.

He had been irritated enough that Dallyn planned to spy on the woman. But this was too much. Spying on her while *he* was with her was insulting.

For a moment there in the garden he'd thought she was aware of the presence. But that was impossible.

He stretched his neck, side to side, trying to relieve some of the tension there and took another drink from the glass he'd refilled. Carrying it and the bottle to his chair, he sat and stared into the fire.

When he'd first realized Dallyn watched, he'd thought to teach him a lesson. He'd kiss her, give the sneaky Fae the show he deserved. But then the curtains opened and he glimpsed her soul yet again. Not calling out for his attention any longer. Quietly watching him, serenely studying him. Waiting patiently.

He took another long, slow drink, feeling the warm liquid glide easily down his throat.

Waiting for what?

One more intriguing question about the intriguing woman he didn't have time for.

It was a damn good thing he was leaving tomorrow. Before it was too late.

Three

"I don't like it any better than you do, Minister, but I can't think of any other way to accomplish what we need to." Lord Daniel Stroud stood glaring across the desk at his superior. "And I'm open to any suggestions you might have."

Lord Humphrey McCutcheon lowered his considerable bulk into his well-used chair. "You know I've none, Daniel, or I'd never consider letting you take this kind of risk." He picked up a worn pipe from his desk and tapped it against his hand.

Daniel knew the Minister had long ago given up smoking, but retained the pipe because handling the thing still gave him a sense of calm.

They both needed some calm at the moment.

"You're confident the information from your source is correct?" Daniel continued to stand, looking down at the older man, who nodded affirmatively.

"You've questioned him since he returned?"

The Minister blinked rapidly, a sure sign of his

frustration to any who knew him well. "I would have, had he returned." He placed the pipe carefully in its holder. "We've lost contact with him completely at this point. Nothing after the first message."

"Damn. That makes it trickier."

"The organization has impeccable credentials, tremendous political and financial backing worldwide. I'd even heard rumors that the head of their board has been considered for the Nobel." The Minister shook his head. "We can't take any chances on this one, Daniel. We have to find proof—absolute, irrefutable proof—before we can make a move of any sort. And don't forget the subtleties we discussed. It's our goal to preserve the integrity of the charity, if possible. Bringing down EHN would be a tremendous blow to countries all around the world that depend on the organization."

"I understand the need for discretion, Minister. And we've no clue who in the inner circle is funneling the money? No idea who the terrorists' contact is?"

"No. Assuming the intelligence is accurate."

Daniel raised an eyebrow in question.

"Yes, yes. I've no doubt it's accurate. Kensington was good at what he did."

The Minister's reference to the missing agent in the past tense didn't escape Daniel.

"If he says it's one of their officers, that he found a link, then I'm confident it's there. Now we need to find it."

"And break it."

"There's not much we can do through this office to assist—officially, at least." The Minister's hand snaked out, stroking the pipe where it lay. "We need to move quickly. The cash flow must be stopped, of course, but this latest . . . this weapon. We cannot allow it to reach the terrorists. We have to identify the persons behind this network and neutralize them."

"I'll put my office to work on it immediately. For a large enough donation, I'm sure the entire board of EHN International will be cooperative. It then will be simply a matter of picking out the one we seek."

Daniel left, taking the elevator up from the secure administrative offices of the little-known governmental agency for which he worked. Reaching ground level, he used his cell phone to call his driver. He had to reach his London offices right away, set things in motion and then get back to Glaston House. There was a tremendous amount of preparation he'd need to put into place before these people invaded his home.

It was almost beyond comprehension. An officer at one of the most prestigious humanitarian organizations on the face of the planet channeling funds to one of the deadliest terrorist groups?

So it would seem. And him thinking to expose his own family to these people. But he was in the best position to do it. With his reputation and social status, no one would question it as they would if a normal operative were used.

Fortunately for him, he had resources and contacts the normal operatives didn't. He was going to need them, because he also had the distinct advantage of knowing what enemy they were really up against.

While the Minister had his operatives investigating all avenues of information for clues to the identity of the people involved, Daniel knew they were actually searching for someone whose power came from outside the Mortal world. Which meant that person could only be identified—and dealt with—by someone whose power also came from outside the Mortal world.

As he stepped off the curb and into the waiting car, Daniel flipped open his cell phone again and hit the speed dial.

If Ian left right away, he could be at Glaston House before Daniel had time to regret his decision to act as bait.

Four

Sarah held down the backspace button, watching the little black line gobble up the words she'd written. Boring, uninspired words. It was times like this when she wished she wrote with a pen and notepad. Crumpling the paper and tossing it across the room would have to be more satisfying than this pale imitation of Pac-Man she'd been engaging in all afternoon. The characters wouldn't speak to her. The story was just beyond her reach, as it had been for months. The only difference now was that she couldn't even concentrate on trying to pull the words out of the ether.

She could only think about him.

Perhaps she should go with that. Use him in her book.

No. Bad idea. She would never fantasize about a real man. Especially not this one. It would be too uncomfortable if she ever met him again.

Which she wouldn't. After all, he told her he was leaving today.

Still, she always ended up with a little crush on her heroes, fascinated by them as she'd never been by the real men she met. She suspected that was why she could write them so well.

That was also why she wouldn't write about Ian. She didn't want to be attracted to him. She wouldn't be fascinated by him. She refused to be captivated by a man who probably suffered from random thoughts about whether or not he'd remembered to call his mother when he looked at her. Well, she amended her thoughts, his older sister at the very least. He was much too young for her.

Besides, Ian was the type of man who was way too tempting. She wouldn't risk her heart, wouldn't risk rejection at the hands of a man again. Once had been enough.

Brad. She had thought herself in love, at least in the beginning. But it wasn't meant to be.

Brad had quickly grown tired of her. Tired of her strange feelings and odd behavior. Tired of waiting for her trust fund to kick in. She should be grateful to him, however. He didn't hang around long enough to turn her into a bitter replica of her grandmother.

Instead he'd only stayed long enough to allow her to learn some basic truths about herself and life. She was meant to be alone.

She stood and walked to the kitchen, unconsciously wiping the tear that trailed down her cheek.

What had she accomplished today? Well, so far the only thing she'd managed was to work herself up into a really good feel-sorry-for-Sarah mood.

She entered the little kitchen Martha had stocked in preparation for her arrival, and opened the freezer door. Not a single container of chocolate ice cream to be found. Now that was a real shame. Self-pity always made her ravenous. Apparently there were several "necessities" she'd need to pick up on her next visit to town.

Since she wasn't getting anywhere with her writing anyway, she decided to cook. Comfort food would make her feel better. It always did. A big, thick hamburger with thinly sliced sautéed onions. Maybe she'd leave off the bread so she didn't have to feel too guilty. Then again, maybe not. At least it wasn't ice cream. She could always go walking later to work off some of the calories.

She pulled out the largest onion she could find and set to work, peeling and slicing. Midway through the task, tears streamed down her face. These were onion tears, not pity tears. Much better than before.

With the last of the outrageously strong onion stirred into a slow sauté pan and a wonderful home-cooked aroma already building, she decided to take a minute for fresh air. She hurried out through the tiny conservatory and across the back porch.

Her eyes still stinging from the fumes and blurred with tears, she stood on the top step waiting for the breeze to perform its magic, making the pain go away.

She didn't notice him at first.

He stood quietly with the sun at his back, right at the edge of the forest that bordered the neat little lawn. Watching her.

"Hi," she called, and put a hand up to shade her eyes so she could see him more clearly.

Big mistake. Onion juice. The stinging tears flooded back. Closing her eyes at the fresh onslaught, she stepped forward, finding only air, and missed the top stair completely.

She threw out her arms to brace herself, fully expecting a face-first landing. She gasped when, instead of dirt, she encountered a pair of strong arms. How he'd made it across the lawn so quickly she had no idea and, at the moment, didn't really care.

She tried to lean back to get a better look at her rescuer. Didn't they grow any unappealing men in this part of Scotland? Apparently not.

He was tall—as tall as Ian. Where Ian was dark, this man was blond, with long hair pulled back in a low ponytail. Where Ian's eyes were a piercing black, his were a deep green.

Wait a minute.

When had Ian become the measuring stick against which she gauged other men?

Still, this man had rescued her. "Thank you."

"Not at all." He tilted his head and appeared to inspect her face. "You're not harmed?"

"No." She smiled at him. "Thanks to you I'm not."

"Then what pain causes you to weep so?"

Before she realized his intention, he loosened his grip and slid his hands down her arms until their hands met, where he clasped her fingers tightly.

No time to prepare, no time to steel herself for the assault of overwhelming feelings.

Feelings that didn't come.

"Onions," she murmured, unable to comprehend yet another contact that brought no pain of unfettered emotions.

"I beg your pardon?"

"I was peeling onions. The fumes . . ."

How is this possible?

"Onions?" He lifted his nose to the air, like a tracking dog on scent. "They are the source of that glorious aroma?"

"Glorious now that they're cooking, maybe, but earlier . . . oh my gosh. My onions." She jerked her hands from his and ran back to the kitchen.

So, she'd be having crispy rather than sautéed onions with her hamburger. At least they hadn't burned.

"They certainly don't look as good as they smell."

Sarah jumped at the sound of his voice, not having heard him follow her into the kitchen. He peered over her shoulder at the stove, his nose wrinkled in distaste.

"I didn't realize there were other guests here." She turned and extended her hand, no longer concerned about what would happen if she touched this man. "I'm Sarah Douglas."

He paused for a moment and then took the hand she offered, but instead of the expected shake, he lifted it to his lips in an old-world gesture, brushing it with a touch as light as a butterfly wing.

"I'm not a guest. I'm a neighbor, a friend of Ian's. My name is Dallyn." He dropped her hand to bend near the stove, sniffing deeply and licking his lips. "Ummm. This smell is wonderful."

"Well, Dallyn, would you care to join me for lunch?"

His eyes lit up, his face breaking into a beautiful smile. "I would like that very much."

Under normal circumstances, she would never have considered inviting a complete stranger to eat with her. But nothing had been "normal" since she'd set foot in Scotland.

Besides, this particular stranger held no threat for her. He was an amazingly good person.

She'd felt it in his touch.

Henry was home, ensconced in the den in his favorite chair.

Ian watched the man fiddle with the remote control, hunting for the program he wanted on television. He was obviously uncomfortable, his face contorting in pain each time he moved too quickly.

"Are you sure yer up to handling this on yer own?"

Henry glared at him. "I willna be on my own. Peter and Martha are here. Go."

Ian turned to leave, but stopped. "You'd be in less pain if you'd take the medication they gave you."

"Fine job of handling things I could do drugged out of my senses." He tossed the remote to the table. "How do you think I'm to figure out what's going on with our guest if I canna feel anything?"

As Ian had expected, Henry wasn't at all pleased with the suggestion that he might have been wrong about Sarah.

"I'm no telling you to stay medicated for her whole visit, Henry. Only for a few days. Until the pain eases a bit."

"Oh, so I suppose you think I'm no up to handling a little pain now."

"Are you planning to act the petulant child all evening?"

"Only so long as you're acting the meddling maiden aunt."

Ian shook his head and sighed. "Even as a child, you never were good with pain, Nephew." He stalked out of the room, not waiting to hear Henry's next volley.

He had packing to do. Then he'd try to reach Daniel again. If he left within the next hour, he could be at Glaston House by midday tomorrow.

Ian threw his suitcase into what passed for a backseat in his vehicle and slammed the door. The car was small and somewhat cramped, but it went very, very fast when he wanted it to, and for that alone he loved it and thought it worth every pound he had paid for it. His auto was one of the things he loved best about this time.

He turned and started toward the side of the house, briefly considering whether or not he should go find Sarah. Say good-bye.

Deciding against it, he stopped with his hand on the gate. It was better this way. Better to leave well enough alone. There was nothing to be gained by prolonging things.

He turned in time to find Dallyn pulling the suitcase out of his car.

"What do you think yer doing?"

"We've a substantially significant event here. It requires an adjustment on our part." Dallyn smiled and headed toward the front of the house. "A change of plans."

Ian reached the Fae as they entered the door, stopping him with a hand to his arm.

"We have a rather significant event emerging at Glaston House as well. I need to leave now."

"You've spoken to Daniel? He's going forward with the plan?"

"Yes. I just got off the phone with him."

Dallyn tilted his head up, eyes closed, like he waited for divine guidance. As if none came, he sighed and turned his penetrating gaze back to Ian.

"Would that I had two of you, Ian. But I don't, so you're staying here for now." He headed toward the library. "Do you suppose we might have a dram of the fine whisky you keep in here? I seem to have a craving for it this evening."

"What do you mean, I'm staying? I just told you I spoke to Danny. I have to get to Glaston House. He's counting on my help."

Ian watched in frustration as Dallyn tossed the suitcase on the floor and strode directly to the recessed bar, taking down three glasses and filling them.

"I suppose Henry is entrenched in front of his infernal telly?"

"We'll talk to Henry when we've finished here. What's going on?" Ian reached out for the glass offered him. Somehow he felt he was going to need it.

Dallyn drained his drink and refilled it before speaking. "I've been observing your little American guest today."

Ian could feel irritation building again. Hadn't last night been enough?

"And?"

"She's quite lovely."

The Fae watched him too closely for this to be a casual comment. He refused to rise to the bait, so he said nothing.

"She's also quite a good cook."

"Where are you going with this?" Ian set his glass on the table.

"I took the midday meal with her . . . lunch, I think she called it." The intense scrutiny continued.

"You did what?"

Dallyn rarely showed himself to Mortals. Ian could barely remember the last time it had happened.

The Fae rolled the empty glass in his hand, staring at it as if he suddenly found its composition fascinating. "Quite the experience, too, since I don't normally find Mortal food to be to my liking."

Now he remembered the last time Dallyn had shown himself. Clearly remembered. Resentment roiled through Ian's blood. "No. But you've frequently found Mortal women to be to yer liking, have you no?"

Dallyn refilled his glass before turning. "Are you losing your objectivity on this, Ian?"

"Losing *my* objectivity?" He shook his head. This went well beyond arrogance. "*I'm* no the Fae who showed myself to a Mortal. That would be you." He picked up his glass, continuing to glare at Dallyn.

The Fae's laughter echoed off the walls.

"I fail to see what's so funny." Ian crossed the room, deliberately refilling his drink from the bottle, giving himself time to calm. It was unlike him to lose control of his temper in this way.

"Exactly. You're failing to see." Dallyn narrowed his eyes. "I didn't show myself to the woman."

"What?" The whisky sloshed out onto his hand as he jerked around to stare at the Fae.

"She saw me standing there, observing her. In my own form."

"But . . . how is that possible?"

"Well *that*, my friend, is what you're staying here to find out."

Sarah and her soul seemed well matched in at least one thing—they both kept their curtains wide open.

Hidden in the deep shadows of the garden, Ian watched her, as he had since Dallyn left. Sunrise was near and still she paced, stopping for short periods of time to stare at her little computer screen before rising and pacing again.

Henry had been ecstatic when they'd spoken to him. Dallyn's discovery had given him a whole new take on the woman. He could hardly wait for the new day to begin so he could meet her. Ian had finally convinced him they should invite her for dinner, allowing Henry to study her discreetly rather than limp down to the cottage at first light for a good stare at the woman.

He, on the other hand, had been staring at her for some time now. Of course, that was different. He needed to come up with a plan to win her trust. A way to discover how much she knew about what she was, what she could do.

Fae blood.

It was the only explanation. She was like him.

No. Not like him. Not a Guardian. She was an innocent who happened to be in the wrong place at the wrong time.

Wasn't she?

If she was, he needed a plan to protect her from the Nuadians. If they learned about her, they could use her to access the Portals. They couldn't cross the water surrounding the Portal, but she could invite them in, lead them across. Her Fae blood would allow her to see the Portals as easily as she could see the Fae themselves.

He watched now as she emerged onto the back porch and moved slowly down to the lawn behind the cottage. She stretched her arms and lifted her face to the approaching dawn like some pagan goddess. Some Faerie goddess.

He needed a plan to protect the Portal from her. Even if she were an unsuspecting innocent, she was still a danger to that all-important doorway to the Realm of Faerie.

She lowered her arms, but remained where she was, barefoot in the damp grass, as if waiting for the first ray of sunlight to bathe her face. A gentle breeze molded the gauzy gown she wore to the soft curves of her body. He was unable to tear his gaze from her.

He needed a plan to protect himself.

Five

"What do you mean, you haven't been back to check?"

Flynn recoiled from the venom in the woman's voice, her unrivaled beauty spoiled momentarily by the viciousness displayed on her face.

"I'm sorry, Adira. She's not been out of the compound alone. I've had my men watching for any opportunity."

"Reynard will not be pleased with your lack of progress on this front, as I am not."

As usual, she exaggerated, giving herself the air of more influence and power than she actually wielded. Reynard didn't share power. Flynn needed only to get around her. To get directly to Reynard. But he'd bide his time until he knew for sure. No point in troubling the Great One with "maybes." That was what Adira was for.

"You should be there now. You must be prepared to take advantage of any chance to verify your suspicion, Flynn. This could be exactly the circumstance we've waited for." She turned her back on him and walked to her ornate chair at the far end of the room. Her red gown billowed out behind her and over the arm of her chair as she sat, almost as if it had a life of its own.

The foolish woman fancied herself a queen, at the very least, though her true position was no more than courtesan to their ruler, Reynard.

"My being there waits only upon this audience with you, Adira. I delayed only to provide the update you requested."

"Then consider the interview at an end. Verify the information as soon as possible and return to me immediately."

Flynn turned and left the hall, a small malicious smile on his lips. Oh, as soon as he knew for sure, he would return, no doubt about that. But not to see Adira.

Going through this power-hungry bitch was an irritation, but if he were wrong, it was much less painful than having approached Reynard with bad information.

And if he was correct? His leader would be well pleased and would reward him handsomely. The smile on his face grew.

It was only by pure accident he had even noticed the woman. That she should be out driving in that storm was odd enough, but he felt strongly she'd seen him. In fact, it had seemed as though she looked for him even after she'd gotten out of her vehicle, as if she'd felt his presence while he watched her from his hiding place in the trees.

He'd know soon enough. Somewhere along the way, there would be an opportunity, and he would be there. Ready to take advantage of it.

He could afford to be patient.

The Brotherhood of Nuada had waited a very long time for an opening like this.

Six

Wasn't letting go supposed to be the hard part? Well, she'd let go. But now she was finding the hard part was leaving it that way. Must be all those years of conditioning.

After the curious visit with her unexpected lunch guest yesterday, Sarah spent the afternoon not writing. Followed by a night of not writing. Oh, she'd tried. She'd even gotten pages down. All of which she'd deleted afterward.

Her imagination wasn't cooperating. She'd start to write about her latest hero, a larger-than-life redhead with devastating blue eyes, but the only eyes she saw when she closed her own were obsidian. The red hair kept morphing into shiny black, curling onto a neck that rose from a pair of shoulders to die for.

Just before dawn, she'd finally thrown in the towel, gone out to meet the sun and surrendered to whatever forces were vying for control of her life. She'd offered up whatever it was the Fates wanted. A blank check. She was committed to this now. She promised not to ignore the feelings. She promised to try to act on them all. She promised to trust them.

Please, please just don't make me feel that.

She didn't need a man disrupting her life again.

She'd had her coffee and her shower and taken off for a long walk. Which had brought her to this place. This crossroads. Straight would take her back toward the cottage. Left would lead to the central gardens. Right would be . . . one of the trails Ian had cautioned her to avoid.

Wouldn't you know it? Right *felt* like the way she needed to go. Like fingers tugging at her. Like she could close her eyes and still see the way.

And who would ever know? Ian was gone. His uncle, freshly returned from the hospital, was unlikely to be out and about. Even if she strayed off the McCullough estate and ran into any of the reclusive neighbors Ian had mentioned, she could simply apologize for wandering onto their land. Surely they wouldn't be as upset as Ian had hinted they might.

She had promised to act on the feelings. The Fates wanted trust?

Here you go.

She put her hands over her eyes and twirled in a circle, throwing her arms out at the last minute to stop herself from toppling over with dizziness. Keeping her eyes closed, she walked in the direction she faced, arms extended out from her sides.

"Sarah, watch out!"

The shout drew her up short. Ian? He was supposed to be gone.

She opened her eyes and found her face within less than an inch of a low-hanging tree branch.

So much for blind trust of the Fates. Maybe this trust thing took practice. Maybe she'd better keep her eyes open next time.

What the bloody hell was wrong with the woman?

He'd watched in amusement as she'd twirled about with her eyes closed, her filmy dress flowing about her body. Even when she'd started down the trail he cautioned her against, he'd still smiled, as she obviously had no idea which direction she headed, off balance as she was from the twirl, her arms out to her sides, eyes closed. Until she'd almost bludgeoned herself on the tree, that is.

"What are you thinking? Is this how you go about gathering experience for yer latest book?" Bloody storytellers. Probably writing about a blind woman or something.

"Hardly," she mumbled, the familiar blush staining her face and neck. "What are you doing here? I thought you left yesterday."

"Something came up. A change of plans." He arched an eyebrow. "Fortunately, I'm still here. And right in time to save yer pretty . . ." *Arse.* He caught himself and smiled before finishing, ". . . nose," and lightly touched his finger to the tip of that nose as he said it.

A shy grin broke across her face. "My . . . nose thanks you. And the body part that I would have landed on right after I hit my nose on that branch thanks you, too."

"Yer most welcome. Actually, I'm out here hunting for you."

"Really? Did you have a premonition you'd need to save my . . . nose?"

"I fear Henry's going to get the credit for that one. He sent me. He's anxious to meet his guest, but since he's still housebound for the next few days, he hoped you'd join us at the manor for dinner this evening. At six o'clock?"

She looked as if she might refuse.

"It would mean a lot to him."

She chewed on her lip and he knew she was considering it.

"And I promise, it's Martha's cooking this time, no any of mine."

That earned him a laugh out loud, her green eyes sparkling in the midday sun. "Okay. You've convinced me. I'll be there at six."

They turned and walked together down the path. When they reached the cottage, he opened the door for her, but blocked her entry with his arm.

"You did notice the track you were on was one I'd warned you might want to avoid, dinna you now?" Apparently his warning hadn't been strong enough before.

"I . . . hadn't really planned to go that direction." She stopped and gave her head a defiant little tilt. "What exactly was it that I needed to avoid on that path?"

"As you go deeper into the forest, it's no marked. You could easily get lost and wander off our property. It's also no cleared, so it can be dangerous. Things like low-hanging branches." He grinned.

The blush returned and he couldn't resist the temptation to tease.

"You should consider a large hat for yer walks, Miss Douglas."

She looked momentarily confused. "And why is that?"

He reached out and tapped her on the nose again. "Because you've gone all pink on yer walk today."

The pink turned an interesting shade of red as it flowed down from her cheeks to . . . He smiled again, this time wondering where the color might stop.

"Six o'clock," she said, pushing past his arm and closing the door.

She'd only brought two suitcases. How hard could it be to decide what to wear for dinner? She'd sworn she wouldn't go through the great clothing swap this time, but it didn't help. She'd even resorted to standing in the middle of the room, eyes shut, waiting for a *feeling* to direct her to the proper dinner apparel. Nothing happened.

Obviously the Fates were fickle in their guidance. She should have expected that after her earlier "Fate" experience.

Three outfits later, she knocked at the door of the manor house.

Peter answered and escorted her to the library, where her hosts for the evening sat on the sofa, heads together, deep in discussion. As Peter announced her, Ian jumped to his feet, a smile breaking over his face.

"Ah, here's our lovely guest now." He strode to the door and, placing a large hand at her back, walked her over to where Henry was seated. "This is Sarah Douglas."

"You must be Henry." Sarah hesitated only briefly

before she extended her hand. It was, after all, expected of her.

"Please forgive me for no standing. It requires a bit of a production at the moment." The older man took her hand between his own, a sincere expression of pleasure on his face.

Henry looked exactly as she had expected, right down to the white hair, rosy cheeks and twinkling eyes.

How he *felt* was another matter entirely. He emanated a positive energy, overflowing with caring and curiosity—the type of feeling she would imagine might be given off by a great healer or scientist.

She ducked her head to hide the grin she could barely contain as she joined Henry on the sofa. Thank heavens she hadn't lost her ability to laugh at herself. All this touchy-feely practice was making her downright fanciful. If she weren't careful, she'd turn into the nutcase Brad had accused her of being.

Henry retained possession of her hand, stroking the back of it as if he held a small puppy. "So, Sarah—may I call you Sarah?" At her nod he continued, "How do you like Heather Cottage?"

"It's wonderful, exactly as you assured me it would be when we spoke."

"I'm sorry I was no here to greet you when you arrived. I trust Ian has been a considerate host?"

Sarah found herself unable to look away from Henry. His gaze bore into her, making her feel as though he were attempting to see to the very depths of her, like a man searching for something.

A grunt from the chair directly across from her broke the spell.

"I'm sitting right here, Henry. It's hardly likely you'll get Sarah to confide my failings in my presence." He leaned forward, arching an eyebrow. "Perhaps you should let it go for the time."

"Perhaps. For now," Henry murmured. Releasing her hand, he sat back, all twinkles again.

A slight frown skittered across Sarah's face. Emotional undercurrents swirled about the room, strong enough for her to know they were there, but remaining just out of her reach.

"You haven't anything to worry about. Ian has been a very thoughtful host. He's gone out of his way to make my stay comfortable." She turned to Ian, pinning him with a look. "And even if you hadn't, if I had any complaints worth bothering your uncle about, your being here wouldn't make a difference. I'd complain if I felt the need." No reason to point out that she wouldn't have complained to either of them. Complaints drew attention to the complainer, and attention was something Sarah had sought to avoid her whole life.

"Dinner is served, yer lordship." Peter's announcement from the door drew their attention.

Ian stood and reached out a hand to her. "May I escort you to the dining room?"

Sarah darted a glance over at Henry, who smiled.

"You go on ahead. Peter will assist me and I'll be right along."

Sarah stopped at the entrance to the dining room, surprised by the old-world elegance. The room sparkled, candlelight reflecting off mirrors and crystal. Ian allowed her to survey the scene before tugging her forward to the table.

"Henry likes the ambiance," he whispered into her ear as he assisted her to sit.

His warm breath stirred over her ear and down her neck, leaving a little trail of electric energy in its wake. Energy she could feel sparking out all over her body. For now, she'd chalk it up to the *ambiance*.

He straightened and moved to take a seat opposite her. "Martha has worked all day to treat you to an authentic Scots meal." A mysterious little smile played over his lips. "I'm looking forward to yer review of it."

Fortunately she'd studied her travel guides and wasn't taken completely unawares. The haggis, tatties and neeps were expected and, amazingly enough, quite good. There was a moment when Martha announced "spotted dick" that had given her pause, but even that turned out to be a fairly tasty sponge cake kind of thing.

After dinner they'd adjourned to the library for snifters of brandy. The McCullough men were amazingly old-fashioned when viewed together like this. Sarah could easily imagine them standing before that same fireplace a century ago exactly as they did tonight. Of course, she would have been exiled with the women a century ago rather than invited to join them for a drink. That would have been a shame. She was rather enjoying her first taste of brandy.

Sarah nodded and sat quietly for a moment, thinking over the evening's details, when one in particular popped into her thoughts.

"Both Peter and Martha called you 'your lordship' this evening. Is that a custom associated with a Scottish clan?"

Ian chuckled. "I believe yer thinking of a Highland laird. Though I was born there and will always be a Highlander, I've few ties to the area now. And I'm no the laird of the McCullough clan."

"So why do they call you that? I thought that form of address was only used for people with titles."

Both men smiled at her now.

"That it is," Henry explained. "Ian's official title is Earl of Dunscore."

"Earl? I had no idea." She turned to look at Ian. "Why didn't you mention it earlier?"

He shrugged. "What would you have me say to you? It's no something I consider verra important, actually. The title came into the family so long ago, it's almost as if it has nothing to do with me."

"So it's a hereditary title?"

He smiled at her, as if considering his response. "Aye. It was awarded as hereditary."

Another sip of brandy warmed her throat and chest, sending residual heat to her cheeks.

"But why is it your title? I mean, if it's hereditary, wouldn't it fall to Henry as the elder McCullough?" She looked from one man to the other.

Ian shifted his position at the fireplace, but it was Henry who answered.

"Other side of the family, you might say."

Both men nodded.

The room was silent for a few moments as Henry made his way to the sofa, waving off Ian's attempt to help him.

"By the way, I understand you met our good friend and neighbor yesterday." Henry had at last managed to get himself seated again, his leg propped on a stool.

"Dallyn? Yes. He stopped by the cottage and introduced himself."

"So he just dropped right in, did he?" Ian spoke without taking his eyes from the fire.

He sounded irritated.

"No. Actually, I was the one doing the dropping and he was there to save my . . ."—she grinned at Ian who had finally turned to watch her—". . . nose. Literally. I missed the top step on the back porch and your friend Dallyn was all that stood between me and a face-first landing." She rolled her eyes. "It wouldn't have been pretty."

"Yes, well, he's ever the hero, is he no?" Ian muttered.

"I believe he dined with you?" Henry watched her closely, continuing after her nod. "I dinna think in all these years he's ever taken a meal with one of my lodgers."

"Really? Well, all I can say is that man was giving off some serious hunger signals. . . ." She stopped when Ian snorted and strode across the room to refill his glass.

"Would you care for another?" He brought the decanter with him to refill Henry's snifter. At her nod, he splashed a bit more into her glass as well.

Henry leaned toward her, and in a stage whisper confided, "It's Ian's belief that Dallyn considers himself quite dashing where the ladies are concerned, though he would not say it about his friend."

"Really? I guess I could see that." Sarah twisted in her seat to look at Ian and was surprised by the dark scowl on his face.

"You should be more careful. Just because some

strange man walks up to yer door, disna mean yer to invite him in for a meal."

"Perhaps not, but when one walks up to my door and rescues me, that should qualify for something."

Ian's scowl grew to a full glower.

Henry had once again claimed her hand, patting it. "I think what Ian's trying to say is that you need to use caution with strangers. You had no way of knowing that Dallyn was a good person."

"Yes I did. He felt good."

Whoa . . . how did that slip out? The brandy must be as strong as it was tasty.

"Aha!" Henry crowed, still holding her hand.

Ian simply stared at her, his face devoid of any emotion at all.

Well, wasn't that exactly what she had known would happen? Wasn't that how everyone reacted when they witnessed her oddities?

Henry let go of her hand and groaned as he shifted in his chair. "I fear I have to forgo much more of our extremely pleasant evening." The man was obviously in pain.

"Have you still no taken any of yer medication?" Ian tilted his head toward the older man, frowning once again.

"No. And considering the amount of brandy I've poured into my system, right on top of the wine with dinner, I dinna believe I'll be taking any tonight." Henry grinned at him like an unrepentant child.

"Then at the verra least, you need to get some rest."

"And so I shall."

Ian assisted Henry to stand and gave him the cane

he was using to get around, calling Peter to help the man upstairs.

"Oh, before I go." Henry cast a mischievous smile Ian's direction. "I think you should escort our lovely Miss Douglas on an evening constitutional. It would do both you youngsters a world of good." In response to Ian's glare he continued, "What? It's quite good for the digestion. I'd walk meself but for this." He pointed down at his knee and, donning an innocent look, leaned heavily on Peter as they made their way out of the room.

Sarah waited until she thought the man would be out of hearing range. "It's okay, Ian, you shouldn't feel you have to take me for a walk." She tried for a smile that wouldn't come as she stood up. "I should leave now anyway. It's getting late. Thanks for a lovely evening."

Ian stopped her before she reached the door, his hands on both her shoulders. She hadn't even heard him move. She made a mental note to avoid after-dinner brandies in the future.

"No, Henry's right. A walk is just what we need. The fresh air will do us both good."

He led her down the hall and outside, where he released her in order to turn and shut the front door.

She closed her eyes for a moment and took a deep breath. It felt like the first she'd had in several minutes. Somehow Ian's fingers on her shoulders had restricted her ability to breathe properly.

That was a new feeling—even for her.

They walked for a while in utter silence, Sarah trying to decide how to broach the subject. She didn't require, or even appreciate, Ian's forced companionship.

It was embarrassing. Although she accepted that Henry was trying to be a good host, she'd rather be alone than to have him force her company on his nephew. Especially now that she knew Ian was someone so important. As if an actual earl had time to waste on her.

By the time they reached the Night Garden, still having no diplomatic words prepared, she decided to make do with the plain, undiplomatic ones running through her head like little joggers.

"I'm impressed by how you go out of your way to humor your uncle, but you don't have to continue to spend time with me because he asks it of you." Her voice breaking the silence sounded overly loud to her own ears.

"I dinna do that." Ian took her hand and pulled her to sit on a bench in the corner of the garden.

"Well, it appears to me that's what you've done. Tonight's a perfect example. You were obviously unhappy with Henry's request that you walk with me, yet here you are." She pulled her hand from his. One more deep breath to keep up her courage to finish this confrontation.

"Just goes to prove that appearances can be deceiving. My irritation with Henry had nothing to do with his suggestion that we walk."

She studied her feet. He might be telling the truth. If only she had the nerve to touch him, she'd know for sure. No, she didn't need proof one way or the other. It didn't matter.

"I've spent time with you because I chose to. Because I wanted to get to know you better." He paused. "Sarah?"

When she didn't look at him, he gently took her chin

in his fingers and turned her face to him. "Sarah. It's important to me that you believe me. I'm no out here tonight because of Henry. I want to be here. With you."

She suspected it was coming. Thought she could see his intention in his eyes. The adrenaline kicked in, giving her plenty of warning to take flight, but she couldn't seem to get her muscles to cooperate with the directive from her brain.

He leaned over and kissed her. Only a light feathering of his lips across hers, yet it packed the power to send her eyes fluttering shut and her stomach plummeting to her toes and back again.

"Come on, Sarah, let's get you home, luv." He stood in front of her, his hand extended, waiting for her to take it.

When had he risen? How long had she sat there with her eyes closed?

She took the hand he offered and let him walk her to the cottage. At the door, he leaned down and touched a light kiss to her forehead.

"Friends?"

She couldn't quite make out his expression in the shadows where they stood.

"Friends," she agreed, a bit breathlessly.

She watched his back, the muscles highlighted as he moved from shadow to patches of light along the pathway to the manor house.

That kiss at the door might have felt like friends, but the one in the garden certainly hadn't.

All in all, it had been quite an evening.

Ian sat in the library, staring into the fire, the book he'd thought to finish lying untouched in his lap.

Before Sarah arrived for dinner, Henry had insisted on rehashing the details of both of Ian's encounters with Sarah's soul. The man had been fascinated. Apparently, for all his contact with souls, and in spite of the numbers he had healed, Henry had never actually seen one.

It had been a first for Ian as well, but that didn't seem to make it any less frustrating for Henry.

Ian knew the man had been trying to look beyond Sarah's barriers all evening, constantly probing and making physical contact. He hoped Henry's little outburst before he called it an evening meant he had gained the knowledge he sought. Ian would be grateful for any insight into the mystery of Sarah.

She had agreed to be friends.

Certainly that would make it easier to discover what he needed to know—if Henry hadn't already accomplished that. And it would make it much easier to keep tabs on her, protect her, if necessary.

So if being friends was going to make everything so much easier, why did the prospect feel so complicated right now?

Ian puffed out his breath, dropping his head back against the chair. The question might be complex, but the answer was really very simple.

Because in the garden tonight, she hadn't felt like a *friend*. She hadn't responded like a *friend*.

He closed his eyes and instantly pictured her as she'd been when he dragged himself away from that kiss. Her face tilted up toward him, her soft lips slightly parted, her eyes fluttering open, momentarily unfocused.

Why had he done something so foolish as to kiss her?

He could rationalize that, in that moment, she had needed to be kissed. But the truth was, when he'd gazed into her eyes, *he* had desperately needed to kiss *her.*

Because the hurt in her eyes had stung him. Because it bothered him she'd misread his reaction to Henry. He could hardly confess that his irritation was due to worry over a rebellious nephew who wouldn't follow his doctor's orders.

He had to regain his normal control, which seemed to slip in the woman's presence. He couldn't afford to get sloppy. He had responsibilities that could not be ignored. And, for now at least, she was one of them.

Tomorrow he would call Danny and decide what to do next. He'd talk to Henry and see what he could learn.

He scrubbed his face with his hands, as if to erase any doubts, any confusion.

Friends?

That would work for now. It would have to.

Seven

"She actually said she thought I *felt good?*" Dallyn grinned at the other two men.

"You needn't let it go to yer head," Ian muttered, resulting in laughter from the Fae.

"And you needn't get your knees out of joint."

"Nose, Dallyn," Ian automatically corrected. "Nose out of joint."

"Ah, yes . . . nose, nose," Dallyn repeated, as if trying to memorize a new fact.

"It's all verra logical, you see," Henry interrupted. "I think she's a Sensor." The man was beaming. He'd been excited all morning about his discovery the night before.

"You *think* she's a Sensor?" Ian reached for a piece of the toast from the rack in the center of the table.

"I'm sure she's a Sensor. I just dinna know how much she absorbs through her touch." Henry paused to refill his cup from the teapot. "I can tell you this, though. However much she's sensing, it's probably no to the full capacity of her abilities."

"What do you mean?" Dallyn leaned forward, arms on the table.

"Ian was correct about her soul no being wounded. Although I've still no seen it." He frowned and glanced at Ian. "I could feel it."

Dallyn looked to Ian in surprise. "Do I understand Henry to mean you've *seen* the woman's soul?"

Ian nodded his response.

"And what did you feel?" Dallyn turned his gaze back to Henry.

"It's been blocked for years while Sarah has apparently denied her abilities. It's that frustration and unhappiness that came across to me when I spoke to her on the telephone. I simply misdiagnosed." He shrugged his shoulders.

"So, why now, I wonder?" Dallyn sat back, steepling his fingers in front of his chin, tapping lightly. "Why has she chosen now, after so many years, to loose the flow?"

"The bigger question for our purpose is, has she decided or has someone else decided for her?" Ian dropped the half-eaten toast to his plate. It suddenly tasted like sawdust in his mouth. "That's what yer really asking, is it no?"

"We can't rule out anything."

"We can rule out any evil intent from that woman." Henry set down his cup. "I'd know if she had it. It's no there."

"Which makes her all the more dangerous. What

better tool to use against us than an innocent?" Dallyn's faraway gaze hardened as he turned to Ian. "All the more reason not to let her out of your sight."

Ian scrubbed at his face. "Verra well. We'll go with this morning's plan. But if, as you suspect, someone on the Nuadian High Council is behind all of this, I'd feel much better leaving her here where she's safe."

Dallyn stood, turning his face up to the sun before looking down at the other two men. "Oh, it's one of them, I've no doubt. Though I may not be the Sensor our little guest is, I feel a strong evil touch. Not on Sarah," he added hastily as he held up a hand. "But if they learn of her, they won't hesitate to use her. Until we know which one of them we're dealing with, she's safer with you than here alone." He turned to Henry, offering a small nod of his head. "No offense intended, my young friend."

"None taken, General."

"A Sensor." Dallyn pursed his lips thoughtfully, his hands clasped behind his back as he studied the floor. "Even in the long ago, true Sensors were rare. The Fates moved them about the Mortal Plain at their own whim, placing them where they needed to be, when they needed to be there, and drawing others to them like pieces on a game board." He looked up and smiled. "Where you find a coincidence on the Mortal Plain, you'll find a Sensor. I have a suspicion things are about to get very interesting for our little guest. Good day, my friends."

Ian watched in silence as his friend disappeared around the curve in the path. "Bloody cryptic Fae," he muttered as he stood.

He had too much to do to simply sit here. They'd

spoken with Daniel earlier. He'd been very clear. Ian must leave for Glaston House tomorrow. The others would be arriving over the next couple of days and Ian must be there to meet them.

Everything now rested on whether or not Ian could persuade Sarah to join him. Of course, he could always use a compulsion, but somehow that seemed wrong to do to Sarah.

Henry's chuckle brought him back to the present. "I'll never get used to someone who barely looks old enough to be my son referring to me as his 'young friend.' "

"You are but a youngster to him, Henry. Dallyn was already old by the time I was born."

Ian glanced back down the path the Fae had taken. The path that led past the cottage and Sarah.

He rose from his chair. Time to go see exactly how persuasive he could be with his new *friend*.

Ian watched the cottage for several minutes before approaching the door. The windows were all open. Though it was early, she was obviously awake, removing that excuse to delay his visit. He was stalling and he knew it, still not convinced this was the best plan. But, as it was the only one they had, he didn't have much choice.

Walking up the path to the entrance, he caught sight of her through the front window. She stood in the center of the room, both hands molded around a cup, staring at the ceiling.

He hesitated again at the door, which stood wide open. She still hadn't moved, oblivious to his presence.

"Sarah?" He leaned his head inside the door.

"Holy sh—" She jumped, spilling dark liquid down the front of her sweatshirt.

"I'm sorry. I dinna mean to startle you."

"Not your fault. I get totally lost sometimes." She smiled and sat the cup down on the end table. "What brings you out here so early in the morning?"

"You do." At her look of confusion, he spread his hands in a helpless gesture. "I have a big problem and I dinna know who else to ask for assistance."

Her eyes went wide. "Is Henry all right?"

"He's fine—it's no that." He looked around expectantly. "May I come in and talk to you about it?"

"Oh."

She paused for a moment and nervously tucked her hair behind her ears, a useless gesture in Ian's opinion since the curls slid right back over again.

"How rude of me. I'm sorry." She held out a hand, inviting him in. "Would you like some coffee?" She started toward the kitchen area.

"I'd no want to trouble you."

"No trouble. I have to refill mine anyway." She gestured at the front of her sweatshirt, then stopped and pulled it off over her head.

Ian's world slowed for an instant, watching her remove the soiled clothing. The little blue T-shirt she wore underneath rose up with the outer covering, exposing a small expanse of pale, flat stomach. As the blue cotton fluttered down to meet the little shorts she wore, he had to clench his hands together to keep from reaching out toward her. He couldn't remember the last time a woman had affected him so strongly in such a short period of time.

"Coffee would be good." He followed her into the kitchen area and took a seat at the table, hoping his voice didn't sound as strained as it felt right now.

She brought filled cups and sat across from him. "Now, what exactly is it I can do to help you?"

"My friend Daniel and his wife are hosting a house party and they've asked that I come down to assist them. Their estate is a bit south of Bristol." He paused to take a sip of his coffee, sneaking a quick look at Sarah to assess her reaction so far. "The guests he's invited are quite important to Daniel. He really wants to make a good impression."

She put her coffee on the table, although she still cupped both hands around it. "So, what would you like me to do? Keep an eye on Henry while you're gone?"

"No, Martha and Peter take excellent care of him." He paused to make sure he had eye contact. "What I'd like is for you to come with me."

"What?"

"I've spoken to Daniel and Nessa about bringing a guest to round out the group. I'd verra much like that guest to be you."

"Why me?"

Time to test Henry's theory about Sarah being a Sensor. He placed his hand on top of hers, leaving it there in spite of the flinch he felt. It would be much harder for her to refuse if she knew he told the truth.

"All the invited guests are bringing their wives. I dinna have one of those." He grinned. "I thought perhaps you'd agree to be my surrogate."

She paused and looked down at his hand on hers. He wondered briefly if she might pull away, but instead she took a deep breath and then looked back at him.

"You're an attractive young man, Ian."

"I'm pleased you think so," he interrupted, still grinning.

She ignored him and continued, "Because of that alone, I'm sure there are many women, all much younger than I, who would be happy to be your *surrogate*."

Her hand trembled under his.

"Perhaps. But, first of all, I'm no as young as you might think." *Not by a goodly number of years.* "More to the point, Daniel and Nessa are close friends. These people and this get-together are verra important to Daniel. I'd no embarrass him by bringing just anyone. I need someone special. I need you to come with me."

Her eyes widened and he bit back a smile of success as he released her hand. Score one for Henry's theory. She certainly appeared to have felt the honesty of his words.

"What's so important about this house party?" She clasped her hands together, moving them to her lap.

He hoped Daniel's cover story for luring their suspects to Glaston House would convince Sarah as well.

"Daniel's got it in his mind to be on the board of directors for this charity group. He's hosting a long country weekend for the men in charge of the organization. Four days on his estate getting to know him and Nessa, determining whether or no Daniel meets their standards. Some relaxing leisure time, a couple of dinners—all the things men of their station expect."

"You don't sound terribly impressed."

"Aye, well, if I'm of a mind to donate time or

money, I do, but Daniel's no the sort of chap to be satisfied with that alone. When he wants to get involved, he throws himself into it completely. Whole hog, I believe you Yanks say. His focus right now is entirely on making it onto this board and, if that's what he wants, I'll do whatever I can to help him." He gave her what he hoped was an engaging smile. "I need you to help me, so I can help him."

"Well . . ."

The little frown on her face and the hesitation in her voice told him she was wavering.

"It would be a great opportunity for you as well. Their estate is only a short distance from some of the places you mentioned you'd like to visit before you go home. Stonehenge, Glastonbury Tor, Avebury. You did say seeing them was important to you, did you no?"

He almost had her now. He bit back another smile. It would be very bad form on his part to add that, with her abilities, he wouldn't allow her within five miles of any one of those places until this current threat was over. Each of them housed their own Portals to the Realm of Faerie. Having her close to the Portal on this property where he could watch over her was bad enough.

"When would we go?"

Got her, like a trout on the hook. "We need to leave tomorrow morning. It'll take us about seven hours by auto—past some of the loveliest scenery England has to offer, I might add. Right down through the lake country. We'll return on Monday. On our way home, we could even do a quick diversion to Wales, if you like."

Her hands were back around her coffee cup, her

thumbs unconsciously tapping together. "I'd really love to see those places, and I don't know that I'll get another opportunity. If you're sure an additional guest wouldn't be a burden for your friends."

He reached out and covered her hand with his own once more. "I've spoken to them about you. I told them I hoped I'd be able to persuade you to come along. They're excited to meet you and they're looking forward to yer coming down with me."

The pause before she answered was almost unbearable. He could see the thoughts churning through her head and the turmoil they caused reflected on her face.

"Okay. I'll do it," she answered at last. Her hand still trembled under his.

"Thank you, Sarah. You canna imagine how much this means to me." He stood. "I've got some things to get ready now, but I'll be by about eight in the morning to fetch you. Is that agreeable to you?"

She looked like a frightened deer, ready to run, but she nodded and stood, sliding her hands into the pockets of her shorts.

He walked down the path to the manor house, turning once and waving since she still stood in the doorway. For now he would concentrate on what he needed to do next, on how to keep everyone safe, on how to deal with the threat.

He would *not* concentrate on how long her legs looked in those little blue shorts, on how soft they would feel. While there were many things he enjoyed about this current century, at this moment female mode of dress was quite high on his list.

Oh yes, this was shaping up to be one long weekend.

Eight

*H*ow did she get herself into these situations? Sarah glanced to her right, sneaking a quick peek at the man driving the car in which she rode. Why did she keep saying yes to Ian?

Because he asked for her help like he really needed it and no one had ever done that before. Because he was honest with her.

Brad had certainly never asked for her help. Nor had he been honest with her. And once he'd had a taste of the uncomfortable abilities she'd lived with since childhood, even the promise of her coming trust fund wasn't enough to keep him around.

Their split had been messy and painful for Sarah, but it was just as well it had happened so soon after their marriage. They'd been young then. As it was, each had moved on with their lives. Separately. The last she'd heard a few years ago, Brad had remarried, finally finding the wealthy wife he'd always wanted. For her part, she'd be happiest if she never saw the man again.

She should never have said yes to him.

And here she was, saying yes to a man all over again.

Why? Partly because it felt like she should, as if the persistent intuitive feelings that plagued her wanted her to say yes.

And, if she were completely honest with herself, she'd have to admit it was partly because she liked to see the hint of a dimple that showed up when Ian smiled. Because she wanted to spend more time with him, even though that was a really bad idea.

More time with him meant more opportunity for him to realize how different she was from everyone else. Worse yet, the more she was around him, the more she liked him. And that would make his ultimate rejection of her that much more painful.

What was she thinking? Ian was too young, too handsome, too normal to ever be interested in her as more than a friend. No, not normal, she reminded herself. The man was practically royalty. So far out of her league that her even thinking about him was sheer fantasy.

Sarah leaned her forehead against the window, watching the passing countryside to clear her thoughts.

The trip had been wonderful so far. Not having to concentrate on driving, she could devote herself to the scenery. Ian had even taken a detour, or diversion as they called it here, to show her a couple of castles, smiling mysteriously when she said she'd love to see one up close. He told her he was certain they'd get a close look at a castle before their trip was over. He also promised that on the way back they could take an extra hour or so to see Melrose Abbey, where Robert the Bruce's heart was buried.

"I think we'd best pull over for some petrol up ahead." Ian jarred her from her current musings. "Do you want anything? A fruit smash or some sweets?"

"No thanks." She'd tried one of the fruit-flavored soft drinks at lunch and found it a bit tart for her taste.

Ian pulled into the service station and grabbed his wallet from the car visor. After removing a credit card, he tossed the wallet down on the console between the seats before heading into the little shop.

Sarah watched his reflection in the side mirror. She smiled, thinking that he certainly did justice to that pair of jeans, when she noticed a couple of young women stop to admire him as he entered the store. They elbowed one another and giggled. No wonder. He was quite an eyeful, and probably about their age. One of the women looked in her direction and Sarah quickly turned her head.

Glancing down, she caught sight of his wallet and a thought suddenly crossed her mind. His license would be in there. And his birth date would likely be on that license. She looked back at the mirror. Ian was still somewhere deep in the interior of the little shop, nowhere near the windows or the front counter.

It wasn't hers. Going through it would be snooping. She didn't snoop. Besides, she had no doubt that she could ask him his age and he'd tell her. And then he'd ask her age.

Another glance at the mirror and then down. The wallet, lying open no more than four inches from her hand, seemed to call out to her. Her fingers twitched, and then eased closer, almost of their own accord. Her eyes darted back to the mirror. Still no sign of him.

Her fingers brushed the wallet. The black leather was soft and warm from lying in the sun. Another check of the mirror. He was at the register, smiling at the girl who was ringing up his purchase.

Now or never.

Sarah turned the wallet around and stared at a small replica of Ian's handsome face, feeling as if his eyes in the picture chastised her. Guilt washed over her and she turned the billfold back around as it had been. But not before checking the date. Barely twenty-eight. Ten years younger.

You knew as much.

She glanced back at the mirror as he exited the shop. One of the two young women who'd watched him, the tall redhead, approached him now, placing a hand on his arm as she spoke to him. He smiled at her as he listened, gifting her with his full attention.

Sarah snapped her eyes away from the mirror. Of course a man who looked like that was going to attract the attention of other women. What else could she expect? Besides, they were simply friends. It didn't matter in the least if he stopped to chat with that redhead. It meant nothing to her.

She drummed her fingernails on the door handle. Enough. She needed chocolate. Now.

She climbed out of the car and headed toward the shop, raising her head in time to catch Ian's quizzical look as she passed him.

"Changed my mind," she mumbled, unwilling to stop and face the irritated gaze of the redhead whose hand still rested on Ian's arm.

The "Sweets" counter held a wealth of unknown candy bars, but there were some familiar names. Sarah reached for a chocolate bar, barely restraining herself from tearing it open then and there. A bottled water would be just the thing to wash the candy down nicely.

She started for the coolers visible at the back of the store when something caught her eye. A rack of paperbacks, and, in the middle of them, a familiar cover.

"Oh my God." She picked it up, running her hand over the face of the book. It was one thing to know your book was going to be released in another country. It was an entirely different matter to see it sitting on a shelf.

"I take it S. J. Douglas is you?"

She jumped at the sound of Ian's voice so close to her ear, the book and her candy bar both hitting the floor.

"I thought you were outside already." She placed a hand over her pounding heart. How had he managed to sneak up on her so quietly?

He straightened after retrieving her things from the floor, amusement clear on his face. Sarah snatched the chocolate from his hands and stalked to the cashier. She noticed on her way to the car that the redhead and her friend had disappeared. Ian joined her a short time later, and they pulled back onto the motorway.

After several minutes of silence, he cleared his throat in what sounded like a mixture of cough and chuckle. She glanced over. If he was laughing at her, she might have to seriously hurt the man. His eyes were straight ahead, not a sign of a smile to be found.

Sarah released a deep breath and relaxed back against the leather seat.

"That's why I dinna recognize it, you see," he said softly. "I believe they're called romantic novels here, no women's literature."

She sneaked a sideways glance at him. His eyes were still on the road, but there was no mistaking the grin that covered his face.

Lifting a hand to her cheek, Sarah wondered at exactly what temperature spontaneous combustion actually occurred. Whatever it was, she had to be close to it right now.

Her skin was finally returning to a normal color.

He should have resisted the temptation to tease, but he found it had become rather enjoyable. Why she'd be embarrassed by what she wrote was beyond him, but he'd pursue that at another time. They'd be at Glaston House shortly.

"So this organization that your friend's so anxious to become part of—what kind of charity work do they do?"

He fought the urge to grin again. She was trying so hard to recover.

"Feed people, mostly. EHN is . . ."

"End Hunger Now," she interrupted. "*That's* the board he wants to be on? Good grief. Those people are some pretty heavy hitters."

"And Daniel wants to be in there hitting right alongside them."

From the look on her face he assumed she was only now realizing what she might be in for this weekend.

"How many people are going to be there?"

"Three of the corporate executives, along with their wives, have been invited for the weekend. As far as I know, they've all accepted. And us, of course. And some of the local gentry will be joining us for a fund-raising dinner." He grinned. "Danny likes to pull out the lords and ladies to impress his visiting Yanks."

"How did your friend convince people like that to come spend four days with him?"

He shrugged. "Money. Lots of it. If the donation's big enough, you can entice almost anyone. Meeting with these men is necessary for Danny to accomplish what he wants."

That, at least, was true. It was the only way to determine which of them wasn't exactly what he appeared to be. Someone at EHN was channeling funds to terrorists. Based on the information passed to Daniel by British intelligence, it had to be one of the men he'd invited here this weekend. Based on what Ian had been told by Dallyn, the one they sought was also a Nuadian.

"And why are we here?"

"Well, I'm here for local color and moral support, one of the lords Danny likes to parade about to impress the visiting Yanks." And to locate their problem and solve it.

"And I'm here for . . ." She left the question dangling while she stared at him.

He gave her his best smile. "The most important thing of all. Yer here for my moral support." *Close to me. Where I can keep an eye on you.* He pointed up ahead. "Glaston House awaits, milady."

She followed the movement of his hand. Her eyes widened and her mouth formed a perfect little circle as she sucked in her breath. He brought the car to a complete stop at the gates, leaning out to punch a button on the black security box.

"Ian McCullough and guest."

The gates slowly opened and he drove through, stopping again just inside so he could enjoy watching her reaction to the sight in front of them.

"This is where your friend lives?"

"Impressive, is it no?" Although called Glaston House, it was actually a fully renovated castle. "I told you we'd see at least one castle up close. We'll be spending the next four days at one."

Putting the car in gear, Ian drove them forward across an ornate bridge. It spanned a slow-moving stream that circled the perimeter of the property, snaking into the surrounding woods. Once beyond the trees, the castle sat in the center of an enormous green rolling lawn, flanked by some of the most intricate gardens in this part of England. Nessa was quite proud of her green thumb.

Ian pulled the car to a stop at the edge of the drive, got out and walked around the vehicle to open Sarah's door. After assisting her out, he hadn't taken three steps before a small screaming body slammed into him, attaching itself to his leg.

"Up, Uncle Ian, up!" The little boy threw his arms around Ian's neck as soon as he was lifted high enough.

"Wills, lad, you've grown like a weed." He gave the boy a tight hug before setting him on the ground. He pointed at Sarah. "This is my special friend, Miss Sarah Douglas. Can you help me make her feel welcome here?" He ruffled his hand through the boy's fair hair.

Huge blue eyes studied Sarah intently before the child walked over to her and extended his hand. "My name is William Daniel Martin Stroud." He grinned at her. "You're Ian's friend, so you can call me Will."

"I'm pleased to meet you, Will." Sarah took his little hand into her own. Her eyes widened and a small gasp escaped, so quiet it might have gone almost unnoticed.

Except that Ian noticed.

Will looked back at him. "Ooooo, Uncle Ian. I like her."

Ian grinned at the little boy. "As do I, lad." He walked over and put an arm around Sarah's shoulders as the child's parents arrived.

He'd warned Daniel about Sarah's discomfort with touching people. He watched his friend reach out and take his wife's hand as they approached. Danny had always been good at remembering the important details.

"You're here at last." Daniel smiled at them both.

"These are my friends, Daniel and Nessa Stroud." Ian tightened his arm around Sarah and looked down at her. "And this is Sarah."

"Welcome to Glaston House. We're so pleased to have you here. Ian's told us so much about you." Nessa smiled at her and then at the little boy still holding Sarah's hand. "I see you've already met Will."

"Yes, I have, thank you. I appreciate your invitation." Sarah smiled in return, but her gaze kept slipping to the child staring adoringly up at her.

"Are we the first?"

Danny nodded in reply to Ian's question. "Although a couple of the officers along with their wives should have landed by now. Anderson is picking them up, so they'll be here in an hour or so, depending on traffic. The others will be coming in throughout the day tomorrow."

"I'm sorry to be such a rotten hostess, but I need to get back to the kitchen." Nessa smiled apologetically, shaking her head. "Our cook is new and I want to make sure everything is on schedule for this evening's reception. Ian, you're in the Caretaker's Cottage, as usual. I take it you can see to getting Sarah settled in?"

Ian winked and flashed a thumbs-up signal. Nessa started back to the house, turning only to call her son to come with her.

Will reluctantly let go of Sarah and ran to his mother, taking her hand and laughing at some quiet remark from her as they crossed the drive.

"Your son is adorable. How old is he?" Sarah watched the two of them climb the stairs to the castle.

"Turned six last month," Daniel answered, pride evident in his voice.

"I'm surprised Will's here. I'd thought he might be with Nessa's parents." Ian didn't like the idea of exposing the boy to this. He'd feel much safer having the child away from here this weekend.

"They aren't back from holiday yet." Daniel rubbed a hand over the back of his neck. "Believe me, Ian, that would have been my preference, but we have a nanny in, one from the . . . uh . . . agency that we've used before."

"Good." With someone in to protect Will, one worry was lessened.

Sarah was still tucked under his arm, quietly observing the discussion.

Ian smiled down at her. "We need to get you settled in so Nessa disna lose all faith in my ability to be useful."

He walked her back to the car. They'd drive around to the cottage to unload their bags.

What he really needed right now was to spend some time alone with Daniel. They had a multitude of details to go over before these people began arriving.

Not the least of which concerned the car that had followed his all the way from Scotland.

Nine

*I*t was a rare thing indeed when fate was so cooperative.

Flynn smiled and shook his head. Parked a discreet distance across the road, he watched through the barred gates as the small group of people gathered at the end of the driveway.

Just this morning he'd been cursing his luck, convinced he risked losing a special opportunity to have his talents recognized . . . and properly rewarded. He'd been so concerned about having to be here, about not being able to continue his surveillance of the woman.

But one did not refuse a task assigned by Reynard himself. At the very least, a personal assignment allowed him direct access. No more working through Adira.

Then fate stepped in.

Not only was the woman off the protected grounds, now she was well within his reach. It was almost as if the Guardian had delivered her to him.

Did the Guardian have any idea what she might be?

But no, he was getting ahead of himself.

It was only important that he discover whether or not his suspicions were accurate. He'd nearly had the opportunity to find out earlier today when they'd stopped. Crystal had done her best to distract the Guardian, to give Flynn time to get near the woman. But before he could reach her, the woman had suddenly gotten out of the car and gone inside the shop, and the Guardian had followed closely behind.

Perhaps he did suspect. Or perhaps he knew.

Flynn's pulse quickened. It was a good sign. No matter. Flynn would know for certain soon enough. He only needed to see if she recognized him. Or if she could see him in his own form.

And if she does?

Well, then it would be time to call Reynard and update him personally.

Flynn rubbed his hands together before putting the car in gear and pulling back on the road. Success was so near he felt as though he could almost reach out and touch it. He cast one last glance over his shoulder as he drove away. The Guardian had taken a protective stance, his arm around the woman.

Now there was something Flynn hadn't considered.

A look of irritation flashed across his face. He prided himself on being incredibly thorough. It was a trait that served him well, making his services especially valuable to Reynard. Yet he'd overlooked this possibility entirely.

Could it be that the Guardian hovered about the woman for personal reasons?

Flynn threw back his head and laughed. This day continued to get better and better. It had been a long time since he'd had the opportunity to challenge one of the Guardians over anything important.

He pulled out his cell phone and flipped it open. No need to wait now. Either way, Reynard was going to love this.

Ten

Sarah hung up the last of the clothing she'd brought with her and sighed before shutting the door to the little closet Ian had pointed out before he left. She had the feeling her wardrobe was nowhere near what it needed to be for a weekend with people like the ones he had described.

And clothing was the least of her worries.

EHN. The name nagged at her. Of course it was familiar; everyone knew about their charity efforts all around the world. But those initials meant more to her. As she recalled, the woman Brad had married was associated with the organization somehow. She wished now she had paid more attention to the article she had read announcing their engagement.

Still, Ian had said that the representatives who were coming were all men. "Corporate executives and their wives" had been invited, according to him.

She took an unsteady breath, determined to calm herself. It was silly to worry needlessly.

Even though she'd already changed, she still had almost an hour before dinner. Daniel told her it would be a garden reception, so she'd opted for dress pants and a sweater. Catching her reflection in the mirror as she walked toward the door, she shrugged. It might not be dressy enough, but at least she'd be warm if the evenings here were as cool as they'd been farther to the north in Scotland.

She opened the door and went downstairs to the main room. Her shoulder bag, housing her ever-present laptop, sat on the sofa where she'd left it when they first entered. She moved it to a small desk by the front door, stopping to look around.

Muted pastel tones blended in the cottage, giving it a comfortable feel. The central room included a small kitchenette area, which Sarah decided to investigate now. A tiny refrigerator held ice cubes, soft drinks and a bottle of wine. A small microwave and a sink filled the remainder of the narrow space, and an electric water kettle perched on the counter that ran the length of the little kitchen.

Sarah turned to examine the rest of the room. The wall opposite the front door was almost completely swallowed up by a large stone fireplace flanked on either side by glass doors. The doors exited out to an enclosed garden area with a small patio table and chairs. An enormous pillow-strewn leather sofa faced the fireplace.

The wall opposite the kitchen was covered in a floor-to-ceiling bookcase broken by two doors, one of which led upstairs to her bedroom. She supposed the other must lead to Ian's room, although his luggage sat inside the front door.

She picked up his suitcase, surprised at how light it was in comparison to her own, intending to put it in his room.

Only to find it wasn't a bedroom at all.

"Wow." Letting go of the suitcase, Sarah nodded in appreciation. This had to be the best bathroom she'd ever seen, even taking into account television commercials and magazine ads. Shiny black marble covered the floor and walls, highlighted by one wall of mirrors and accented with towels and candles in a rich red. She walked to the tub and ran her hand over the edge. It looked like a swimming pool in comparison to her tub back home. She could imagine how the room would shimmer with all the candles lit, bouncing light off the mirrors.

"Welcome to *Lifestyles of the Rich and Famous*," she muttered.

She left the room, taking the suitcase back to the front door. Hands on her hips, she looked around to see if she'd missed something. Maybe this wasn't the Caretaker's Cottage where Nessa had indicated Ian would stay. Maybe Ian had simply dropped off his luggage here.

Remembering an unexplored door in her bedroom, she turned and went back upstairs. There were three doors. The first was to the small closet where she'd put her things.

The next opened into a bathroom she'd discovered earlier, quite modest by the standards of the one downstairs. She backed out. The last door opened into another closet, much larger than the one she'd used, with clothing already hanging.

Men's clothing. No wonder Ian's bag was so light.

It appeared he had a full wardrobe of clothing here. There were even shoes lined neatly on a rack toward the rear of the closet.

It would seem that she had found Ian's room.

She had a flashback to meeting her hosts and remembered Nessa's remarking that Ian had told them so much about her. Now she wondered exactly *what* he'd told them. It was a question she fully intended to have answered.

"Sarah?" Ian's voice echoed up from downstairs.

Talk about timing.

Narrowing her eyes, she turned to the stairs. This would be as good a time as any to ask him.

Reaching the bottom, she found Ian carrying a grinning Will.

"Look who I found sitting outside our door."

As soon as he swung the child to the floor, Will ran to her, throwing his arms around her legs and hugging tightly. She thought of her first meeting with the boy and how she'd been flooded with wave after powerful wave of joy flowing from him. It was almost enough to make her miss Ian's reference to *our* door.

Almost.

"Hello, Will. Come to visit?"

The boy nodded but glanced sheepishly at Ian.

"Escaped to visit is more like it, eh, Wills?" He scooped up his bag and started upstairs, turning at the last minute. "I'm no sure where his nanny has gotten to, but we'll deal with that when we get to the main house. Do you mind entertaining our wee guest while I get ready?"

She shook her head. "No problem."

He arched an eyebrow and gave her a slow smile. "You look lovely. I'll be down in a bit." With that he turned and took the stairs two at a time.

"Come on, Sarah." Will tugged at her sleeve. "Bunches of butterflies live in this garden. I want to show you."

She smiled and allowed the child to pull her outside as she heard the shower turn on upstairs.

Apparently her question would have to wait until later.

"Are we ready?"

Sarah jumped at the sound of Ian's voice.

After shutting the patio door behind him, he joined her and Will. The three of them set out for the main house, the little boy holding Ian's hand.

Sarah studied Ian from under her lashes. As usual, he looked like he'd stepped off a magazine page, right down to the damp ends of his hair curling at his neck against the silky material of his ivory sweater.

She quickly looked away when he turned his head to speak to Will.

"What happened to yer new nanny?"

"I wanted to visit Sarah." The boy didn't meet his gaze.

"And?"

"I asked for Hide and Seek." Will's face lit with a mischievous humor. "When Nanny covered her eyes, I left." He shrugged his little shoulders.

"You know, with all the strange grown-ups here this weekend, I'm thinking it would be much better for you to stay close to Nanny."

The little boy nodded. "But I wanted to see Sarah.

I like her. You said I should help make her feel welcome," he reminded.

Ian's eyes sought out Sarah's over the top of the child's head. He appeared to be holding back a grin. She could understand why. This was one determined six-year-old.

"Wills, how about if I promise to bring Sarah up to yer room to say good night, and I make sure you get to visit with her each day we're here. Will you stay with Nanny then?"

The boy looked up at Sarah, catching her hand with his free one. "You'll do that? Come to see me each day?"

"Of course I will. I'd like that very much."

Will's smile at her response was accompanied by a pulse of emotion so strong Sarah thought for a second her knees might buckle. She had never experienced such amplified emotions from any other person as she received each time she touched this boy.

The child tightened his grip on her hand, calmly watching her with big eyes. "And you'll come to say good-bye before you leave?" Ian stopped, giving the child his full attention. "We promise."

"Okay, Uncle Ian. It's a deal."

They had reached the garden and soon heard voices. Daniel and a young woman appeared around the first bend in the mazelike path.

"Look, Nancy, you only have one thing to do for the next few days. Is it too much to ask that you do it? He's only six. With your training, I'd think you could maintain surveillance on one small six-year-old." Daniel ran his hand through his hair, which was already quite disheveled, as if his hand had followed the same path many times in the last few minutes.

"Daddy!" Will ran to his father, who bent to pick him up, hugging him close.

"Wills came out to the cottage for a visit." Ian exchanged a look with Daniel as his friend handed the child over to the nanny. "But he's promised no to do it again without his nanny. Isna that right?"

"Absolutely." Will grinned at all of them. "You'll remember to come say good night?"

"Absolutely," Ian echoed back as the boy and his nanny turned toward the house.

Ian dropped back beside Daniel on the narrow path, leaving Sarah to walk alone in front of them. She could hear them talking quietly behind her. Even when it sounded as though the men had halted, the buzz of their whispered conversation becoming too indistinct to follow, she continued forward, drawn by the sound of laughter ahead.

Coming to the end of the path, Sarah moved onto the terrace before she stopped to survey the scene in the garden courtyard. It was beautifully set up, delicate chairs in groups of twos and threes around a small central pond. Large iron stands held multiple candles, which, along with strings of lights, shed a subtle illumination over the gathering. Soft music floated through the night air, delivered by unseen speakers.

Nessa stood at a food-laden table on the opposite side, speaking to two women. Sarah suffered a small twinge of embarrassment when she saw the other women wearing dresses, but pushed it down in favor of practicality as she realized the temperatures were already dropping.

To her left, at the far end of the pond a bar had been set up, complete with a smiling bartender. In front of it stood two men whose backs were to her, their heads lowered, deeply involved in a discussion. They turned, drinks in hand, and one of them raised his head, glancing her direction.

She froze, unable to look away, recognition jolting through her.

His eyes widened in surprise and then narrowed as he sauntered her direction.

"Oh, shit," she breathed, feeling her stomach drop. Her worst fear had come to pass. Her ex-husband was here.

Ian scanned the group from the edge of the courtyard. He listened to Daniel's initial assessment of the men who had arrived—the men whose files they had discussed in detail earlier today. But his friend's words faded into background noise as he watched Sarah standing several meters in front of him.

The rounded neckline of the cream-colored sweater she wore exposed just enough skin to emphasize how soft and feminine she looked. Very touchable. Especially with her loose curls brushing right above her shoulders. Like spun gold. His fingers flexed as he thought of running them through that hair.

Stay focused.

She distracted him and that was dangerous. For all of them. He couldn't afford to let that happen.

Centering himself, he was immediately aware of a difference in her. The unnatural rigidity of her stance telegraphed her tension across the distance.

He wondered that the entire group didn't see it, but no one else seemed to notice. He tracked the direction of her gaze. The man she watched smiled as he approached her, but there was nothing friendly in his expression. He reminded Ian of a fox stalking its prey—not particularly large, but quite fearsome for its sly behavior.

Ian studied him. He was a fit-enough-looking man, probably in his mid- to late-forties, with light brown hair. He exuded the type of confidence that comes from years of controlling other people.

Ian held up a finger to stop Daniel's running commentary. "Who's that? The one headed toward Sarah."

"Bradley Tanner. He's the one I was telling you about." Daniel frowned. "Why? What is it?"

"I'm no sure."

Lowering his head, Ian blocked out his surroundings and concentrated. The distance was no challenge for someone with his abilities. Enhanced hearing was only one of the gifts of his Fae blood. Once he blocked out all other distractions, he could hear their conversation clearly.

"Well, well, well. If it isn't the Ice Queen herself."

Ian jerked his head up in time to see Sarah's face color and her arms tighten around her middle in the self-protective gesture he'd come to associate with her.

"Brad." Her tone was tight and clipped.

"I must say, I'm surprised to see you here. Are you with someone?" He took a drink from the glass he held, his smile turning malicious. "Hard to believe anyone here would want something like you to warm his bed."

"I can see you haven't changed at all." Sarah glared at the man.

"Why should I? I wasn't the nutcase. You were. So, have you found yourself some ancient Brit who'll put up with your crazy nonsense?"

A wave of resentment washed over Ian and he started forward. A waiter passed and he snagged two glasses of champagne off the tray. Whoever the bloody bastard was, he wasn't going to get away with speaking to Sarah like that. It might not be fashionable to challenge the bugger to a duel in this day and age, but there were other ways to handle him.

"I take it that's a no? As I recall, you weren't comfortable with people, didn't want them touching you." He took another drink and then sneered. "Oh wait. I remember now. It's only *men* you're no good with."

"Really?" Ian interrupted. Catching Tanner's eye, Ian flashed a humorless smile as he joined them. "And here I was thinking she was quite good."

He moved close behind Sarah, ignoring her flinch when he pulled her back against his chest. A shiver passed through her as he carefully wrapped his arms around her, both glasses held out in front of them.

"Sorry I'm late, luv." He leaned down to kiss her neck, just below her ear, nuzzling for perhaps a moment longer than necessary. Never taking his eyes from the other man's, he inhaled deeply, enjoying the feel and the scent of her. "I stopped to get yer champagne. Who's yer . . . friend?" He continued to stare at the man as she accepted the glass with a trembling hand.

Before she could answer, the man extended his hand. "Brad Tanner, chief financial officer for EHN International."

Ian met it with his own. "Ian McCullough."

"*Lord* Ian McCullough," Daniel interrupted. "Earl of Dunscore."

Focused on the man in front of him, Ian hadn't even noticed his friend join them. He smiled as Tanner's eyebrows rose. Titles occasionally served their purpose. Especially with men like this one.

"And how exactly do you know *my* Sarah?" He emphasized the word, watching as the other man's jaw muscle twitched. Sarah stiffened in his embrace just before Tanner answered.

"Because she used to be *my* Sarah. We were married. Briefly." His smile didn't reach his eyes.

"Not briefly enough," she muttered.

Ian tightened his arm around her, allowing his fingers to caress her shoulder. Better that than allowing his fingers to squeeze the man's neck, which is what he'd prefer to do right now. Ladies were not meant to be treated so thoughtlessly, particularly not in public.

"Well." He shrugged carelessly, though it took effort. "We all make mistakes."

He'd made one, for instance. He'd judged Sarah to be naïve, unsure of men based on lack of experience. It appeared he'd been wrong. She was unsure of men based on *bad* experience. Now that he'd met the man she'd been married to, it made perfect sense. If she'd ever had any self-confidence, this idiot had done his best to destroy it.

The pain and embarrassment he'd seen in her eyes the one time she'd looked up ate at him still. He slid his hand from her shoulder up to her bare neck, tightening his grip so she couldn't pull away, using his thumb to stroke small gentle circles under her ear-lobe. The exact spot where he'd kissed her.

Finishing his champagne, he concentrated on serenity, on how much pleasure he found in touching her. He allowed it to fill his mind, ignoring the conversation around him. Henry had judged her to be a Sensor, and Henry was rarely mistaken. If that were the case, the emotions would flow through his fingers into the very core of her. He knew the instant she felt it. The trembling stopped and she relaxed against him, her head tilting away, allowing his thumb greater access. He doubted she even realized she'd moved. But he was acutely aware of it.

As was Brad Tanner, if his stony expression was any indication.

The second man had joined them, Daniel introducing him as Paul Stephenson, chief operating officer for EHN. Ian shook his hand, but didn't relinquish his hold on Sarah. The man was older, with gentle eyes. Ian was almost willing to bet this man wasn't connected in any way to what they were looking for.

But Tanner? Ian would enjoy his being involved.

"So, McCullough, what kind of work do you do?" Tanner's eyes flicked from Ian's face to his hand on Sarah's neck and back again.

"My properties take up most of my time. At least the time I'm willing to devote to work." Tanner seemed like a man easily influenced by wealth and title. Ian was willing to use that.

"My wife, Marlena, is over there." Pointing at the appetizer table, Stephenson spoke quietly to Sarah. "Would you like me to take you over and introduce you?"

"No," Ian answered for her. "Thanks, but I'll do that. We've neither of us had anything to eat since morning, so that looks like the spot for us. If you'll excuse us, gentlemen?"

The grateful smile Sarah gave him as he steered her across the courtyard disappeared when they saw the men following a short time later.

Nessa had already started introductions, beginning with Marlena Stephenson, a tall matronly woman with a ready smile. She turned toward her other guest, a statuesque young woman with long blond hair and pouty red lips.

"And this—"

"This," Brad interrupted, putting his arm around the younger woman as he arrived at the table, "is my wife, Nicole." He smirked as he brought his gaze up from his wife to look at Sarah. "Isn't she lovely?"

"Oh, Bradley . . . stop it," Nicole giggled. "Call me Nicki. Everyone does." She turned and batted large brown eyes in Ian's direction, placing a hand on his shoulder. "Nessa here tells us you're an honest-to-God duke."

"Earl, actually," Ian corrected, pleased at the irritation that flashed across Tanner's face. He decided that Sarah must have noticed it as well since she discreetly smothered her chuckle in a cough.

"Daddy will really get a kick out of that." Nicki smiled at the group, allowing her hand to drop to her side. Exchanging her empty champagne glass for a full one as the waiter passed by, she favored the whole group with another of her blinding smiles.

"Daddy?" Ian turned a questioning look toward the woman's husband.

"Alexander Storey," Brad filled in. "Nicole's father is the founder and CEO of EHN. He and Mr. O'Dannan arrive tomorrow."

"Mr. O'Dannan?" Ian had begun to feel a bit like a parrot, but he had his own part to play. After all, as a social guest of Daniel's, he wouldn't have any reason to know who these people were, even though Daniel had briefed him on all of them when he'd first arrived. All except this O'Dannan.

"Personal executive assistant to the chairman of the board. I've only just heard from him this past hour," Daniel added. "If all goes well, Mr. Servans, the chairman himself, might even join us for our big dinner event." He smiled at everyone gathered and lifted his glass in a toast, playing his role to the hilt. "Even on such short notice, several willing donors have already agreed to attend. And I've offered to up my own donation if the chairman joins us."

"Money's about the only thing that'd bring that man out," Marlena muttered under her breath, and her husband frowned in her direction. She shrugged and turned away from the group, refilling her plate from the selection at the table.

Ian held back his smile, thankful for his superior hearing.

"We're so excited about your little weekend, aren't we, Bradley?" Nicole gushed. "When I heard we were going to be spending four days partying with real royalty here, I simply agonized over which designer to wear." She handed her empty glass to her husband. "Bradley, honey, could you find me another one of those?" She turned back to the others as her husband headed to the bar. "But then I figured it really wouldn't matter 'cause none of y'all shop in Dallas like I do, so I'm bound to be wearin' somethin' different from what all of y'all are."

Airhead. Wasn't that the term he'd seen used on Henry's telly? This particular version of airhead couldn't be over twenty-five if she was a day. He studied Brad as the man brought back his wife's drink and handed it to her, a smug look on his face.

The topic of conversation had changed to the availability of challenging golf courses in the area, with the women discussing shopping in the nearby towns. Sarah remained quiet, his arm still around her shoulders.

"Ian, what say we take these two over to Mendip for a round of golf first thing tomorrow? We can be back before the ladies are even up." Daniel grinned at him, knowing how much he hated the game.

"Of course. Ring me up at the cottage in the morning." It would be a good opportunity to see what they could learn about the rest of the board of EHN from their guests.

Ian felt Sarah rise on her toes and lean into him. He tilted his head down to her.

"When does Will go to bed? We did promise to say good night," she whispered, her breath flowing warmly over his ear and down his neck.

He could have simply responded, but he caught Brad watching them and chose instead to pull her close. Answering into her opposite ear gave the impression he was embracing her and, in fact, gave him the opportunity to do exactly that. An opportunity he found himself more than willing to seize.

"We'll go now," he whispered back.

He wasn't sure if he was more pleased with the way she shivered in his embrace or by the expression of irritation that passed over Brad's face.

He looked up and smiled at the group. "Sorry to leave such good company, but Sarah and I need to call it a day. We're both tired from our long drive down."

"Oh, but it's still early," Nicki protested.

"I'm sure that, unlike you, my dear, Sarah needs her sleep." Brad squeezed his wife's shoulder, a victorious half smile on his lips.

"It's no *sleep* she's leaving for," Ian murmured just loud enough for Brad's benefit. He grinned as they walked away. It felt good to see the smile wiped right off that smug face.

Will had been waiting for them when they'd reached his room, determined not to fall asleep until they arrived, as if he feared they might not come. By the time they'd tucked him in and given him good-night kisses, his little eyes had closed and his breathing was slow and even. Sarah had never seen anyone go to sleep so fast.

She took a deep breath as they walked slowly across the plush carpet of lawn, Ian holding tightly to her hand. Her mind swirled with the tumult of emotions she felt. She should pull away, but the contact gave her comfort and she wasn't willing to give that up just yet. It had been an unsettling evening. Unsettling? It had been horrendous. Seeing Brad, hearing him again had opened old wounds she'd thought long closed. All the humiliation she'd felt so many years ago flooded back.

Only Ian's presence had saved her tonight. He had

been there for her through the whole of it, smoothing her path. Sooner or later she would need to deal with what had happened, answer the questions that would surely come.

"I'm sorry for all that . . . scene tonight, Ian. I know it must have been uncomfortable for you."

She attempted to pull her hand away, but he held on to it, using it to pull her closer to him. Tucking her under his arm, he stopped and looked down at her.

"I dinna feel at all uncomfortable." There it was, that devastating smile again. The one that made her breath catch in her throat. "In fact, I rather enjoyed myself."

"Enjoyed yourself?" She shuddered. "Well, I want you to know that I appreciate your stepping in like that." They were walking again, his arm still around her. "I was so shocked to see Brad here, I couldn't think at first. I had heard that his wife was somehow connected with EHN, but I had no idea he worked for them, let alone was one of their executives. Had I known, I wouldn't have come."

"Then it's my good fortune you dinna know. I'm grateful to have you with me, regardless of what happened back there. That's no yer fault."

"Still, you pretty much saved me from making a complete fool of myself."

Ian chuckled, tightening his arm in a little hug. "It took no great effort on my part. But you do realize the consequences of what we've done, do you no?" He looked down at her again, his hand moving from her shoulder to her neck.

"Consequences?" Did that come out as a squeak?

"Everyone assumes we're a couple now."

"Oh."

"So I'm afraid we'll have to continue our little pretense."

"Oh."

He'd done it again. Robbed her of her ability to make conversation that consisted of more than one syllable. Must have something to do with his thumb moving in that little circle under her ear as it was now. As it had earlier. Relaxing her. Calming her.

The cottage was directly ahead. Hadn't she wanted to ask him something about the cottage this afternoon?

Wait a minute.

"Is this the Caretaker's Cottage?"

"Aye. That's what it was used for long ago, so they continue to call it by that name."

"But there's only one bedroom," she blurted out, turning to look at him.

"Aye." An enormous grin covered his face. "You noticed that, did you?"

"Should I assume your friends already thought we were a couple?"

He shrugged, sliding his hand down to her shoulder. "It appears as though they did. I'd planned to ask Nessa about a change of rooms at the reception, but I got a wee bit distracted. I'm afraid we'll have to leave things as they are now."

"How could they have made a mistake like that? I thought you said you'd told them about me."

He ducked his head in a sheepish gesture. "I did tell them about you, but I guess they jumped to their own conclusions." His hand slid back to her neck.

"You see, Sarah, in all the years I've been coming to stay at Glaston House, I've never brought a woman with me before."

They'd reached the cottage, but instead of going inside, Ian pulled her to sit next to him on the bench outside the front door.

"It's a fine evening. Much too fine to go inside yet. What say we stay out for a bit and enjoy the stars."

Leaning his head back against the wall of the cottage, he closed his eyes and they sat silently for several minutes. She had begun to wonder if he might have fallen asleep when he moved his arm to her shoulders, his fingers lightly caressing her neck.

"How long were you married to him?"

Finally the question she had expected. "Officially, about a year. But in reality, it was only a few months. I think we both knew right away we'd made a mistake."

"A mistake?"

"Yes. I was young, and we rushed into marriage without taking the time to really know one another. It was all such a very long time ago." She closed her eyes and shook her head, trying to ward off the memories. She'd never spoken of this with anyone. That had been a horrible time for her.

Brad had no patience for what he considered her psychotic behavior. No concept of her actually being able to feel his emotions each time she touched him. When she'd tried to explain, he'd thought her insane. And once he found out how long he'd have to wait to have access to her trust fund, he was done with her. Even after all these years, with only a little effort, she could still recall exactly how his contempt and greed had felt the first time she'd touched it.

"How old were you when you married?"

Her eyes flew open. She hated the whole age discussion, but she had been the one who opened the door to it when she allowed herself to talk about that part of her life. She sighed in resignation. It would have come up sooner or later anyway. "We married the year I turned twenty-one."

Ian snorted. "Disna seem to me that was so long ago."

Of course he'd think that. He was only twenty-eight. It seemed a lifetime ago to her.

"I should never have married him. My grandmother tried to convince me I was making a horrible mistake."

"Then why did you do it?"

She took a deep breath. It had taken her years of soul searching to figure out the answer to that question. And even longer to admit to it.

"I thought myself in love. I thought Brad would save me from . . ." She stopped herself. She couldn't tell him the whole truth. Couldn't tell him she had yearned for someone who would understand and accept her for what she was. Someone who would shield her from the emotions of others. "From growing old alone."

"And how is it yer grandmother was the one to try to change yer decision to marry?"

"My mother and I lived with her. Then, after my mother's death, it was just the two of us."

"How old were you when you when yer mother passed?"

"Six."

"And yer father? Why dinna you go to live with him?"

"My parents split up shortly after my birth. I didn't know my father at all. He came to see me once after my mother's death, on my seventh birthday. I remember being surprised that he even knew it was my birthday, since I'd never seen him. We sat in my grandmother's parlor while he asked me questions, trying to get to know me, I guess. Anyway, a month or so later, an attorney showed up at our front door, informing us my father was gone and I was his only heir. Grandmother claimed the money was the only reason Bradley had for marrying me. As it turned out, she was right."

She shook her head, attempting to rid herself of the empty feelings those memories carried with them. "But I was so sure I could make it work." So sure that when she told him about her differences he would understand and accept her as she was. So sure that the intuitive warnings she had were as wrong as her grandmother. "So, I married him."

His hand slid to her neck, the warmth of it comforting her. "I've found over the years that even my mistakes teach me something. Did you learn from that experience, luv?"

"Oh yes." She paused, willing the tears not to fall. "I learned the importance of honesty. I also learned you can't make something real just because you want it badly. Sometimes you must accept things as they are." She had learned to accept that because of her differences she would always be alone.

"I see."

She wondered how much he did see. His thumb started its marvelous circular pattern under her ear and soon she leaned her head back against the wall next to his. Her eyes drifted shut and her body relaxed in the peaceful quiet.

She jumped when he once again broke the silence.

"By the way, when you were being so observant about the cottage having only one bedroom?"

He turned to look down at her, catching her eyes, and she felt a blush building on her face, heating the area of her neck covered by his fingers. She knew he must feel it as well.

"Did you also happen to notice the bloody big sofa in the great room?"

She nodded.

"Good." He leaned back against the wall and stared up at the starlit sky. "Because that's where I'll be sleeping. If you need to find me for any reason."

"Oh."

Damn. Reduced to single syllables again.

Eleven

*I*an blinked, working hard to keep his expression completely impassive. He was sure someone would notice if he pounded his fist into Tanner's arrogant face. After all, it was a beautiful, bright morning and they were in the middle of one of Britain's more exclusive golf courses.

"So I can only assume you haven't slept with her." Brad smirked his direction. "Or maybe you have and that's why you're so quiet this morning." The man stepped up to the tee and took his shot.

Quiet?

His opponent understood nothing, not even how to recognize his own danger. A good warrior was always quiet while contemplating the manner of an enemy's demise. In all his years, he had never been one to boast before a battle or to brag about his intentions. He quietly planned, then stepped forward and acted.

The man smiling in front of him made him wish

for a return to the old ways, to a time of swords and dungeons. He would have made quick work of Bradley Tanner in those days. There were some distinct disadvantages to this century.

"Well, which is it?" Brad stood in front of him, adjusting his glove.

"A gentleman disna discuss his private affairs in this setting." Ian gritted his teeth.

Paul and Daniel had already taken their turns and stood a distance away. Ian doubted they'd heard the exchange.

Brad shrugged. "Well, she's got money now, but you don't look like the kind who needs her money bad enough to put up with that." He slapped Ian on the back. "She's an Ice Queen, McCullough. Stiffens up and sucks all the enjoyment right out of sex. She can't stand to be touched, but I'm sure you've already found that to be the case." The smirk on his face broadened. "Or you will very soon."

Ian's muscles tensed across his shoulders and his eyes narrowed. He fought to consciously relax his grip on the club he held. "Perhaps it was naught but her poor choice of partner in the past."

Brad shrugged and turned, heading down the green.

Daniel joined him at the tee as Brad and Paul continued on to where their balls had landed. "So, what's your impression of those two?"

"Stephenson's no the one we're looking for."

"I agree. His is a gentle soul. What do you think of Tanner?" Daniel immediately grinned and held up a hand. "And I'm not asking on a personal level. That's fairly easy to see."

"Tanner's a bloody great fool. Too much so to my way of thinking to be the contact." He shook his head. "As much as I'd like it to be him. No, the one we're searching for has no yet arrived."

Ian returned the club he held to his bag, choosing another in its place.

"What are you doing?" Daniel frowned. "I know you hate this game, but you're much better than that." He pointed at the club Ian held. "You'll slice something awful with that one."

"Aye. I suppose I might at that."

"You're not going to hit your target."

"I'm thinking you misjudge my target."

Ian lined up his shot and swung at the ball, a smile creasing his face as he watched its flight.

Down the green a shout went up as the small white projectile slammed into Brad Tanner's back.

"Oh, that's a bloody bad shame." Ian's eyes sparkled as he looked at his friend. "Poor chap. That must be frightfully painful."

"It's a damn good thing I don't really want a position on their board, with you doing your best to bugger the whole deal." Daniel shook his head. "I hope you're happy with yourself."

"As a matter of fact, I'm feeling much better than I have all morning." Ian grinned at him.

"Come on. Let's go collect our charges and get back to Glaston House. The next two will be arriving shortly after lunch."

"Do you think you can handle them yerself for a bit? I've a short errand to run when we get back."

"Of course. Anything I can help with?"

"I dinna think so. I've decided to take Sarah shopping." At his friend's raised eyebrow he continued. "After seeing the other ladies last evening it's occurred to me that my guest might end up feeling uncomfortable in the casual clothing I encouraged her to bring."

"I take it you were able to convince her to stay at the cottage with you."

"As a matter of fact, I was able to lay blame at the broad doorstep of misunderstanding, and then, with the whole Tanner issue, the matter resolved itself."

"It's odd, don't you think?" Daniel's forehead wrinkled in thought. "This woman showing up on your doorstep and now her ex-husband being here? It's quite the coincidence."

"Dallyn warned of exactly this sort of thing, in his own cryptic way. He said that Sensors drew to them others who need to be there."

"Well, let's hope that she draws the one we need. At least the way things have worked out you'll be able to keep a close eye on her, regardless of who shows up."

"Exactly."

And the time he'd be "forced" to spend with her would simply be a bonus.

Sarah awoke and stretched, unsure for a moment of where she was. She watched the tiny bits of dust dancing in the sunbeam shining through the window over her bed and gradually the evening before came back to her. Memories of Ian's coming to her rescue sent shivers to her toes, a part of her wanting his act to be real. Then she thought of what—who—he'd rescued her from.

"Damn."

Throwing back the covers, she sat up in bed. Brad was here. The one man she'd hoped never to see again in her entire life. And she was trapped in this place for three more days. She sighed and climbed out of bed, heading toward the bathroom. She needed a shower and a strong cup of coffee to face that terror again.

After a quick shower, she slipped on a pair of jeans and a T-shirt, but paused as she passed the mirror on her way out the door. The T-shirt probably wouldn't be up to par for the group of people she'd be around today, but it was either that or one of the two sweaters she'd brought along. She had only that and the summer dress she'd worn when she'd gone out with Ian, and she still had three more dinner gatherings to dress for.

She shrugged and padded downstairs. She wasn't going to spend her whole weekend worrying about what people thought of her. Well, in all honesty, she probably was, but she refused to give in to it before coffee.

A quick glance into the great room told her Ian was already up and gone, but the smell of fresh coffee filled the empty space. Next to the coffeepot, she found a tray holding a cup, sugar and cream, a fresh rose in a vase of water and a folded piece of paper.

He didn't miss a thing.

She poured her coffee and took the tray out to the garden, sniffing the flower before settling into one of the chairs and propping her bare feet on the other. She savored her first sip and opened the paper.

The note told her he'd gone golfing, but hoped to

be back before she had a chance to finish her coffee. He promised a surprise when he returned.

She smiled and laid the paper on the table, thinking about the man who had left the note. Ian's handwriting was elegant, laced with old-fashioned flourishes she didn't normally think of as typically masculine. Yet the note, like the man himself, felt entirely male. Tentatively she reached toward the paper again, brushing it lightly with her fingertips.

How much could she feel if she really tried?

When she touched a person, skin to skin, an awareness of all their emotions flooded into her. When it had first begun, as a child, she had thought everyone felt that way. That everyone also had the little voice in their heads that warned them not to go near a particular dog, or to avoid a particular person because he was bad, or to hurry home from school in time to warn someone about something that was going to happen.

Her grandmother had quickly dissuaded her of that notion, accusing her of being "strange" like her father.

She had spent the rest of her life trying to distance herself from those things. Trying to hide them, make them go away.

The voice had receded until a few months ago, when it came back loud and clear, insisting that she spend the summer in Scotland.

The awareness that came through touch had never gone away. It had grown stronger, no matter how she fought it, until she learned to avoid touching people as much as possible. Recently, since she'd promised to give herself over to the Fates, she'd found that the awareness was no longer limited to people. When she touched objects, she felt faint impressions of those who had handled them before.

If she thought of these afflictions as powers, she would have to say it was almost as if her powers had begun to grow.

Closing her eyes, she flattened her hand against the note, clearing her mind and breathing deeply.

The note felt warm under her hand. She sensed a fleeting touch of impatience. Had Ian been in a rush when he wrote this? Her fingers began to tingle, even warmer now, and her brow furrowed. What was that swimming around, just out of reach? She could almost see him writing, see him smiling. Her breathing sped up as she felt the heat of temptation seeping off the paper into her hand. Temptation and desire.

But whose emotions was she sensing? His or her own?

"Sarah? Are you all right?"

At the sound of his voice, her eyes flew open and she jerked her fingers from the paper as if burned, quickly clasping both hands around her coffee cup. With her sudden movement, the paper fluttered to the ground unnoticed.

Had he seen what she'd been doing?

"Morning. I'm fine. Good game?"

A small shrug of his shoulders, and an almost guilty smile preceded his response.

"I suppose. It did have its moments."

He disappeared through the doorway, reappearing shortly with his own steaming cup. Gently he swept her feet up in order to sit in the chair she'd been using as a footrest. When she would have moved them to the ground, he tightened his hold, positioning her feet in his lap after he sat.

"You found my note?"

She could only nod her reply. His thumb was working a slow magic on the sole of her right foot. The sensations his fingers produced were so exquisite that only by clenching her jaw was she able to prevent a moan from escaping.

His ministrations switched to the left foot.

"Are you ready then? For my surprise?"

"Your what?" How could she possibly be expected to answer, or even think, when he was doing that to her feet?

"Surprise." He dropped her feet to the ground and stood, taking her hand and hoisting her to stand. "Come on, lazybones, go get yer shoes on. I've a surprise all planned that I'm sure you'll enjoy." He gave her a little push toward the door.

It was difficult for her to imagine anything she would enjoy more than what he'd just been doing.

"Ian McCullough and"—he paused, turning to her with a satisfied smile before completing his announcement to the black metal box—"Miss Sarah Douglas."

He continued to smile as he drove through the gates and slowly headed toward the castle.

"You see? I am no the chauvinist you named me. I announced the both of us."

Sarah rolled her eyes. "I'm afraid that one little act does not absolve you of today's crimes. I told you. I cannot let you pay for those things."

"But I already paid for them." If anything, his smile grew larger. "And lunch as well, I might add."

"Only because you tricked me."

Ian's surprise had turned out to be a day trip to Bristol, to some very exclusive dress shops Nessa had recommended. He'd managed to get her out of the cottage without her purse by telling her they were only taking a short ride.

"And you lied to me."

His smile disappeared. "I did no such thing."

"You said you had something to show me . . . only a short ride."

"And that was completely true. Technically. I wanted to show you the shopping district in Bristol." He favored her with another of his grins. "Even you must admit it was a short ride compared to the one down from Scotland."

She huffed out her breath in a half laugh. "You're impossible."

"That's much better." He pulled the car to a stop at the far side of the drive. "You were so quiet after lunch and on the drive here, I feared you were really angry with me." He turned serious black eyes on her, holding her captive with the power of his gaze. "I'd do almost anything to avoid that, Sarah."

"Well, don't think you're off the hook yet. I do intend to repay every penny you spent on those dresses."

All she'd have to do is figure out a way to determine exactly how many pennies, or pounds as the case may be, he had actually spent. He'd apparently given the store clerk quite a nice tip to ensure she didn't tell Sarah the amount of the sale. Perhaps Nessa could give her a guesstimate based on her experience with the stores.

Of course, who paid for what and being a liberated

woman was the least of her problems right now. After
what she saw at lunch, she was still struggling with
the concept of being a sane woman. Liberation would
have to take a backseat to sanity any day.

"Sarah? Did I lose you again, luv?" Ian was leaning
across the center console, only inches from her face.

"I'm sorry. I'm a bit distracted."

The slow smile, the one she'd secretly dubbed The
Heart Stopper, began to work its way across his face.

"Aye, well then, best I take advantage of that while
I can."

In the space of a heartbeat he closed the small distance between them, his mouth brushing softly over
hers. Then he pulled back from her and lifted his hand
to her face, stroking his thumb across her lower lip.

"Now we're both a bit distracted."

Sarah couldn't think, much less respond, as he
climbed from the car, coming around to open her
door.

"I'm going to take Nessa's packages from the bak-
ery round to the back. I'll meet you at the cottage
later?"

She nodded her agreement, not quite able to form
sounds.

"Do you want me to carry yer things up to the cottage when I come?"

This time she shook her head and watched him
grin as he balanced the stack of boxes they'd brought
back, each filled with the delicate pastries Nessa had
ordered for tonight.

Her lips still tingled and she unconsciously ran a
finger over them as she watched him walk around the
back of the building, effortlessly carrying his load.

There was surely something she was supposed to say to him—something about how he shouldn't be kissing her like that. But her brain couldn't come up with the words. Perhaps her body, traitor that it seemed to be where Ian was concerned, had placed her brain on lockdown.

Serious brain malfunction.

Maybe that could explain what she thought she'd seen outside the restaurant today. It wasn't a rational explanation, by any means, but she'd tried to come up one of those all the way back from Bristol without any success.

Either way, she was beginning to have some serious doubts about her sanity on all counts. Because it wasn't sane to allow herself to get lost in pretending to be someone special to a man like Ian McCullough. And it was most certainly not a sane act to think she'd seen that man watching her from outside the restaurant. Especially not since she was so certain he was the same man she'd seen before. The same one who had jumped over her car during the rainstorm her first night in Scotland.

Sarah cut through the side yard on a path she hadn't taken before on her way to the cottage. She was pleasantly surprised to find herself in a cozy play area.

"Sarah! You came to visit me just like you said you would." Will jumped up from the sandbox where he had been busily occupied. "What's that?" He pointed at the packages she carried.

"Dresses. Ian took me shopping." She put the packages on a bench and seated herself.

Will climbed up next to her, immediately claiming her hand as he sat down.

"Don't you like the clothing?" He snuggled close, putting one small arm around her waist, the other still holding her hand in her lap.

"Of course I do." She looked down to meet his intense gaze, surprised that she'd had no reaction to his touch this time. "Why would you think I didn't?"

"You're unhappy." He squeezed her hand. "I feel it. Like you can." His head snuggled against her side.

"What?" She felt her breath catch in her lungs.

"I'm like you. I never met one of us before."

"One of us?" Her voice wavered. What was this child saying?

The reproachful look he gave her was eerily adult. "We feel things. Things about other people. About what they're like, what they feel." He patted her back. "Didn't your mommy and daddy tell you it's okay, Sarah?" He waited, his large blue eyes fixed on hers.

"No," she whispered, his words hitting her like a punch to the stomach.

"We're special." The little hand continued to pat her back. "It's because of our ancestors."

"Our ancestors?"

He nodded. "The Faeries. We have their blood. So we're special."

"Faeries," she repeated skeptically. "Little winged butterfly people?"

Will giggled. "They aren't like that at all. They might want you to think they look like that, but they really don't. And we would see them the way they really look." He shrugged his little shoulders. "It's in our blood. It's who we are."

Faeries. What an imagination. Still, how did he know about the feelings? She didn't discuss that with anyone. Not anymore. Not since . . .

"Will, did you hear one of the grown-ups talking about this? One of those people who are here visiting your mom and dad?" Surely Brad wouldn't talk about that. Not after all this time.

"No." At her look of doubt, he continued, "Feel me, Sarah. You'll know I'm telling you the truth. We're the same. We're special." He squeezed her hand, staring at her earnestly.

She closed her eyes, allowing the feelings to flood her. There was no question about it.

"I believe you, Will."

Rising to his knees, he threw his little arms around her neck and hugged her tightly. "It's okay, Sarah. We're special," he whispered.

What was her world coming to? She felt more confused than she could ever remember. From the fright of seeing that man outside the restaurant to Ian's kiss in the car, things were simply moving too quickly for her to grasp today. And now this oddly mature little boy with his eerily accurate knowledge of something she worked so hard to hide. It all had her almost seriously considering the imaginary Faerie ancestors living in the mind of an inventive six-year-old.

"Have they arrived yet?" Ian lounged on the leather sofa in Daniel's study, holding a large glass of lemonade.

"Only Storey. The aide, O'Dannan, is flying in separately. He'll be here later this evening."

"Until you mentioned him last night, I'd no heard anything about this O'Dannan. There was no file, nothing at all on him in the intelligence we looked at."

"I'm aware of that. Makes him all the more interesting, doesn't it?"

"Aye, that it does. Along with this chairman, this Servans. There's something about that name worrying at the back of my mind."

"Something more than the lack of information on him?"

Ian nodded slowly. Something he'd seen, something he'd read. He just couldn't place it, but it would come to him in time.

"Have you heard of him before?"

"I'm no sure. What about this Alexander Storey? As I recall, he's the head man at EHN, is he no? What's your impression of him?"

Daniel shook his head, disappointment clear in his expression. "I don't think he's the one, Ian. From what I hear, some financial deal forced him to the side, putting the new chairman in the driver's seat, though he's rarely there."

"From what you hear?" Ian raised an eyebrow.

"Yes. From my new top secret undercover agent." Daniel smiled. "Nessa told me. It seems Marlena Stephenson gets very talkative with only a few mimosas under her belt."

"She talked about it in front of Storey's daughter?" Ian frowned.

"No. When Brad returned from our game this morning feeling . . . uh, under the weather"—Daniel rubbed at his nose, obviously hiding a grin—"Nicole had the driver take her into town shopping. I don't suppose you ran into her?"

"No, we dinna."

"And your shopping day went well?"

"It did." Perhaps too well. The thought of Sarah's lips, her soft breath as he'd kissed her in the car brought a smile to his face. A kiss he shouldn't have taken, but one he couldn't regret. He shook his head. He had to stay focused on the matter at hand. Not on Sarah.

"Has Tanner recovered from our wee fairway accident?"

Danny shrugged. "I haven't seen him all day. I suppose he'll be at this evening's festivities."

"That's more the pity. I had rather hoped he'd be indisposed this evening and spare me his company."

"Spare you, or is it Sarah you're thinking of?" Daniel leaned back, propping his feet on the small table between them.

"His behavior toward her was quite unacceptable last evening. I simply prefer she not be upset like that."

"And why is that, do you suppose, Ian? Why would her being upset bother you so?" Daniel's eyebrow had lifted in question. "Could it be you're losing your objectivity where Sarah's concerned?"

"Why the bloody hell is everyone so convinced that my objectivity is suddenly endangered?" Ian abruptly stood from the sofa and stalked to the window to look out. "First Dallyn, now you." He shook his head.

"Perhaps because we can see what you don't." Daniel rose and followed his friend to the window, placing a hand on his shoulder. "I see how you look at her."

Ian continued to gaze out the window. From here

he caught sight of Sarah and Will walking together toward the Caretaker's Cottage. Will was carrying one of her packages, holding her hand. They stopped and she leaned down to speak to the boy, her blond curls brushing against the fair hair of the child. Ian shook his head, and closed his eyes briefly before turning from the captivating scene.

"What exactly are you trying to say?"

"I'm simply asking you to remember what you risk, what you stand to lose." Daniel dropped his hand and walked back to his chair, picking up his lemonade.

Neither man broke the silence for a few moments.

He was well aware of what he risked, and he had no intention of failing to honor his oath. Though there were moments when he was with Sarah. Moments when he could almost imagine his life being different.

"If you had it all to do again, Danny, would you do it differently? Do you regret yer decision to give it all up?" Ian watched his friend closely.

"I've no regrets at all, Ian. I'd gladly trade the few extra powers I was given and all eternity for whatever time I might have with Nessa and Will." His brow furrowed. "But there's a big difference between you and me. I'm not the one who promised my dying father I'd serve as a Guardian."

The memory of Larkin's death still hurt, even after all these centuries. His father, a full-blooded Fae, had been one of the last to die at the hands of the Nuadians in battle. The last battle prior to the Great Spell that prevented the Fae from fighting in the Mortal Plain.

Ian had been there waiting when they'd brought

his father into the Hall. Pain etched deeply on Larkin's face, he'd held on long enough to reach his son. To ask—no, demand—his son's promise to guard the Fountain of Souls and the humans living in the Mortal Plain. Only in that way, he'd said, could his death be avenged. Ian had given his oath without thought. It was, after all, his beloved father.

"I'm pleased you've no regrets at yer choice. I, too, believe you made the correct decision. And yer right, Danny. There is a difference between us. But the difference is that you found yer Soulmate. Mine disna exist, so I've no reason to dishonor my oath." He turned and looked out the window again. The lawn was empty.

"How can you be so sure of that?"

Good question. One he used to think he could answer easily. But not now. Not since he'd met Sarah.

Twelve

"Why have you waited until now to tell me about this?" Though he hid it well, Reynard was furious. He'd been surrounded by incompetence since the beginning of time.

"I wanted to . . . I thought it would be best to make sure, Great One, not to waste your time with—"

"And you have proof of this now?" Reynard's question cut short the explanation. He didn't want to listen to the man's excuse. It was always excuses. From all of them.

"Not exactly. But I believe she saw me."

Reynard breathed out an impatient huff of air, pulling the phone away from his ear, while he worked to maintain his composure. *Fool.*

"Another thing. She's with the Guardian. He hovers around her. I think . . . that is, I suspect it may be personal for him."

Now this was an interesting development.

"Which Guardian?"

"Ian McCullough. He guards the Portal at—"

Reynard interrupted again. "I know which Portal he and his brother's descendants guard." He leaned back in his chair, thoughtfully stroking his chin. "McCullough. You're right, Flynn. This is most interesting."

Flynn's panicky laugh grated on his nerves, but he didn't show it. Never show weakness to underlings.

"It's why I decided to bring this directly to you now. This is important, I thought. Too important to take back to Adira, I thought."

"Adira?" That caught his attention. What did his mistress have to do with any of this?

"Yes. I brought the matter to court, but she said I shouldn't bother you until we knew more. That I should . . . I should come back to her with my findings. But now . . . now that I believe it's so much bigger, I knew I should come directly to you." The man cleared his throat, betraying his nervousness in yet another manner. "Adira will be very angry with me."

Something potentially this big and she'd said nothing to him? What was she up to? The lovely Adira, Courtesan of Nuada, would have some explaining to do.

"Don't worry about Adira. I'll deal with her." *I will most certainly deal with her.* "Back to this woman. I want to know for sure whether or not she is of the blood. Do whatever it takes to verify it. The situation you describe proves nothing conclusively. I'm not impressed with what you think, Flynn, only what you know to be fact."

"I'll work on that, Great One."

"No. You'll do it, not work on it. Otherwise you'll

deal with me. And I assure you, I can be much more unpleasant than Adira could ever dream of being."

He paused to listen to the quickened breathing on the other end of the line. Obviously Flynn understood his assignment and the consequences of failure. Flynn had been a useful agent in more than one situation, but he always required the proper motivation. Reynard was more than happy to provide it.

Flynn's voice quavered when he spoke again. "We'll need to decide how to deal with the Guardian. I could—"

"No. You'll do nothing. There's very little you can do against a Guardian. Not in the Mortal Plain. We have no power there. I'll need to think on this. In the meantime, you might tell them I'm bringing my . . . my brother, yes, my brother. That will do."

Ramos. He would be perfect.

"As you wish, Great One."

A female Mortal descendant of the Fae blood. She would have the ability to lead him across the protected waters and through a Portal into the Realm of Faerie. Once there, he was only a thought away from the Fountain of Souls and eternal life. Once he had achieved that, his ultimate goal was within reach. Complete control of the Realm of Faerie. He'd see the High Council on their knees before him, begging for his mercy.

As they'd made him beg.

Could Flynn be correct about this woman? Reynard wouldn't accept any mistakes with this. Not like the last time. He'd searched too long. Although there must be many such women, they were difficult to locate. Long ago, he'd spent a lifetime in the search.

And now, to have one handed to him like this? The only thing better would be to find one who was the Soulmate of a Guardian. There was nothing better than an opportunity to make a Guardian suffer.

Unless it was the elimination of a Guardian.

"Oh, and one more thing, Flynn."

"Anything, Great One."

"You might practice calling me Mr. Servans."

Thirteen

"*I* can do this. I can do this." Sarah watched herself in the mirror as she repeated the words like some deranged cheerleader.

She would not be intimidated by that man. She'd lived through marriage to him, she could certainly live through a dinner party with him. What could he possibly do to her? Other than call her names, question her sanity and generally embarrass her. She could survive that. She'd survived it before.

She was stronger now. No longer a dewy-eyed girl to be disappointed by what she had seen at the time as his betrayal of her. He meant nothing to her now. There was nothing he could say that could wound her anymore.

Unless he told Ian about her. About how different she really was. About the things she felt.

She didn't want Ian to learn about her. Didn't want to see him look at her as everyone always did when they heard her secrets. The disbelief, the pity, the avoidance.

She shook her head. Brad would have no reason to do that. Surely he wouldn't go out of his way to create a scene in front of the people he worked with or his young wife.

Would he?

Or had he already spoken to someone about her? A conversation that little Will had overheard?

The child's knowledge of her feelings still rattled her. There had to be some logical explanation. She had only to discover what it was.

Another glance at the mirror assured her that at least she wouldn't have to worry about being dressed inappropriately tonight. Ian had excellent taste in clothing. She wore the less formal of the two dresses he'd chosen for her, this one a snug green silky dress under a shimmery gossamer covering that flowed around her body with each movement. She was a little uncomfortable that it followed her curves quite so closely, but even she had to admit it looked pretty good.

"Is there no some classic American joke about how long it takes you women to get dressed?" Ian's voice drifted up from the lower level of the cottage.

"Several of them," she called back, turning from the mirror and starting for the stairs. Pep rally was over. Time to head out to the big game.

She came to an abrupt halt at the bottom of the stairs as Ian emitted a long, low whistle.

"And worth every minute of the wait." He nodded appreciatively. "It looks even better on you now than it did in the shop. You're a vision tonight, Sarah."

"Thank you."

She was sure he would have complimented any

woman he escorted, but his words warmed her. And the look on his face when he took her arm at the door made her feel as lovely as he claimed she was.

Her flattery-induced euphoria lasted until they reached the terrace and the party already in progress. She wasn't sure whether she was more uncomfortable with the angry daggers shooting their way from Brad or the looks of unabashed curiosity coming from his baby-faced wife.

"Wait here."

The words Ian breathed in her ear triggered a moment of near suffocating panic when he dropped her hand and walked away. But he returned carrying two glasses of champagne before she could react.

I can do this.

He placed his hand low on her back, and once again his breath brushed against her ear as he leaned in close.

"Relax, luv. Dinna let him get to you. You've nothing to fear."

She stiffened. "He doesn't frighten me." Technically true. It was only what he might say that frightened her.

"Of course you dinna fear him."

Ian's light chuckle against her ear sent chills down her back and heat rushing to her face. Was it even possible to feel hot and cold at the same time? Possible or not, she did.

From the quickly averted gazes of the other guests, Sarah realized how their actions were being interpreted. Ian was doing this intentionally, to foster that impression, to help her. To bolster her self-confidence in dealing with her ex-husband and the others.

Why was he doing it? It didn't matter anymore. Just as she'd given herself permission to relinquish control to whatever higher powers were responsible for her "feelings," she now gave herself permission to enjoy this moment in her life. An opportunity to have a man like Ian pretending to be attracted to you came along more rarely than . . . what? More rarely than Will's imaginary Faerie ancestors showed their faces. She'd be a fool not to take advantage of the adventure.

She turned her face to his and smiled.

"Thank you," she whispered, closing the small gap between them, brushing her lips lightly across his.

Her own actions might have shocked her had she not found his unexpected response so astonishing. Astonishing and thoroughly enjoyable.

His eyes widened in surprise a second before the grin forming on his mouth traveled to them. The hand at her back pulled her tightly to him and he turned the kiss from the light touch she had intended into something else altogether—something that stole all thought of where they were until the sound of a throat clearing next to them brought her back to reality.

"Bravo, old man." Danny stood next to them, grinning. "But perhaps you could hold off until after dinner is served?"

Ian pulled away, but continued to hold her gaze. "Perhaps." Turning to his friend, he mirrored Daniel's grin. "But dinner had better be spectacular."

The hand at her back loosened, guiding her across the terrace.

Sarah breathed deeply, working hard to keep her

trembling legs moving forward. She was keenly aware that the tremors racing through her body had nothing to do with the open stares of the other guests and everything to do with what she had just experienced.

Ian's response to her had been honest and open, clearly transmitting his emotions. He hadn't been acting. His kiss was filled with desire. Desire for her.

I can do this?

Her cheerleader seemed to have deserted her.

"Dammit, Ian, you're not listening to a word I've said." Daniel slammed his glass down, the contents spilling out onto the gleaming cherrywood of the old desk.

"Aye, Danny, I am." Ian turned from the glass doors to look at his friend. "Dallyn says there's movement in the Nuadian energy field." He turned his gaze back to the terrace, pausing to open the doors a crack. With only a little effort he'd be able to hear the conversation he watched so intently.

"This is important," Danny grumbled as he wiped at the spill on his desk.

"Important, aye, but it's no unexpected. Dallyn has said all along that one of the Nuadian High Council is involved. Sooner or later, we knew there would be movement in the energy field." He glanced back again for a moment. "It means our wait is almost over. Soon we'll know who it is we're facing."

"Yes, well, not at the rate we're going. That assistant, O'Dannan, arrived earlier this evening, but sent word down claiming he was too tired to join us tonight. And then he announced that the chairman, this Ray Servans, is bringing his brother with him. I'm telling you, Ian, it doesn't feel right. It's not any of the men we've interacted with so far, I'd bet my estate on it."

"You dinna have to bet anything. We already know it's none of them. When our man shows up, I'll feel it. I know my own kind."

Ian only half listened to Daniel's continued discussion of the possibilities. He believed in concentrating his efforts on what was real, what was at hand. Possibilities meant nothing until they materialized, until they were on his field of battle. And once they were? Then he'd deal with them, neutralize them as he always had.

For now, he was much more interested in what Brad Tanner was saying to the small group gathered around Sarah. He didn't like the looks of that. Opening the door wider, he slipped through, listening intently before he approached.

"I don't care what it looked like, princess." Tanner leaned into his wife, speaking loud enough to be heard by the whole group—loud enough that Ian didn't need to use any special effort to hear the slurred speech.

"She's a cold fish, completely frigid. And I, of all people, should know. Shouldn't I, Sarah?" He turned, lifting his glass in salute, sloshing the contents over the side. "My Ice Queen, I called her. My Virtual Virgin." He shook his head. "Not an actual virgin, mind you. I saw to that, and pretty damn well, too, I might add." He chuckled and lifted his glass for a drink, looking surprised when he found it empty.

His wife tugged at his sleeve, casting apologetic

glances at Sarah, who stood still, frozen in place, as the others looked on in obvious embarrassment.

"No, Nicki here can vouch for me on that count. I'm damn good in bed, but this one"—he swung his glass toward Sarah—"this one is like screwing the dead, completely incapable of enjoying sex."

"Oh, Sarah, I am so very sorry." Nicole moved toward her, hands lifted helplessly. "It's the painkillers he took for his poor back. I warned him not to drink after taking the meds, but I'm sure you must remember how stubborn Brad can be." She shrugged.

"So I wonder what excuse she uses for his being an ass all the rest of the time," Marlena Stephenson murmured to her husband, who looked down, attempting to hide the smile on his face.

"It's why she writes those freakin' romance books," Brad interrupted. "Because she can't do it, she writes about it. Fiction all the way in her case." He snorted, laughing at his own joke, and turned toward the bar, snagging a filled glass.

Ian reached her then, putting his arm around her shoulders. He'd expected trembling, but found nothing. She felt as frozen as she looked, staring straight ahead at Tanner, her cheeks a flaming red.

Rage grew, dancing through his blood, causing his hands to curl into fists. With effort, he relaxed them. The man was thoroughly intoxicated, barely able to stand on his own.

"I believe it's time, Mrs. Tanner, that you help yer husband retire for the evening. Allow the alcohol to work its way out of his system."

Either that, or he wouldn't be responsible for what was about to happen to Bradley Tanner.

"I'm not going anywhere, Lord Boy Toy." Brad threw his glass to the ground, where it shattered, pieces scattering around his feet. "Unless you think you can make me go." He leaned toward Ian, belligerently thrusting out his chin. "You want to try to make me go?"

"Daddy," Nicole shrieked as she turned to an older gentleman standing quietly on the edge of the group.

Alexander Storey stepped forward, putting an arm around Tanner's shoulders. "Why don't you let me help you back to your room, Brad?"

"No. I'm fine. I'm enjoying myself. I can take him. I work out." He stumbled against the older man.

"Paul?" Storey motioned to Stephenson, who hurried forward. Between them, they managed to assist Brad inside, Nicole trailing in their wake.

Marlena Stephenson reached out a hand, touching Sarah's arm to get her attention. "Don't pay any mind to him. He's always unpleasant, although I don't think I've ever seen him quite this bad." She patted Sarah's hand. "Do you truly write romance, my dear? I love romance novels. I simply devour them. Have you been writing for long? I wonder if I might have read something of yours."

Sarah stiffened and then sighed before answering, as if resigned. "I've been writing for several years."

"I find her writing to be quite good." Ian smiled down at her as she turned to him, a surprised look on her face. She hadn't realized he'd bought the book she'd dropped in that little shop. "Of course, I am only reading my first one and I do admit to being a wee bit prejudiced." He looked back at the women. "She writes as S. J. Douglas."

"No," Nessa squealed, grabbing Sarah's hand. "I have your latest book on my nightstand right now. I can't believe you've been here this long and I didn't know who you were." She glanced accusingly at Ian. "And you didn't say a word to me."

Marlena stood back and nodded appreciatively. "I'm impressed, Sarah. As a matter of fact, I have all your books back home. I love your heroes. They're so . . ."—she gave a little shiver—"alpha male." She smiled mischievously, tilting her head. "I guess now that I've met the prototype for them, I can understand why."

"Oh, no, I—" Sarah started to protest, but Ian cut her off.

"Why, thank you, Mrs. Stephenson. I appreciate the compliment. And now"—he dropped his hand to Sarah's waist—"I think my little author and I will hit the buffet table. I seem to have worked up quite an appetite. If you'll excuse us?"

He guided her to the opposite side of the stone pond, where the buffet had been arranged. He'd filled their plates and found a bench at the far edge of the terrace for them before she finally spoke.

"Thank you for coming to my rescue. Again."

He shook his head slowly as he sat down next to her. "I dinna do anything that any other man would no have done in my place."

"Oh really? Because I could swear there were other men standing around, and none of them stepped forward to stop Brad."

"Well, I did say 'any man in my place.' None of them were lucky enough to be yer escort this evening."

"You and I both know that doesn't have anything to do with it. You would have stepped in to prevent any woman from being treated that way, wouldn't you?"

He shrugged his shoulders. "Perhaps I'm simply no as tolerant as other men."

"No, that's not it." She tilted her head, narrowing her eyes. "There's something terribly gallant about you. Something old world. As a matter of fact, now that I think about it, I can see why Marlena would assume that I patterned my heroes after you."

"And why is that, luv?"

"Well, just like my heroes, you're a pretty take-charge kind of guy."

He nodded. "Go on."

"You're chivalrous, considerate and extremely helpful."

Another nod. "Continue."

She sat back, a confused smile on her face, as he'd expected. "More? What else would you have me add to that list?"

"Well, so far you've described every boy scout in the country. But according to what I've read in yer book so far"—he raised an eyebrow—"if I'm *just* like yer heroes, then I'm also quite handsome, verra strong and verra brave." He paused, looking to her for confirmation before continuing.

"Yes, I suppose those are traits I could attribute to you as well."

He couldn't hold back his mischievous smile as he picked up where he'd left off on the list of his supposed qualities.

"Let's see, I'm also unbelievably sexy, and—what

was that other one? Oh yes . . . absolutely irresistible
to the heroine."

She lowered her eyes to the plate in her lap as
color crept into her cheeks. "Yes, well, but you must
remember, my heroes are only fantasy."

Ian took the empty plate from her hands and put it
on the ground next to his. When he turned back to
her, he placed a finger under her chin, lifting her face
to look into her eyes.

"That, sweet Sarah, is what a good hero excels at—
fulfilling yer every fantasy."

Her eyes widened as they fixed on his and he felt
the slightest tremble against his fingers. Hard to believe in this moment that he had ever thought her
anything less than the most beautiful woman he'd
ever met.

When she spoke, her voice held the same light
tremor as her body. "If I didn't know better, Ian Mc-
Cullough, I'd think you were flirting with me."

"What makes you think I'd no be flirting with you?"

She lifted her chin from his grasp and looked back
down at her hands clasped nervously in her lap before
once again meeting his gaze. This time it was defi-
ance he saw there.

"Well, for one thing, because I'm too old for you."

As if that would matter, even if it were true. He
threw back his head and laughed, drawing looks from
the other couples around the terrace.

"I'm serious, Ian." She stood and looked down at
him. "I'm too old for you to be considering any kind
of romantic . . . anything with me."

"I dinna care. Yer age disna matter to me." He rose
to stand.

"It does too matter. I'm . . ." She paused, drawing in a deep breath and closing her eyes for moment. "I'm thirty-eight, Ian. You're a full decade younger than I. That's an enormous difference."

"It's only numbers, Sarah."

He pulled her close and lowered his head to hers, nuzzling his lips against the spot under her ear that he'd already discovered sent shivers through her body.

He should stop this game quickly, while it was still a game, but she was vulnerable now. Not only the kind of vulnerability he saw in her eyes, but the kind that came from everyone watching. She couldn't pull away when this was the behavior the observers expected, and he knew it. Counted on it. Used it.

"Meaningless numbers, and some unreasonable obsession you have with age that we'll revisit at another time." He straightened and slid his thumbs to either side of her neck, moving them in the small circles that seemed to relax her. "That's a promise."

He knew she felt the truth in his statement when her eyes widened and her mouth opened slightly as if she would protest.

"But for now, we've a little boy we've pledged to tuck into bed."

She nodded and he tightened his grip, bending over her again and pulling her close to gently kiss her lips.

Somewhere along the way, what he'd intended as no more than playful banter had turned entirely serious. He'd only thought to build her self-confidence, to help her feel more sure of herself, but to his surprise, he found he'd meant every word of what he'd said.

"And like yer heroes, my sweet, I never break a promise."

Instantly she tensed and pulled from his grasp. He allowed her to go, to reclaim her distance.

Ian didn't actually consider himself to be hero material as she'd suggested. He did, however, think of himself as an excellent warrior. And, like every good warrior, he understood the importance of choosing his battles wisely.

He would wait for the right time and the right place to engage in this particular battle.

"What were you giggling about?"

Sarah tucked her feet under her as she settled into the enormous leather sofa in the great room of the cottage. She watched the muscles beneath the tight silk T-shirt Ian wore ripple across his back like the famed Nessie in her loch. All the while, she tried not to remember that this sofa was currently doubling as his bed.

"I dinna ever giggle, woman. It's no a manly thing to do." He rose from the hearth and dusted off his hands, leaving the fire he'd just lit. "I laugh or I chuckle, but never giggle."

He grinned and picked up the bottle of wine he'd retrieved earlier from their little fridge, holding it up for her inspection.

She examined the label, a task made more difficult since the only illumination in the room came from the fire and a shaft of moonlight glinting through the massive French doors that flanked the fireplace on either side.

"What am I looking for?"

"It's Danny's own vineyard he stocks our icebox with. Cheap bugger." His grin turned to a huge smile as he uncorked the bottle and sniffed. "Ah, but lucky for us, the people he hires to tend the place and make the wine know what they're doing."

"I didn't realize people had vineyards here in England." She reached out to take the glass he handed her.

"His vineyard's in France." At her look of surprise he continued. "Aye, he's been a busy boy over the years, with interests all over the continent. And still he's managed to snag himself a lovely wife and have that fine son."

"Will is such an unusual child. But very loving, isn't he?"

The boy had hugged her neck and kissed her good night before they'd left his room tonight. He'd also taken the opportunity to whisper a reminder to her that she was special and should be happy.

"Aye, that and quite advanced, too. Sometimes you'd think him an adult trapped in that small body. He's verra intelligent, that lad." He grinned again as he sat close to her on the sofa. Very close. "He is, after all, my godson, so I like to think I can claim some of the credit."

"He does seem unusually mature at times. And he certainly has a vivid imagination." She sipped her wine and tried to convince herself that she could not feel the heat of Ian's body seeping through her dress where his leg touched hers.

"A vivid imagination? What makes you say that?"

"This afternoon I spent some time with him in his playground. We had a long talk, and he told me he's descended from Faeries." She ran her finger around the rim of her glass, wondering why the boy's comments had disturbed her so deeply.

"He told you that, did he?"

"Yes. And that I am as well." She turned to look at him. "Quite an imagination, huh?"

"Did he tell you what makes him think yer both descended from the Fae?" Serious dark eyes caught and held hers.

Ian had asked earlier tonight why she believed a relationship between them wouldn't work. It was time she was completely honest with him. Then he'd have his full answer.

"Because we both can . . . um . . . feel things, sense things. Things about other people. About how they feel." She watched him, wondering, fearing, how he would react.

"And can you, Sarah? Can you sense things about how other people feel, what they think?" The dark gaze still didn't leave hers.

She paused, trying to determine what censure might lurk in those beautiful eyes, waiting to pounce if she answered honestly.

"Yes," she whispered, though her mind screamed for her to deny it. It was time for honesty. She had to know what he really thought of her.

"Then perhaps you truly are a child of the Faeries." He smiled and placed his glass on the table behind the sofa, then took hers from her hand and placed it next to his. Turning back to her, he lifted both hands to her face, cupping them there, just below her ears.

"In this light, I could easily mistake you for a Faerie goddess."

"I meant it, Ian. I can sense things. Don't you think I'm odd, or weird, or crazy, or . . ."

"Shhh." He moved his thumb over her lips. "I dinna think yer anything but enchanting."

He pulled her close, replacing his thumb with his mouth—a light brush across hers at first, then something more insistent, his teeth nipping at her lower lip.

"No." She put her hands on his chest and pushed him away. She couldn't do this. He couldn't possibly want her—not the real her. Not once he stopped to think about their differences. Not once he realized she was serious about what she'd told him. "I told you before. This can't work. We're too different."

She started to wrap her arms around her middle but he caught her hands, moving them to his chest, where he held them trapped. Trapped over his rapidly beating heart.

"Because of what you feel or because of the numbers, Sarah? Is that it? Is that why you think this won't work? Then now's the time I promised. The time to revisit yer age obsession. Why does it matter to you so? Would you care if I were older than you?"

"But you're not."

"Answer my question. If I were fifty or sixty or even older, would it make any difference to you?"

"It's not the same with men, Ian. All men want younger women. And they all want women who don't go around sensing what everyone feels."

"Not all men want that."

"All the men I've known."

"Then all the men you've known have been bloody great fools. And I assure you, Sarah, of all the things I am, I'm no bloody great fool." He tightened his grip on her hands. "I dinna have a problem with what you feel. And I've told you before, yer age is of no consequence to me."

Sarah watched, mesmerized, as he transferred his grip on her hands so that he held them both tightly with one of his, while with his other he tugged his shirt free from his pants. Then, reclaiming one of her hands in each of his own, he placed them on his chest, under his shirt and held them there against the warmth of his bare skin.

"You said you can sense things, things about how people feel. Then feel me, Sarah. Feel me and know that I tell you the truth. I dinna care about the numbers. And I dinna worry about yer ability to sense my thoughts. I welcome it."

She relaxed her hands against his chest, and he let go of her. Her fingers explored the unfamiliar terrain, settling in the crisp hair. She closed her eyes and reached out with her mind, searching. Determination hit her first, followed by honesty. Her age really didn't matter to him at all. More important, he didn't think her strange. He found her fascinating. She continued to reach out and suddenly she found a wellspring of emotion, one so strong it swept the others away until only it remained, flooding her, flowing through her.

Her eyes flew open in surprise. "You want me."

"Aye." His hands moved to her shoulders. "More than I've ever wanted any woman."

There was no doubt this time that he was going to kiss her and for a moment she froze.

"Wait. I have to warn you, Ian. Brad always said I

should come with instructions. I'm not very good at . . . I can't . . ." She struggled for the right words. She was terrible at this. Brad had told her so. The staggering emotions of her partner would inundate her mind, paralyzing her. If they went any further, she'd disappoint him and she desperately hated that idea.

"Bugger Brad. I'm no a man who needs instructions." His eyes sparkled with his intent.

He crushed her to him, his mouth coming down on hers, tender but demanding. The tip of his tongue danced against her mouth, darting side to side until she willingly parted her lips.

Her hands, still caught against his chest, moved up toward his shoulders, her fingers filling her with delight at the tactile sensations they fed her mind as they made their journey upward.

Waves of frustration rolled over her, and she realized with a shock they were her own. Frustration at having her hands stopped in their travels, trapped in Ian's shirt, unable to reach those magnificent shoulders she longed to trace with her fingertips.

A tiny moan and Ian pulled back from her to search her face.

"I'm caught," she breathed.

A grin, *the* grin, spread over his face as he leaned away from her long enough to pull his shirt over his head and toss it to the floor.

"Better?"

"Oh my. So much better."

His chest was wonderful, like a fantastic unyielding landscape, undulating in the firelight with each movement he made. It should be photographed.

"So very much better."

It should be studied, it should be . . . She lowered her head to that sumptuous chest and sucked his nipple into her mouth, running her tongue round and round the dark little nub.

"Holy Mother of God," he groaned.

Clasping his arms tightly around her, he rolled them from the sofa to the floor, cushioning her drop with his body, a move that plastered her to the length of him. Her head cradled to his chest, she could feel the proof of how much he wanted her pressing against her stomach.

His hands slipped under her arms and pulled her up the length of his body until her face met his. He kissed her mouth briefly before burying his face in her neck, alternating kisses and tiny, painless nips with his teeth in the sensitive area where her neck met her shoulder.

Her long skirt had tangled and slipped up in the tumble from the sofa. His hand, slowly skimming up her thigh, encouraged it higher and higher until at last her legs were free of the restrictive material, allowing her to slide a leg to either side of his body. Straddling him, she used his chest to push herself up to a sitting position.

The long, hard length of him pressed against her intimately. She could feel movement as, locked away from her by only a few thin layers of material, he grew larger still. She felt tension in the muscles of his chest as she ran her hands from his stomach to his shoulders and back again.

He watched her, their eyes locked on one another.

His hands, which had stilled when she'd straddled

him, started moving again, skimming over the shimmering material of her dress, up her stomach, and across her breasts, where they lingered just long enough to draw a sharp moan from her when his thumbs, his magic thumbs, slowly circled her nipples.

They continued on then, moving to her shoulders, as he used his unbelievably spectacular abdominal muscles to sit up. Pulling her to him, he lowered his head, encasing the tip of her breast in his mouth, sucking through the silky material of her dress and bra. His tongue moving back and forth, his teeth gently nipping.

He was a wonder to her. She'd never felt any of this, anything like this in her life. There was none of the pounding need and self-absorption she'd experienced in the past. None of the greed and contempt she had felt in Brad. There was only warmth. The warmth that came from desire and caring. She was surrounded by it, immersed in it, floating in it.

She closed her eyes and burrowed her hands into his hair as she'd wanted to since the first night she'd seen him. She buried her nose against those same dark locks and inhaled deeply, taking in the clean, masculine scent of him. She kissed the top of his head as he continued to spark feelings in her body with his mouth at her breast.

She felt as if she might explode at any moment—a feeling so good—she feared she might scream.

When she opened her eyes and saw the grinning face staring at them through the glass door, she did scream.

Her figment was back.

Fourteen

"Have you forgotten your oath so soon, my son?" His father stood tall above him as he had in Ian's youth, a disappointed frown on his brow.

"No, Father, I remember and honor it. Always." He heard his own voice as it had been in his childhood.

"Take care that you remember your vow to protect the Mortals, else the day come when you're forced to choose."

"I am ever conscious of my oath, Father."

Larkin turned away, shaking his head sadly. Bright sunlight glinted off the shining silver armor he wore, blinding Ian for an instant. And in that instant, his father disappeared.

"Come back," he cried aloud, waking himself. He lay on the sofa, his covers kicked to the floor in a tangled heap. When he stood and looked around the room, the reality of where he was returned to him.

It had been a dream.

He scrubbed at his face. Some nice strong coffee would drive away the cobwebs from his brain. He'd only taken a couple of steps toward the little kitchen when his foot landed on something sharp.

"What the bloody hell?" He leaned over and picked up the offending object, a high-heeled shoe. Sarah's shoe.

He thought of when he'd seen it last, as she slipped if off just before tucking those lovely feet under her when she sat down on the sofa. Last night. Just before he'd lost control and everything had gotten completely out of hand.

He carried it with him to the counter, tucking it in the waistband of his pajama bottoms before putting the coffee on to perk. Sarah thought he made it for her each morning, and he hadn't the heart to confess that it was his own little vice, an addiction picked up on one of his visits to the States many, many years ago.

His shirt still lay on the floor where he'd tossed it last night. With his freshly brewed coffee in hand, he walked over and picked it up, flipping it over his shoulder on his way out the glass doors to the patio.

After setting down his cup, he walked over to have a look around the French doors. He and Daniel had checked the area last night, but found nothing. He was hoping something would show up in the morning light.

Ian was convinced that whoever was stalking Sarah was no figment of her imagination, especially after she admitted that she'd seen the same man in town yesterday watching them while they had lunch. Her description of the man she'd seen through those doors last night seemed very like Daniel's description of the elusive Mr. O'Dannan.

Later this morning, he planned to walk up to the manor house and make a point of meeting the man. If he was the one spying on Sarah, then Ian had a score to settle with him. First, for frightening her so badly. Second, for ruining what had been a very promising evening.

Ian smiled and picked up his coffee, enjoying his first sip.

Although logic told him he couldn't afford any involvement with Sarah, to his warrior's mind last night had felt like the right time and the right place for what had almost happened.

He refused to tarnish that now by worrying about what a bad idea it was to let his relationship with her go any further. She was a forever type of woman and he couldn't afford to be mixed up with one of those. His forever was already spoken for. He knew what he needed to do. He just wasn't sure if he could do it—or, more accurately, not do it.

The interfering Peeping Tom had simply prevented something that shouldn't have happened anyway.

Ian walked to the door where the mystery man had stood. The only thing out of place was a crumpled piece of paper wedged under the roses. He leaned over and picked it up, hoping it might be some type of clue, but it was only the note he had left for Sarah yesterday.

There were no other signs. No footprint of any kind marred the soft dirt on either side of the doors. But he had no doubt someone had been there, and with the vibrations he was sensing so fresh, that left only one possibility. Their voyeuristic visitor was Faerie. A Nuadian Faerie.

Thinking of the Fae brought the memory of his father and the dream rushing back to him.

He sat down at the small iron table and propped his bare feet on the chair across from him, savoring his coffee once more.

It was only a dream.

Only a dream? Who was he kidding? His dreams were never just dreams. Every single dream he'd ever experienced had come to pass at some point. This one was a warning. They always were.

Now he merely needed to figure out what it warned of before something terrible happened.

The smell of coffee tickled at Sarah's nose, pulling her from the safe cocoon of sleep. She stretched and sat up. Heat flooded her face as the memory of last night washed over her.

The memory of Ian.

He made her feel things, want things she'd never felt before, never wanted before. Was this how it was supposed to feel, those things she wrote about but had never experienced for herself?

She crawled from the bed and headed downstairs, drawn by the fresh-perked aroma filling the cottage.

At the foot of the stairs she paused. Ian was nowhere to be seen. She continued to the counter and poured her coffee, determined not to think about last night—not Ian, not the face in the door—none of it.

Her good intentions lasted only until she turned from the counter and caught sight of Ian through the open glass door. Her heartbeat quickened until she could feel the blood pulsing through her body. Even doing something so mundane as sitting, he was majestic.

The early morning sunlight shone on his bare chest, highlighting his muscles with each tiny move. He ran his hand across a piece of paper on the table, flattening it, over and over, his brow wrinkled as if in deep thought about what he saw there. Then he took a drink from his cup and leaned back in his chair, his eyes closed.

Sarah couldn't stop staring at the scene in front of her. Couldn't stop remembering. Her fingers could feel the soft texture of the dark hair that curled against his neck. When she breathed in, she could still smell the heady masculine scent of him.

In that moment she admitted that she wanted him as badly as she knew he had wanted her last night. Ian McCullough had touched her, the real her, like no one she had ever known.

But while she wanted him, she was terrified of that wanting, terrified of him. Just as he had the power to make her feel things she'd never felt, he also had the power to hurt her as no other ever had.

Her father's rejection had come as no surprise. He had left his family long before her mother's accident. She was surprised more than anything when he came to visit, still the beautiful, tall blond god she remembered from her mother's stories. For a long time after, she liked to pretend it was longing she'd seen in his green eyes when he took his leave of her, but eventually she accepted the truth, and she felt no pain as she went on with her life.

Her grandmother, embittered by her own husband's desertion, was angry at the role life had given her—angry at having to raise her daughter's child. Sarah never had any illusions about her grandmother's wanting her. She always knew the woman raised her as a duty, not out of love. That early knowledge enabled her to steel herself, to protect her emotions.

Even in her marriage, she'd managed to keep an important part of herself separate, tucked away and untouched. Brad had been able to embarrass her, to disappoint her, to make her doubt her own worth, but never to really damage the core of her. When their marriage ended, she picked herself up and continued on.

Sarah turned and headed back up the stairs. The hand holding her coffee shook.

Ian was different.

If she let him in, when Ian walked away she might not be able to pick up the pieces and go on.

Ian had the power to break her heart.

"What do you mean, he's gone?" Ian turned to glare at his friend.

"Exactly what I said." Daniel glared back. "Gone. As in no longer here. I stopped by his room this morning and when I got no answer to my knock, I let myself in. Nothing to show the man was ever here except for his note."

"How the bloody hell did he manage to leave without anyone knowing? How did he get through yer security?"

"How the bloody hell should I know?" Danny asked pointedly.

"Sorry." Ian's shoulders slumped. "I've no call to yell at you. I'm frustrated."

"From what I saw when you called me down to the cottage last night, I don't doubt that you are." Danny watched him expectantly.

"That's a subject no open to discussion. What excuse did he give for leaving so soon?"

"None, really. His note merely relayed his regrets at being called away."

"If he was the one at the window last night—"

"From Sarah's description of the man," Daniel interrupted, "I'm certain it was Flynn O'Dannan who stood outside the cottage."

"I checked carefully at first light this morning. There was nothing. No prints in the dirt, no smudges on the glass, not a leaf disturbed. Nothing."

"You think he's our man? The one we've been looking for?" Danny sat down hard in his chair.

"No." Ian sat down across from him. "I think he's the *Fae* we've been looking for. Or at least one of them. I felt him on everything he'd touched. He might cover his tracks, but he canna cover his essence."

"And now he's gone, and we have no idea where." Danny leaned back in his chair, closing his eyes. "This whole time wasted."

"No necessarily. There are still others coming. I'd suspect O'Dannan was naught more than the advance scout."

Daniel sat quietly, obviously thinking over the possibilities. "A scout?"

"If it were me, I'd want to send someone in advance of my arrival. Someone to verify who is here. Someone to verify the lay of the land."

"Makes sense. So tell me. What exactly did their 'scout' see in that cottage last night that frightened him away?"

"There was nothin' he could have seen that had anything to do with this operation. Last night was purely personal."

"I'm sure it was," Daniel murmured, a frown wrinkling his forehead.

"I'm warning you, Danny, we'll no be talking about my private life."

"Well, perhaps we'd better, because something certainly frightened that man away."

"I dinna think so." Ian stood and pulled an object from his pocket. "I'm thinking fear has nothing to do with it. I'm thinking the scout simply did his job. I've a bad feeling it's all about Sarah."

"You've lost me, Ian. I'm not following you here."

"Think about it. What if this O'Dannan was at the window as a test, simply to verify whether or not Sarah could see him? She said it was the same man who'd watched us at lunch. The same one she saw outside Thistle Down when she first arrived. What if O'Dannan was the one who followed us down from Scotland?"

Danny nodded slowly. "He did arrive in a car similar to the one you described." He stood up and faced his friend. "If, as you suspect, he's Fae, Sarah's scream last night would prove without a doubt that she'd seen him. And that would be a dead giveaway of her lineage."

"It's how we found out, her seeing Dallyn in his own form. And I've no doubt but that O'Dannan is Fae."

"Then Dallyn was correct. They're going to try to use her."

"That and more. I suspect Henry was right as well—that she has abilities she's no even aware of." Ian extended his hand with the paper he'd fished from his pocket. "Have yerself a look at this."

Daniel took the paper his friend offered and glanced up questioningly.

"It's a note I left for her yesterday. When I came back to the cottage, she was sitting outside, surrounded by a red glow, her hand upon this paper."

Daniel hesitated, fingering the note. "I don't understand. You saw an aura around her?"

"No, it was no an aura. The verra air around her glowed red, charged in some manner. Yet she seemed to be totally unaware of it."

"Ian, this is incredible. Here in the middle, this looks like . . ." He stopped and looked up, amazement clear on his face.

"Aye." Ian took the note back and lightly ran his finger across it.

There in the center of the paper was a handprint. Sarah's handprint. Burned into the paper.

Fifteen

There. Right there on his knee. A smudge of dirt next to the perfect crease in his beige Armani pants.

Reynard pulled a pristine white handkerchief from his breast pocket and dabbed at the offending spot with short, irritated strokes. It must have come from the door when he'd climbed into the vehicle. The Mortal Plain was such a dirty place. He hated that about being here.

Not much longer now.

"I still can't believe the fool didn't realize he'd have to leave after what he did."

He looked up at the young man who spoke. Ramos lounged comfortably in the seat across from him, looking as if he'd been born in a limousine. Reynard smiled at the thought even as he amended it. The young man had not been born in a limo—only conceived in one.

"It's because, as you say, Ramos, he's a fool." He dabbed again at the smudge before stuffing the handkerchief into the ashtray. It was ruined now. Dirty. "Flynn could think of no other way to accomplish his task." He shrugged. "It's of no consequence to us now. He'd be useless in the next phase anyway. That's why you're here."

"As always, Father, it is my honor to serve you." Ramos bowed his head, shining black hair sweeping across his shoulders at the movement. When he looked up, laughter danced in his pale green eyes. "And my pleasure."

"So eager to face a Guardian, my son?"

Excitement lit those eyes for only an instant before Ramos's mask was back in place, hiding whatever emotion the man might feel. Reynard thought, not for the first time, how very like him his son was. Pity he was half Mortal.

"I look forward to releasing a Guardian's soul, Father."

"You want me to think you enjoy only the end re-sult? I find that hard to believe."

This time Ramos made no effort to hide his smile. "I relish the whole of it—the joy of the chase, the thrill of the challenge. And if along the way I can bring misfortune to a Guardian, well, it's like dessert after an excellent dinner."

Reynard regarded his finely manicured nails before looking up at his son. "The woman is the key. We mustn't forget that. If Flynn was correct and the Guardian has claimed her, you do realize that taking her from him would cause him great distress."

"Not only do I realize it, Father, I'm counting on it."

Yes, so very like himself.

"Don't forget you're my *brother* during this visit, not my son."

Ramos laughed. "Yes, the fact that we look the same age might be a little disturbing to the locals. Don't worry, Father. I won't let you down. Have I ever?"

"No, you haven't. Of course, I've never asked anything this important of you before."

Unflinching pale green eyes fixed upon his. "I'm quite aware of that. It's because of what I am. Because I'm not a . . ."

The annoying chirp of Ramos's cell phone interrupted their conversation.

"Yes?" His eyes met Reynard's. "One moment." He placed the small telephone to his chest. "It's Qasim. His man in London wants to know when you'll deliver the . . . item they're expecting."

Insignificant Mortal. Although he had served his purpose, Qasim was no longer necessary. Once he had the woman . . .

"Tell him there will be no delivery. I've no more time to waste on his petty problems."

Reynard settled back against the soft leather seat and sighed deeply, his son's conversation with the Mortal merely background noise to his thoughts. No longer would he need to deal with the annoying Mortals and their fanatic causes. No longer would he have to depend on the release of souls from their pitiful Mortal hosts to extend his life and keep him young. A female descendant of his people was within his reach. The real thing this time.

He glanced at his son from beneath lowered lashes. Ramos didn't know about Qasim's cause, nor the true nature of the items they provided the man. While Reynard trusted his son to deal with the vague details and the Mortals involved, he could never forget that Ramos was half Mortal himself. And Mortals had an irritating habit of getting emotionally involved in causes, forming attachments to other Mortals, to annoying ideals of right and wrong. Most inconvenient.

Still, his son had proved his worth on many occasions. His gift of inner sight had worked to ferret out traitors Reynard might never have found on his own. More important now, Reynard's people were unable to battle on the Mortal Plain. But his son was not fettered with such a restriction because he was partly a child of the Mortal Plain—a half-breed. He was the Nuadian version of a Guardian. Reynard's secret weapon. A weapon he had chosen at last to unleash.

If only he could have sired a girl child. While all descendants of the Fae had the ability to see their people in their true form, only female descendants could also see the gates to the Realm of Faerie. Males could see them only after they had been escorted through a gate once.

A daughter would have solved the problem long ago, but female children, rare for all Fae, were completely denied the outcasts. His people. The Nuadians. Yet another injustice he'd repay the High Council for when he made his way back.

Once he had control of this woman, this descendant of his race, it would be just a matter of time until he was back in his beloved Faerie Realm, standing at the Fountain of Souls. Just a matter of time until he dipped his hand into the fountain, drank his fill and immersed his body in the life-rich waters, insuring his immortality and continued youthfulness.

Just a matter of time until time itself wouldn't matter at all.

Sixteen

"There's something very bad here."

The child's whispered warning had caught Sarah off guard as she'd hugged Will good night. The whole day had been so uneventful, it was as if last night had never happened. As if she'd not seen that man standing at the door, watching. But Will's words brought it all back.

"What do you mean? What is it?"

"I don't know. I only know something very, very bad is close to us. Can't you feel it? Something bad is going to happen." Big blue eyes had regarded her seriously. "You should stay close to Uncle Ian. He's strong like my daddy, you know? He'll protect you."

Even here, standing at the edge of the ballroom, watching the people gathered for this evening's party, Sarah couldn't get the words out of her mind. Obviously Will had more than his share of imagination, but the little boy had seemed genuinely frightened when he spoke to her.

Though she felt embarrassed now, sitting at Will's bedside she'd been grateful for the long evening gloves Ian had insisted on buying for her to wear with this dress. The flow of feelings from the child were always so much stronger than those she had ever experienced from any other person. Even through the gloves she had felt tendrils of Will's discomfort. She couldn't imagine how strong it might have been had he touched her bare skin.

She nervously scanned the crowd, searching for Ian, feeling silly at the relief flooding through her when at last she spotted him at the bar waiting for their drinks. He was deep in conversation with Daniel and completely oblivious to the speculative looks and outright stares of the women standing in line around him.

Not that she could blame them. Dressed in the form-fitting tuxedo he'd pulled from his closet tonight, with the lights of the chandeliers glinting off his dark hair, he looked like her idea of every woman's fantasy. And when those black eyes glanced up and met hers across a crowded room as they did now . . .

A shiver traveled through her body, leaving chill bumps in its wake. One side of Ian's mouth curved up in a smile before he looked away, as if he knew the effect he had on her.

"And this beautiful lady must be the famous author I've heard about?"

Sarah started at the deep male voice so close behind her. Absorbed as she'd been in observing Ian, she hadn't heard anyone approach. Turning, she found her face only inches from a broad, tuxedo-clad chest. She stepped backward, giving herself some space from this stranger, and looked up into a pair of pale, turquoise green eyes framed by a wealth of shiny black hair falling over the wide shoulders of a very handsome young man.

The image of Dallyn instantly flashed through her mind. How odd the two men could strike her as so similar. Ian's unusual neighbor was blond and light like a sun-drenched day, while this man was dark, like a clouded, moonless night. If anything, this man should make her think of Ian, whose coloring was so similar. But he seemed nothing like Ian.

"Well, I certainly don't know that I'd say 'beautiful' or 'famous,' but she is an author." Brad, wearing his usual contemptuous sneer, accompanied the man, with Nicole following closely behind.

"Have a care, Tanner. I don't respond well to men who thoughtlessly insult innocent women. Sometimes those men even get . . . hurt."

The snarl in the stranger's voice elicited yet another shiver in Sarah, this one altogether different from the one she'd experienced while watching Ian. She backed up another step, and flinched as he reached for her hand, once again grateful for the gloves.

Color drained from Brad's face and he mumbled what she thought might be an apology before excusing himself to go to the bar.

Capturing her gaze with his own, the stranger brought her hand briefly to his lips, his warm breath curling over her skin, even through the cloth. She couldn't seem to look away from his eyes.

"I don't think your brother would appreciate the tone you took with my husband any more than I do. I expect you to apologize at once."

Nicole's demand broke the hold this stranger had on Sarah's attention. She looked at the woman, surprised by the unexpected authority in her voice. The helpless young girl persona had completely disappeared, replaced by a woman who was entirely accustomed to getting her own way in all situations.

Sarah only briefly wondered which was the real Nicole before the dark stranger spoke again.

"I am Ramos Servans," he said, still holding her hand, completely ignoring Nicole as if she'd never spoken. His voice, deep and cultured, slid over her like silk across smooth skin.

"Did you hear what I said to you? Are you going to go apologize to him now?" Nicole crossed her arms in irritation as he kept his back turned to her. "Or do I need to go find Rey?"

"Don't think to make him choose between us, Nicole. You will lose. You're merely a pretty distraction to Reynard—I am blood." He turned now, his teeth gleaming white as he flashed a hard smile her direction. "And believe me when I say blood runs thick in our family."

Nicole flinched back as if struck. "We'll just see about that," she said, turning sharply and striding away.

Ramos focused his attention back on Sarah, his face once again relaxed and friendly, as if the disturbing little exchange had never taken place. "I am enchanted to make your acquaintance, Sarah Douglas."

"How do you know my name?" Sarah attempted, without success, to reclaim the hand Ramos held.

"You will find I'm a very thorough man. I make it my business to discover every detail about anything that captures my attention." He brought her hand to his lips once more before releasing her. "And you, my dear Sarah, have most certainly captured my attention."

Her face colored hotly as he watched her with an amused expression.

"Really? And how did I manage to do that?"

"Why, simply by being your own unique self, my sweet." He glanced over her shoulder and a look of irritation flitted quickly across his face, an expression she might have missed had she blinked in that instant. "The orchestra begins, I believe. Of course you'll favor me with a dance?"

Music had begun and couples were drifting toward that end of the room.

"I don't really dance, I'm afraid."

He dismissed her statement with a flick of his wrist. "For now, I've business to attend to with my . . . brother." Yet again he claimed her hand, brushing his lips lightly against it. "But be assured, before the night is over, I will return to claim my dance with you, Sarah Douglas."

She watched in confusion as he moved through the crowd before disappearing through the terrace doors. The whole episode, though lasting only a short time, was quite unsettling.

"And what was that all about?" Ian stood at her side, holding two glasses. Offering one to her, he turned to look in the direction where Ramos had disappeared. One inquisitive eyebrow was arched when he turned back to her, waiting for her answer.

"I'm not sure." The most honest answer she could give.

Ian's breath huffed lightly and he took a drink from his glass. "Then perhaps you could at least tell me who he is."

"I'm not sure of that, either." At his dark look of irritation, she laughed. "Seriously, Ian, I know nothing about the man except his name."

"Aye? From all the hand kissing I saw, I would have assumed you knew the man well."

"No." Was Ian jealous? He sounded jealous. "He came over with Brad and Nicole, but he and Brad had a disagreement. They left and he stayed."

"Well, if he disna get along with Tanner, he canna be all bad." He smiled for the first time since joining her. "What's his name?"

"Ramos Servans."

His eyes narrowed and his body stiffened. She'd never seen Ian rattled before, but he certainly was now.

"Servans?" He recovered quickly, pausing to take a deep breath. "Stay away from him, Sarah."

"What?"

"Trust me on this one, luv. You dinna want to be around that man. Neither him nor his brother." He drained his glass and placed it on the tray of a passing waiter.

"I didn't think you knew him." Ian's attitude was so unexpected, she was unsure of how to respond to it.

He shook his head. "I've no met either man yet. Though I've heard of them."

"Well, Ramos seemed nice enough to me. Maybe you should actually take the time to meet these men before you start warning other people away from them."

He captured her hand and smiled. Taking her drink from her, he placed it on the tray of another passing waiter and then began to pull her toward the music.

"Oh, have no fear, Sarah, I've every intention of meeting them both."

They worked their way through the guests to the opposite end of the room, where several couples were already moving together to the alluring beat of the slow melody the orchestra played. He stepped into the flow of bodies, pulling her with him.

She stopped and shook her head. "I'm really not much of a dancer, Ian. I don't think I can do this." She couldn't possibly. Not here. Not in front of all these strangers.

"Och, Sarah. Come to me, darlin'. Close yer eyes and relax," he murmured as he drew her close, enfolding her in his arms. "Yer a Sensor, luv. Let yerself go. Feel the music."

Her arms slipped around him as if they'd a mind of their own. Muscles in his back flexed and released under her fingers as his body began to move in rhythm with the music and, pressed so close against him, her own responded. Before she even had time to think of anything other than how good he felt next to her, she was dancing.

She closed her eyes and melted into Ian, losing all track of time. The music flowed, one melody into the next, without a break. It didn't matter. Nothing mattered. The sensual combination of soft music and Ian's hard body moving against hers was like warm honey slowly pouring over her senses. She simply wanted it to go on without end.

Ian's body abruptly stiffened and moved slightly away from her as he turned. She opened her eyes to find Ramos Servans standing next to them.

"I've come to claim the dance you promised me, Miss Douglas." He held out his hand.

Ian's eyes glittered dangerously, his fingers tightening at her waist.

Sarah blinked rapidly, trying to clear her mind of its sensory overload. "I don't believe you two have met. Ian, this is Ramos Servans. Ramos? Ian McCullough." She looked between the two, not missing the fact that neither offered to shake hands with the other.

In fact, as unlikely as it seemed, she had the distinct impression of two warriors sizing one another up, squaring off on the field of battle.

"Whisky. Straight. And keep it coming."

Ian emptied the glass and slammed it to the bar, motioning to the bartender for a refill.

"Lucky thing your bloodline gives you immunity to the effects of alcohol."

"I dinna know about that, Danny. I'm no so sure I'd no rather prefer the effects right now."

His friend stood at his side, both of them watching the dance floor.

"If it's any consolation, my friend, she doesn't look like she's enjoying herself as much as when she danced with you."

Ian snorted. "Verra little consolation, with the way he's holding her. I doubt you could pass a piece of paper between them."

"Pass a piece of . . . ?" Daniel slapped him on the

back. "Hell, Ian. When you were out there, if we'd put that piece of paper anywhere near the two of you it would have burst into flames."

When Ian only glared at him but didn't reply, he continued, "Yes sir, flames. Hot enough to incinerate. Almost as heated as the looks you're sending their direction right now."

"I'm that obvious, am I?" Ian dipped his head and smiled sheepishly.

Daniel studied him for a moment before answering. "In all our years together, I don't remember ever seeing you like this."

Ian shrugged. If Danny only knew what an understatement that was. Ian himself didn't understand all the feelings he was having. But he certainly recognized anger when he felt it. And watching the couple swaying together on the floor across from him, he felt anger flow through his body like the blood through his veins, pumping and surging with each breath he took. With each movement of Ramos's hand on Sarah's back.

Sarah herself was a vision in gold, from her hair to her toes. Only her eyes sparkled in contrast. Gold set with emeralds, he amended his thought. Priceless.

He'd known the gown was meant for her the minute he'd seen it in the shop. The same color as her hair. When he'd insisted on buying it for her, all he could think of was how she would look dressed in it. Now that she wore it, he couldn't seem to think of anything but how she'd look as it came sliding off, the silky material gliding down her legs, pooling around her feet.

"There he is. He's arrived."

Daniel's elbow to Ian's ribs took him by surprise, pulling his focus from the woman on the dance floor.

"What? Who's arrived?"

"Servans."

"I've been watching Servans." *With his hands on my Sarah.* Where had that thought come from?

"No. That's only the brother, Ramos. He has nothing to do with EHN. I told you that earlier. He couldn't possibly be the connection." Daniel cast a withering look his direction. "Snap out of it, old man, get your mind back to business. Over there, by the door. Look at him."

A tall blond man in an impeccable white Armani tux stood at the entry to the ballroom, one hand carefully arranged in his front pocket. Ian recognized the designer's work. He wore it himself. He, however, had better taste than to wear white to a function like this or to pose like a model on the runway.

Danny was right.

Ian might be only half Fae, but he could spot a full-blood anywhere. And he would bet any one of his estates that the man in the doorway was a full-blood Fae. He'd know for sure when he got closer.

As he watched, the man surveyed the crowd with the haughty arrogance of a king looking over his peasants, his eye at last lighting on whatever or, more likely, whoever he sought.

Following the direction of his gaze, Ian spotted the couple on the dance floor. Ramos had seen his brother's entrance and was moving toward him, his hand at Sarah's back, propelling her forward. It was them Reynard had looked for and he headed in their direction, satisfaction showing on his face.

Ian angled his way through the crowd, intent upon intercepting them, Daniel at his back.

"What are you going to do?" Daniel elbowed past an older couple, smiling to excuse himself.

"I dinna know yet. But I do know what I'm no going to do. I'm no going to allow that Fae any time alone with Sarah. There's no telling what he might say or do to her. Or worse, how his presence might affect her."

He silently thanked the eager salesgirl who'd been so focused on making an additional sale when she'd brought out those gloves.

"At least with the gloves she'll no touch him," he muttered, pushing past a young woman who seemed quite fixed on gaining his attention.

"Perhaps she should."

Daniel's comment brought him to a halt. "What are you saying?"

"You're so certain they want to use Sarah against us. It's possible she could be our key to learning about them. To confirming what Servans is, what he plans to do."

Ian started forward again, speaking over his shoulder as he went. "I'll no do that to Sarah. She deserves better than to be used by any of us. She's a woman, no a weapon."

"Think about it. That's all I'm saying."

"No. And that's all I'm saying." He hurried forward, leaving Daniel behind.

"Ian." She murmured his name and smiled up at him as he reached out to touch her shoulder, reclaiming her from Ramos.

Unexpected relief filled him as she snaked her arm

around his back. He pulled her close and, tucking her tightly to his side, he touched his lips to the top of her head, breathing in the scent of her. He looked up to find two sets of green eyes fixed on his every move.

Reynard spoke first. "Ramos, you must introduce me to your lovely lady friend and her companion." He closed the distance to Sarah, capturing her hand and bringing it to his lips.

"Sarah Douglas, this is my . . . brother. Reynard Servans."

How interesting. Ian's eyes narrowed in thought. The pause had been slight, but he'd caught it. Very like the one he always suffered when he tried to introduce Henry as his uncle.

"*Enchanté*, mademoiselle." Reynard pressed another kiss to Sarah's hand.

"Are you . . ." She paused, her head tilted to the side as she spoke, her eyes narrowing as she glanced back and forth between the brothers. "Are you French?"

"No, my lovely lady. My home is currently in Switzerland. I simply find French to be the most civilized language man has invented. Certainly the only one suitable for greeting a beautiful woman such as yourself."

"Well, thank you." She turned to the brother, who had made the introductions. "I can see it runs in your family."

He acknowledged her comment with a smile and the barest dip of his head.

"But you sound completely British."

"Though our family estate is in Switzerland, Ramos has lived in London since he left for school many years ago." Reynard dropped her hand and turned to Ian. "And this would be . . . ?"

"Ian McCullough." He introduced himself, choosing not to offer his hand or his title. Neither were necessary.

Reynard didn't offer to shake either, instead clasping his hands behind his back.

"I've heard of you," he murmured.

"Good."

So, the game playing would be only thinly veiled. That was as it should be. He remembered now why the name struck a chord. Hearing the man lived in Switzerland had connected it for him. He'd come across it in his reading. He didn't need Sarah to confirm what this man was. Their search was over.

"Reynard Servans. Welcome to our home." Daniel picked that moment to join the group, accompanied by Nessa. A new round of introductions ensued, followed by Daniel calling over a waiter and offering glasses of champagne all around.

"A toast." Daniel held up his glass. "To a prosperous year of fund-raising and success in feeding those in need."

Each of them lifted their glass, clinking them together in the middle of their little circle. As they did so, Daniel's glass tilted, the bubbly liquid pouring down Sarah's arm.

"Oh my word, Sarah. I feel like such an ass. I'm so sorry." Daniel looked around, motioning for a waiter.

Ramos pulled a handkerchief from his pocket and wiped it down Sarah's arm, soaking up the better part of the champagne.

"No, no, it's okay. Here." She pushed the wet

handkerchief away with a smile. "Well, I guess you won't actually want to put that back in your pocket. But thank you for trying to help."

Ramos shrugged, tossing the wet square of linen onto the waiter's tray.

"I feel so bad about this." Daniel reached toward Sarah. "Here, let me help you get that wet glove off."

Ian glanced sharply at his friend. Had Danny's face not turned an unaccustomed shade of pink, Ian might have suspected, in light of their last conversation, that he'd done it on purpose.

"I'll have one of the maids rinse it out for you," Nessa added.

"Oh, don't go to any bother, please. It's fine, really," Sarah responded, peeling the clinging, wet material away from her skin. Once it was off, she stretched out her arms and looked down at them, laughing. "Perhaps I'll set a new fashion trend wearing only one."

Before she could lower her arms, Reynard withdrew a handkerchief from his pocket and dabbed at the beads of liquid left behind. Her head snapped up and she started to pull back, but he captured her hand, continuing to wipe the moisture from her skin.

At the contact, Sarah gasped, and Ian turned to see her eyes huge with shock and her mouth open, as if frozen in a silent scream. Then she crumpled.

He caught her just before she hit the floor.

Blackness. Swirling tendrils of evil rising from a slimy pitch blanketing everything. Cold curling around her fingers, sliding up her arms, reaching for her face. Suffocating her.

"No." A piercing scream in her mind, it was barely a sigh as it left her lips, but it was enough to wake her. Enough to save her from the evil terror threatening to consume her.

Sarah opened her eyes, unable to comprehend where she might be. The pain hit immediately. She blinked several times in an effort to get the little fragments of images to stop hopping around, to stop banging on the back side of her eyeballs with their sharp little hammers. Her head throbbed until she gave up and closed her eyes. Lying there breathing was the best she could hope for at the moment.

But she found no peace in the dark behind her eyelids. The malevolence waited for her there. It had receded, but even now it writhed in the distance and she knew, without a doubt, it would come for her again.

Gradually hushed angry whispers penetrated her consciousness. She worked to slow her panicked breathing, to listen, hoping one of the speakers could save her.

"Dinna I tell you I'd no risk her touching that vile creature? What were you thinking to do such a thing, especially when you knew how I felt?"

Was that Ian? It was so hard to tell with all the pounding in her head.

"We needed to see what would happen. Now we have all the confirmation we sought." A long pause, then the voice sounded calmer. "I suspect you're simply not thinking clearly on this. If the positions were reversed, you would have done the same thing. You know it."

Daniel? What had Daniel done to make Ian so

angry? If only she could concentrate. But the black continued to grow and slither there in the corner of her mind, seeping ever closer, distracting her.

"No. Here's what I know. Tomorrow morning, I'm putting Sarah in my car and I'm leaving here. You deal with them. I'm done. I'm driving straight back to Thistle Down, and I'm no stopping until I've crossed the waters where I know she's safe from them."

"Ian, be reasonable. You can't . . ."

"For the first time since we started this I am being reasonable. I should never have brought her near them. My mind's made up."

"Dallyn won't be pleased."

"Dallyn can bloody well go bugger himself, for all I care. I'm done with it. All of it."

A door slammed and the noise jarred her head, inciting the hideous roiling mass that threatened her, encouraging it to move forward.

She tried to sit up. Almost at once, hands were on her shoulders, gently pushing her back. Hands sliding down her arms, fingers feathering over her face.

Comfort, concern, fear, protectiveness. All swirling together, wrapping around her in a defensive cocoon, sheltering her in warmth, driving back the evil.

Ian.

She reached for his hand and captured it with her own, pressing it to her cheek.

"Rest for now, luv." His free hand stroked her hair. "Yer safe here. I'll see to that."

"What happened?" His touch strengthened her and her voice returned. She opened her eyes.

"I suppose that's a question I'll be asking you." His soft smile warmed her.

This time when she pulled herself up to sit, he assisted her.

"I'm not sure. I remember pulling off my glove and then Reynard started to wipe at my arm . . ." She stopped speaking as the full memory washed over her.

Pure evil. Worse than anything she'd ever known. Worse than anything she'd ever even imagined. All coming from Reynard.

Ian saw it in her face, or sensed it—she didn't know which. She didn't care. His strong arms enfolded her, pulling her close.

"I've never felt anyone that evil in my whole life." She pulled back from him, just enough to look up at his face. "It was awful, Ian. His touch . . ." How could she make him understand what she'd felt? "I still feel it on my skin. I see the evil, actually see it, every time I close my eyes. Horrible black writhing pools of it."

He said nothing, but tucked her head against his shoulder and lightly stroked her back, holding her close, driving the horror away.

Until she looked up and saw the glass doors and the impenetrable shadows that lay beyond them. A tremor ran through her whole body. Those same doors that had framed the awful grinning face last night.

"Lie back and try no to think anymore. We'll talk later, when you've rested and you feel stronger."

"I can't relax here, Ian. Not with those doors. Not when I keep thinking that at any moment that man could be there again. Watching."

He seemed to understand her fears and, although he'd assured her this afternoon her stalker was gone, that she had nothing to worry about from that quarter, he didn't argue with her now.

Instead he stood and lifted her into his arms, carrying her up the stairs as if she weighed nothing at all. Kissing her on the forehead, he gently deposited her on the bed.

"Sleep well, luv. I'll be down the stairs if you need me."

Alone? He was going to leave her alone? She couldn't fend off the blackness by herself. It only went away when he was there.

"Don't."

He stopped, his hand on the doorknob, and turned, looking at her questioningly.

"Please don't leave me alone."

He took a deep breath and walked back to her, sitting down beside her on the bed.

"Verra well. Get yerself ready for sleep and then call down to me. I'm going to double-check all the doors so you've nothing to worry about. All right?"

She nodded and quickly climbed off the bed as he stood and left the room.

She might value her independence, but, just this once, she was willing to do anything, even meekly follow instructions, to ensure she didn't have to spend the night alone.

Flipping on the bathroom light, she noted with disgust that she was even paler than usual, emphasizing dark smudges under her eyes. Fear certainly hadn't done anything to improve her looks.

She shook her head as she slipped out of her beautiful new dress. Turning the hot water on full blast, she lathered her arm, and scrubbed until it turned pink.

Maybe she should give up and go home early. Her writer's block showed no signs of abating in spite of what she'd expected when she came on this trip. She couldn't find the words to put on paper any better here than she had at home. She wasn't accomplishing anything, except scaring herself silly. At least there wasn't anything like what she'd experienced tonight back home in Denver.

Of course, there wasn't anything like Ian in Denver, either.

"Ian?"

Her soft voice floated down the stairs and he looked up. She waited at the top of the landing, like a child too frightened for bed.

A child with the face and body of a Faerie seductress.

He groaned at the amount of skin exposed by her little shorts and T-shirt. At her tousled curls begging for his touch. At her lips . . .

No.

She needed him for an entirely different reason than the one he was contemplating right now. He joined her on the landing, taking her hand and leading her back into the room. He flipped off the light and led her over to the bed.

"Aren't you going to change out of your tux?"

Big innocent eyes reflecting the moonlight that shone through the window regarded him as he tucked her into bed and climbed in beside her, she huddled under the covers, he sitting on top of them.

"This is fine, for now."

He'd taken off his jacket and tossed away the tie,

loosening the top buttons of his shirt in the process. That was enough. He needed the protection of his modern-day armor for the coming battle.

Clear your mind. Stay focused on the task at hand. He placed his arm around her and she snuggled against him, falling asleep almost immediately. He looked down at her face, calm and serene in sleep. Touchable. Kissable.

He would not let his thoughts go there. She needed only comfort and protection from him on this night. Nothing more. He'd give her that, and only that, even if killed him.

And at this moment, it felt as though it very well might.

Seventeen

She was trapped, unable to move.

Sarah came awake with a jerk. After her last forty-eight hours, she fully expected the worst when she opened her eyes.

What she found was about as far from the worst as she could possibly imagine.

Ian's face was only inches from hers, his lips parted slightly in sleep. His darkly shadowed cheeks, so freshly shaved last night, seemed to call out for her touch. When she tried to lift her hand to give in to that touch, she smiled, recognizing what had caused her to dream of being trapped.

One large muscled arm and an equally muscled leg draped across the bedding covering her body. She hadn't just dreamed of being trapped—she was! But it was by the most pleasant of bindings.

Unable to do anything else, she closed her eyes and enjoyed the feel of his body wrapped around hers. She inhaled deeply, allowing his clean masculine aroma to fill her senses. After years of trying to avoid touching others, for the first time she could remember her mind cried out at her current inability to touch, at this unaccustomed lack of sensory input. She wanted to free her hands from the blankets that bound her, to run them over his skin, to know what he felt. To feel what he felt.

She opened her eyes and found him watching her, a little smile playing around his attractive mouth.

"Good morning." She waited for him to respond, but he said nothing.

His smile grew, lighting his eyes until, at last, he lowered his lips to hers, claiming them.

"Yer a fair bonny sight for a man to wake up to."

Her heart pounded and she tried to calm herself enough to answer.

"You aren't so bad yourself." It was intended to be light and playful, but it sounded much too breathless for that. Blame it on her heart, beating much too fast. Surely he could feel it pounding, even through the pile of blankets pinning her beneath him.

He silently watched her eyes for a long moment, then kissed the tip of her nose and rolled off of her and out of bed.

"Climb out of there and get yerself going. By the time you make it out of the shower, I'll have a lovely pot of coffee waiting downstairs." With that, he walked out, shutting the door behind him.

Good Lord. First he melts her insides and turns her legs to jelly, then he expects her to get up and shower.

Oh well. At least coffee would be waiting for her downstairs.

Coffee and Ian.

How could it get any better than that?

Ian stared at the stream of dark liquid flowing into the glass carafe, but his mind wasn't focused on the little machine or even on the fragrant brew it created for him. His thoughts had traveled upstairs, hovering outside the steamy little room from which the sounds of running water issued.

When had he become so indecisive, so reluctant to lay claim to what he felt was his?

Rolling off Sarah, leaving her bed this morning without answering the need he saw shining in her eyes, had been one of the most difficult things he'd ever done. He had wanted her desperately.

He wanted her still.

Was there any way to reconcile the two halves of his life? He was sworn to be a Guardian, but the call to be with Sarah was like nothing he had ever known. The desire to protect her, to possess her was overpowering. In her arms, he forgot everything, wanted for nothing, knew peace at last.

It was as if she were his Soulmate.

The one intended for him had been lost during one of the final battles on the Mortal Plain over six hundred years ago. An innocent young girl he'd barely known, her soul ripped away by an unfated death at the hands of a Nuadian renegade seeking to prolong his own miserable life.

Ian closed his eyes and hung his head, willing his mind not to replay the horrors. Those souls forced from their hosts before their time were shattered and hurled into chaos. Many never made it back to the Fountain of Souls to be reborn. It had happened so often during those times. So many soul couplings broken for all eternity.

In the centuries since, he had never once backed away from a battle or shirked his duty. Never once doubted his destiny. Never once doubted he would spend his eternity alone as a Guardian, protecting other people's Soulmates.

Until Sarah entered his life.

And now . . . he doubted. Doubted his destiny, his path, himself.

He poured a cup of freshly brewed coffee, watching the ripples that formed in the liquid as the last drop hit.

It could be he struggled with this demon doubt for no reason. She might yet refuse him. She could turn her back on him, walk away, and all this internal battle would be for nothing.

He glanced up as the sound of running water stopped. He set his cup on the counter and headed for the stairs.

There was one way to know for sure. One way to end the doubt.

Sarah took the oversized white towel from the heated stand and wrapped it around her body, tucking the corner into the top above her breasts. The thick terry cloth was soft and warm and felt wholly self-indulgent. She was going to look for one of those racks when she got home.

She tugged at the smaller towel she had placed

about her wet hair before she climbed from the shower and, bending over from the waist, used it to scrub at the moisture in her hair.

When the bathroom door opened, she jerked upright, stumbled backward and would have fallen into the tub if not for Ian's quick grab.

"What are you doing in—"

He cut her question short by pulling her to his chest and covering her mouth with his own. After a moment, she didn't care that she hadn't finished her question; she was no longer interested in whatever his answer might have been.

Her only thoughts were of him and the way he felt. Of how badly he wanted her. Of how badly she wanted him.

He held her tightly to him as his kiss moved from her mouth to her chin to her neck.

"Sarah," he whispered, his breath heating the droplets of water that trickled down her neck.

She had every intention of answering, but her only response was a breathless moan. It was enough.

He covered her mouth again, his tongue demanding the entrance she had no desire to deny him.

One arm slid down and under her legs, and he swept her from her feet, their kiss remaining unbroken as he carried her from the bathroom to the bed they'd shared platonically the night before. This time when he laid her down, he covered her not with blankets, but with his body.

She should be worried about what her wet hair was doing to the pillow under her head, but she didn't really care.

Couldn't care when he caught at the corner of her

towel and lifted it. The wrap gave way and loosened, sliding down under the guidance of his hand, his skin warm against the wet chill of her own.

Couldn't think as he lowered his head and blew on the drips that trickled from her hair to her breast before lapping them up with his tongue.

"Oh my God, Ian. What are we doing?"

"What we were born to do," he whispered before running his tongue up the side of her neck, capturing more water droplets.

He still wore his dress shirt from the night before, the top few buttons undone as they had been when he'd joined her in bed. As she'd drifted off to sleep, she'd marveled at how sexy that looked, how she'd like to undo the remaining buttons.

Her fingers trembled as she reached for those buttons now. She grappled with the tiny bits of plastic, irritated that the buttonholes seemed to hide in the decorative tucks running down the front. When she tugged at the cloth, and growled in frustration, he pulled up and away, rising above her to his knees, straddling her body.

He grasped the front of his shirt with both hands and ripped it open. The tiny buttons made little clicking sounds as they rebounded off the wall and the bedposts, headed for who knew where. Next his tattered shirt sailed through the air to join the buttons somewhere on the floor.

The sight took her breath away. She'd written just such a scene in one of her books, but her words were nothing compared to reality. It was magnificent. *He* was magnificent.

She reached for his waist, her fingers fumbling at

his zipper, but he stopped her, his hands closing over hers, pressing her against the hard length of him.

"I dinna think so, luv." He grinned down at her. "I'm a wee bit excited, so we'll be wanting to let the metal down verra carefully. It's perhaps best I do that."

"Okay, you do it." She tightened her fingers around the bulge that strained against her hand, slowly rubbing down and back up again. The bulge twitched and grew even larger under her touch. "But you'd better hurry."

It seemed like only seconds before his pants joined the tattered shirt somewhere off the side of the bed.

He gently slid one arm under her back, lifting and supporting her weight as he pulled the towel from around her and tossed it away.

"Christ, but yer a beauty." He ran his hand slowly across her stomach and over her hip.

"Hardly. I'm sure you've seen more . . ."

"Shh." He stopped her with a finger to her lips. "Dinna ever doubt what I tell you, woman."

Opening her lips, she nibbled at the finger with her teeth before running her tongue down the length of it. At his groan, she took the finger into her mouth, sucking hard.

"It's a dangerous thing, to tease a man like that, luv," he rasped, but didn't move his hand.

She smiled her answer, switching to a second finger, nibbling and sucking as before.

His growl made her giggle. A giggle that quickly died in her throat when he moved over her, his tongue tracing along the side of her breast before taking her nipple into his mouth. His tongue swirled around and around, and then he began to suck, all in an exact imitation of what she'd done to him. Every nerve in her body tingled in response.

"Ohh," she sighed. This was unbelievably wonderful. He continued on to the other breast, repeating the process as she felt a need growing in her depths.

He moved his hands down her sides to her hips and then under, grasping her thighs and lifting as he slid his body into place over hers.

She locked her ankles behind his back, marveling at how he fit against her body so perfectly.

"Sarah," he whispered as she looked into his eyes, so dark she almost thought she could see her reflection there.

He kissed her, soft and tender little kisses, over and over as he slowly rocked his swollen head against her sensitized opening, stroking and building the need in her.

"Sarah," he breathed against her skin before running the tip of his tongue around her ear, sucking on the lobe as he eased himself just barely into her opening.

He stopped, held himself still, moving no farther.

She grabbed his shoulder, tried to push herself against him, but he held her firmly in place.

"Patience, luv. We'll get there." Though his words were calm, his voice sounded strained.

"No patience," she panted. *Now now now now now!* her brain screamed.

He chuckled and moved a fraction forward before withdrawing.

She gasped, digging her fingers into his arms.

When he entered the next time, he pressed farther before withdrawing.

She actually moaned, the loss felt so great.

As he entered again, he slid his hands down under her bottom and pulled her to him, plunging himself deeply into her body. He stilled, breathing heavily as he held her close, raining gentle kisses on her face, over her eyelids and back to her lips.

She trembled from the sheer joy of it.

He withdrew, but only part of the way now, driving back into her again.

She tightened her legs around him, lifting to meet his next thrust.

His pace increased, as if in tune to the frenzy building inside her body. Over and over until the tension built to a breaking point. And as she broke, all the little muscles in her body clenching and tightening around him, carrying her to a place of ecstasy where she'd never been before, she heard him whisper again.

"My Sarah."

Then he found his own release and collapsed beside her, pulling her close to him, kissing her still damp hair as she buried her face against his chest.

Never, not once in his entire life, had he experienced anything even close to that.

Ian tightened his hold on the woman in his arms.

He no longer doubted. She was meant to be his. His to love, his to cherish, his to protect.

Her protection was his first priority. He would take her back to Thistle Down, where she would be safe. Then he would figure out what he needed to do next, how he would deal with this discovery.

"Sarah?"

"Mm?"

Her vague little noise and satisfied expression filled him with joy, sent the juices of victory flowing through his body.

"We need to get packed, luv, and get on the road." He sat up, pulling her up with him. She smiled at him and he very nearly pushed her back down.

Instead he climbed from the bed. "I'm going to shower while you have yer coffee. Then I'll load up our things and we'll be off."

"Okay." She stretched and moved her legs over the side of the bed. "Then we can stop and say good-bye to Will on our way out."

"No." Servans could still be there and he wouldn't have her anywhere near that Nuadian beast again.

"What?" Her smile turned to confusion.

"I said no. I'll no have you exposed to that man again."

"Servans, you mean?" She paused, closed her eyes for a minute and then smiled. "He must be gone. I can feel it. It's perfectly safe for me now."

"I'll no take that chance."

"Ian. I wouldn't want to bump into that man again either. I wouldn't go if I thought there was any chance he was still there. But he's gone. I told you. I would feel the evil if he were still there. Besides, we promised Will."

Perhaps she was right, but it didn't matter. She was his to protect now. "No. Will is going to have accept our change of plans. I forbid you to leave the cottage by yerself."

"You *what?*"

"Just you sit tight, luv, while I go catch a shower. Yer no to step outside that door without me."

She said nothing, so he leaned over and kissed her on top of her damp curls before he walked into the bathroom and turned on the water.

Sometimes the old ways were best. She might be angry with him now, but she would get over it. He would do anything to keep her safe. Anything. Even risk her being angry for a little while.

He can't tell me what to do.

Sarah stalked out over the lawn, headed toward the main house. Granted, Ian had rescued her from abject humiliation more than once over the course of the past three days, and they had just shared an experience she still could hardly believe, but she would not allow him—or anyone else—to order her about like that. Telling her she wasn't allowed to leave the cottage by herself.

" 'Sit tight, luv,' " she mimicked in a false baritone, scrunching up her nose in distaste. " 'You're not to step outside that door without me.' Well, I don't think so. I don't think I'll be taking orders from you or anybody else today. And I don't think there's anything you can do about it," she muttered, but she glanced over her shoulder toward the cottage and quickened her pace all the same.

She shook her head in confusion. Everything had been so wonderful and then, all of a sudden, he'd turned into this time-warp reject of a chauvinist, ordering her around like he had a right to.

It wasn't happening. She had made a promise to Will and she fully intended to keep it.

Reaching the front door, she lifted her hand to knock just as the door opened and she once again found herself nose to chest with Ramos Servans. This time the chest in question was covered in a white polo.

"Sarah," he said, pleasure lighting his face. He grasped her arms and pulled her to him for a tight hug. "I've been worried sick about you. No one around here was willing to tell me anything about your condition after McCullough carted you away last night."

She froze, not quite sure what to expect. No uncovered skin on her arms, thankfully. She relaxed a bit.

Holding her away from him, he studied her face. "I don't see any ill effects from your little fainting spell. In fact, you look quite good this morning."

"I feel good this morning, thank you."

A grin lit his face. "Yes. You *do* feel good." The grin turned speculative. "I wonder . . ."

He interrupted his own comment to pull her close again, lowering his mouth to hers. When she opened her mouth to gasp in astonishment, he took advantage of the situation, his tongue darting in quickly to dance around her own.

He let go of her, his grin back in place. "Yes. Well, that answers my question. I'll be seeing you, Sarah." Leaning down, he picked up the suitcase she hadn't noticed before and walked past her.

Fragments of thoughts scampered through her mind, all of which began with *What the hell . . . ?* but she didn't manage to verbalize any of those.

"What question?" She was rapidly learning that

what came out of her mouth these days frequently bore little relation to what was in her mind at the time.

A white limousine pulled into the drive, a uniformed man jumping out and opening the door before taking the suitcase. Ramos turned back to her, grin still in place.

"I simply wondered if you'd taste as good as you look and feel." He lifted a hand to wave as he climbed into the car, but leaned out at the last minute. "And you do, by the way."

Sarah stood, hands on her hips, watching the car drive away. If she took every unusual event she had lived through in her whole entire life, she doubted she'd have enough to equal what she'd experienced since she'd stepped off that plane in Glasgow.

After more than thirty years of feeling every single emotion of every single person she came into physical contact with, suddenly everything she had come to expect had turned upside down.

Since she'd been here, she'd bumped into so many people whose touch was like none she'd ever experienced before. From the all-encompassing evil of Reynard Servans to the vague all-over goodness of Dallyn. Now she could add Ramos Servans to that list of unusual encounters.

Shaking her head, she turned to find an intense pair of blue eyes looking up at her from the doorway.

"The very person I came to see." She reached out and ruffled the already messy blond hair on Will's head.

"You should be with Uncle Ian. Where is he?" He looked at her reproachfully as he reached for her hand, pulling her into the foyer and down the hall toward the back of the house.

"Taking a shower." How did this boy constantly make her feel like the child in their encounters?

They entered the kitchen and Will led her to a small table where two bowls were already filled with cereal. A pitcher of milk sat between them.

"He's going to be angry with you." The boy shook his head as he took a seat. "Eat your breakfast."

"This is mine?"

He nodded. "I knew you were coming."

"Oh really?" She sat down and reached for the milk. "I thought you said we were alike. I don't know what's going to happen before it does. How come you do?"

"I don't know what's going to happen before it does either. But I know the way you feel and I felt you getting close."

Why fight it? Will had more improbable answers for her improbable questions than anyone she'd ever known. She decided perhaps she should listen.

Will smiled and gave her a classic little-boy look, a roll of his eyes. "I said you were like me, Sarah, not exactly like me. Your mommy and daddy didn't tell you any of the stories, did they?"

"No, honey, they sure didn't."

"None of us are exactly alike. It depends on which of the gifts we have. See, in the beginning, when Faeries and men lived together in our world, the Fae were very powerful. They each had all the different gifts. But after the Great Spell, their powers didn't work the same in the world anymore. Since we only have *some* Fae in us, we only have a little bit of their gifts."

Cereal crunching was the only sound in the kitchen as Sarah thought that over.

"What's this Great Spell?" She took another big bite and waited for her teacher to finish with his own mouthful.

"Duh. It's what the Earth Mother did to stop the fighting in our world."

"There's still plenty of fighting in our world, junior."

The eye roll again. "Yeah, but that's only Mortals." He took another bite and Sarah waited patiently. "It was really bad in those days and the Mortals were taking the worst of it. I mean, think about it. The Fae were stronger, smarter and had all those special skills. Mortals didn't stand a chance. So the Earth Mother fixed it so the Faeries couldn't fight when they were in the Mortal Plain. Boy, my dad says that really made the Nuadians angry." He laughed and wiped a trail of milk from his chin, followed by another large bite.

"Who are the Nuadians?"

Will's eyes grew very large, and for a moment she feared he might have tried to swallow too much in that last bite. Finally he answered.

"They're the bad guys. The really bad guys. They're Fae who messed up everything in the Faerie Realm by trying to take over. So they got kicked out. That's why there was all that fighting that the Earth Mother had to stop. They gave themselves a new name when they got here to the Mortal Plain. Nuadians. For Nuada of the Silver Hand, a king of the Tuatha de Danann."

"So, let me make sure I have this straight. We live on the Mortal Plain, yes?"

"Yes."

"And the Faeries aren't here anymore because they live in this Faerie Realm. Right?"

Will nodded and continued to spoon cereal into his mouth. "But they're here sometimes," he mumbled around his food.

"Okay. Well, if these Nuadians are Faeries who got kicked out of the Faerie Realm, where do they live?"

The little boy shrugged. "Here, somewhere. They can't get through the Portals."

Breakfast was finished in silence as Sarah considered which of the two of them was actually the better storyteller. She may be the fiction writer, but the child sitting across the table from her had her beat when it came to imagination. He had an amazing fantasy world going on in that little head.

She also considered her strange response to the boy. His feelings passed to her more strongly than any she'd experienced before. She suspected it might be because of the connection she felt to him. A connection she chalked up to his being such a loving child.

Sarah stood and reached over to ruffle his hair again. "You're going to be a force to be reckoned with one day, William Daniel Martin Stroud."

"I know." He stood on his chair and put his arms around her neck, giving her a hug. "What are you going to tell Uncle Ian?"

"About what?"

His slowly shaking head and the little *tsk-tsk* sound

he made had her smiling until he answered her question.

"About that Ramos man kissing you."

"I hadn't thought to tell him anything about it."

"Why aren't you going to tell him?"

"Because it meant nothing. And, anyway, it's not like he'll ever know about it."

"He'll know."

"Well, even if he did, why would it make any difference to him?"

"Because I'm no fond of sharing, that's why."

At the sound of Ian's voice, Sarah spun around. He filled the doorway, looking larger than she remembered from just an hour ago.

Larger and much, much angrier.

The longest seven hours of her life.

Ian hadn't said three sentences to her the entire drive back to Scotland. When they'd stopped for gasoline, he'd waited for her to get out of the car and go into the little shop, staying close, but saying nothing. Even this afternoon, when they'd arrived at Thistle Down, he'd silently carried her bags to the cottage, leaving them inside the door. He'd hesitated, just outside, and she'd thought he might turn and speak to her at last, but he didn't. He'd walked away without a word.

Sarah sat at her computer, the blinking cursor mocking her continuing inability to communicate with her inner muse. Some great author she had been for the last six months. Nothing. She had nothing.

She placed her index finger on the lighted OFF button and pressed, with only the tiniest twinge of guilt as the screen went to black. Leo, the computer guru at her favorite repair shop, had warned her repeatedly about how bad it was to do that, but the action gave her some perverse sense of control. At worst, she would mess up her computer. Not like it was doing her any good anyway. Not like she was messing up anything important. Not like she was messing up her whole life.

"Ha. I think I might have done that already."

Honestly she couldn't understand why Ian was so angry. She hadn't done anything wrong. Sure, she'd left the cottage when he'd told her not to, but, if anything, she should be the one who was angry at that. Not him. Where did he get off telling her where she could and couldn't go?

It couldn't be Ramos, could it? It made no sense that he'd be jealous, and yet one of the last things he'd said had been that remark about not sharing. Even if that were the problem, she hadn't kissed Ramos; he had kissed her. When he had, she'd felt . . . nothing.

Literally nothing from the man, as if he somehow held all his emotions tightly locked away. Nothing from her except surprise and confusion that he'd done it. Certainly no attraction. Not at all like when Ian kissed her.

When Ian kissed her it felt right, like she was complete. A whole person. But there was no point in going there now.

She rose from her chair, walking aimlessly through the cottage and out the back door. With no particular destination in mind, she strolled across the lawn and into the gardens, finding and following the main path until eventually she came to the crossroads.

Once again she felt the strong pull to wander down the fork Ian had warned her against, but she resisted, going only as far as the tree she'd almost collided with on her first trek down the path. She knelt, running her fingers over the bark, trying to understand what force drew her in this direction. The tree gave her no answers.

"Maybe there are no answers," she whispered as she turned to sit. Her back cradled against the broad trunk, she closed her eyes. "Maybe it's just Will's Faeries calling to me."

"That verra well may be."

Sarah's eyes flew open at the quiet sound of his voice. Ian, framed in the glow of the sun at his back, stood by her outstretched feet, looking down at her.

She raised her hand to shield the glare from her eyes. "I didn't know you were anywhere around. How did you sneak up on me so quietly?" Her eyes had been closed only a minute.

"I dinna sneak. Call it a talent . . . or a gift." He shrugged and then put his arms behind his back, bringing to Sarah's mind a soldier at parade rest. "We need to talk."

"About?"

"Dinna make this more difficult than it already is, Sarah."

"I'm not trying to. What do we need to talk about?"

Ian sighed deeply and squatted down to her eye level, reaching out and taking her hand between his two. "Everything that's happened. Faeries and feelings, danger and safety. Trust. We need to talk about us."

"Is there an 'us' to talk about?" She asked the question, not sure she wanted the answer, regardless of what it would be.

"I guess that's what we need to talk about." A small, almost forced grin flitted across his face as he rose, pulling her to her feet. "Henry's out this evening, dining at the home of a lady friend. Come up to the main house tonight and have dinner with me. We can talk then."

"I don't know, Ian. I don't know what to say."

"Say yes."

"No, I didn't mean about dinner. I meant—"

"I know what you meant," he interrupted. "But for now, say you'll have dinner with me. We'll worry about the rest of it tonight."

This time the smile he bestowed on her was genuine. It dazzled her, beguiled her into smiling in return.

"Seven?"

"Okay." How could she refuse him? "Dinner at seven."

He lightly kissed the back of her hand before striding away down the path in the direction *she* wasn't supposed to take.

Sarah watched him disappear into the thick foliage, shaking her head. Dinner and a talk, that's all it would be. A chance to clear the air so they could go back to being friends.

Was that really all she wanted?

"Yes," she said out loud in an attempt to reinforce the thought. "Dinner and a talk. That's all. No 'us.' Only dinner and a talk."

But it was Shakespeare's line about the lady

protesting too much that bubbled through her mind as she made her way back to the cottage.

"So it's Reynard we're dealing with. Was there anyone else—any other Fae with him?" Dallyn was perched on a tree limb a couple of feet off the ground, his back resting against the trunk.

Ian paced back and forth in front of the Portal. "No one but Ramos, though he's no a full-blood. There was another Fae there earlier. Spying on us, I believe."

Dallyn stilled on his perch. "Do you have any idea who it might have been?"

"He goes by the name of Flynn O'Dannan. Why?"

"Ah. Flynn." Dallyn nodded as if to himself, seeming to relax again. "No reason. So, you left Reynard at Glaston House?"

"No, he was already gone. He apparently left right after Sarah's collapse, while Danny and I were still at the cottage."

"Why didn't you deal with him then and there when this first happened?"

"I think you know the answer to that. There were too many innocent bystanders."

"And Sarah to look after." Dallyn swung down off the limb, coming to stand in front of Ian.

"Don't be thinking to complain to me of that. Yer the one who put her under my protection. Yer the one who insisted I take her with me and expose her to that vile horror." He shook his head and started to pace again. "I should have refused in the beginning. I should have left her here."

"And what would you have done had he come here

instead while you were at Glaston House and she here alone, unprotected?"

"She would have been safe here."

Dallyn's laugh was short and without humor. "Don't deceive yourself, young Ian. You make a serious mistake if you think a Fae of Reynard's power can't find a way around your defenses."

"No." Ian felt the intended sting of rebuke in Dallyn's address to him, but he refused to give in to it. "No. The only mistake I made was in listening to yer plan to put Sarah in jeopardy. I'll no do that again, General."

Dallyn walked toward the Portal, stopping to glance back before he entered. "Consider well your actions. Each small movement in the pond results in ripples, each ripple having far-reaching consequences."

Ian shook his head and turned his back on the Fae, heading down the path toward the manor house.

"We'll speak of this tomorrow, Ian."

He heard the Fae but didn't turn, didn't acknowledge the comment, as he stalked angrily toward home.

Ponds and ripples and consequences.

They all spoke in riddles. The more important the message, the greater the riddle. Even after all these years it still irritated him that he'd yet to meet a full-blood Fae who would just say what he meant.

"Pardon?"

Ian had been looking right at her across the dining table, watching her delicious pink lips move. Unfortunately he had no idea what words had come out of them. He'd been watching her all through dinner, so consumed with the sight and smell of Sarah that he couldn't eat. He had no desire for the food in front of him, only for the woman who sat across the table.

She wore the same pale gauzy gown she had the morning he'd secretly watched her in the yard. Even now the thought of how she had looked with the first rays of sunlight glowing around her, the breeze molding that dress to her body, warmed him, stirred his own body to life.

"I was asking if you'd changed your mind about our talk? You've been remarkably quiet all evening for someone who wanted to discuss . . . everything."

He bit back a smile at her carefully chosen words. There hadn't been much conversation throughout dinner. He'd found himself oddly reluctant to begin with Martha serving the meal and then separated from them only by the door between the dining room and kitchen. She had cleared the table a few minutes earlier and they were relaxing over their wine.

"Sorry. I'm thinking a bit more privacy might be in order." He glanced at the door to the kitchen with a raised eyebrow, turning to find her looking in the same direction.

"Agreed."

"I know," he said, rising from his seat. "Bring yer glass and come with me." He clasped his glass and the wine bottle in one hand, catching up her hand with his other.

He led her to a back door and out into the gardens behind the house, down a side path to a cozy gazebo covered in climbing roses. They ducked inside, where a continuous bench lined the walls. A small table sat in the center with a lamp hanging down from the rafters above it.

After setting the bottle and his glass on the table, Ian lifted one of the generous cushions covering the bench to reveal a hidden drawer. He removed a box of matches and pulled the lamp down to light the candles it held.

"Privacy at last."

He smiled and watched her slip off one sandal so she could tuck her leg under her when she sat. The gauzy gown settled around her, and he noticed for the first time as he sat next to her tiny threads in the material that reflected the glow of the candlelight.

He topped off both their glasses and leaned back against the cushion, still undecided how much to tell her. Enough to ensure her safety, certainly, but how much would be enough? He didn't want to go too far. Too much could be overwhelming and she'd never believe him.

She sipped her wine, then put the glass on the table and turned to him. "Where do you want to start?"

The time to plan his speech had passed.

"When did you first start to have those feelings about people?"

She took a deep breath, and her arms slipped around her middle, the self-protective gesture he'd seen so often. She scooted back, putting distance between them, facing him. He'd let her have her space for the moment.

"Is that what this is all about? My feelings?"

"No, luv, that's only a part of it. I told you, we need to discuss everything."

He couldn't stand the look of hurt in her eyes, couldn't stand the thought he had caused that hurt. He set his own glass away and, reaching down, he captured the foot she'd left on the floor and lifted it to his lap, removing her remaining sandal in the process. He started a slow circling massage with his thumbs on the sole of her foot.

"Was it about the time you turned seven, by any chance?" Her head snapped up, the look of wariness he saw confirming what he already suspected would be true.

"How did you know that?" Barely a whisper of sound.

"It's the age when the gifts normally manifest themselves. Seven."

"Gifts?"

"The gifts of yer heritage, Sarah. Gifts of yer blood."

She tried to pull her foot away, to sit up straight, but he wasn't ready to relinquish control of it yet. He wasn't ready to break the physical contact either. He wanted to touch her. When her forehead wrinkled in a frown he barely managed to resist the urge to smooth it away.

"Oh, please tell me we are not talking about Will's Faeries here, are we?"

Without releasing her foot, he leaned forward and handed her glass back to her before resuming the slow massage.

"Just listen and think about what I'm telling you, about a mysterious people whose stories have been told for centuries in widely different cultures all around the world. Strangely similar stories of powerful beings who appear to Mortals only when and where they choose to, in a variety of shapes and sizes. Sometimes they're helpful, sometimes harmful, depending on the story. They're called Fatua in Italy, Fées in France, Amazula in Africa, Tylwyth Teg in Wales. To the Irish they're known as Tuatha dé Danann. They're the Phi race of Thailand, the Lele of Romania, the elves of Scandanavia. Even yer own Native Americans have a variety of names for these beings."

"Those are just fairy tales," she scoffed, her eyes widening as she realized what she'd said.

"Aye, they are that, luv. Tales of the Fae. A race more ancient than you can imagine. Though they dinna live with us anymore, they are still among us. They still live through many of us."

"No." She shook her head slowly. "That's too fantastic, Ian. It's bad enough coming from a six-year-old, but surely you don't believe that fantasy yourself."

"Accept it for the moment, just for the sake of argument. We'll come back to yer believing it later." He held up a hand to silence her protest. "Will told you of the great internal war of the Fae and how some of them were banished from their home, aye?"

She nodded, the look of skepticism still strong in her eyes.

"Those are the ones who are a danger to descendants of the Fae. To you."

"Look, Ian, even if I did believe there were actually something as extraordinary as Faeries at one point in history, I certainly can't accept that I descend from them. There's nothing at all special about me."

"Oh, aye," he taunted. "Yer a normal woman, walking the face of the earth, touching people and knowing everything they feel. Everyone can do that, can they no?"

She had no reply, so he answered for her.

"No. Everyone canna do that. Yer special. You've Fae blood in you. And as a result, yer in danger from those evil ones who roam the Mortal Plain, looking for a way back to the Faerie Realm so they can continue the destruction they started all those centuries ago."

"Why would they want me? What could I possibly do for them?"

"You've the power to see the Portals they need. With you they could find their way back into the Faerie Realm. Once that happens, life as we know it here, now, will be altered."

"Okay, if what you say is true, then why is Will able to feel things? Didn't you say all those Faerie gifts kick in when you're seven? *He's* barely six."

"I told you seven is the age the gifts normally manifest themselves. On the rare occasion a child is born who's more powerful in the gifts for one reason or another. Will is such a child."

Her head bowed, she stared at her hands in her lap for what seemed an eternity to him before looking up. "And you know all this how?"

"Because I am Fae as well."

"I thought you said you were a Highlander?"

"I am. My mother was a daughter of the laird of the McCullough clan. My father was full-blooded Fae."

She stared at him incredulously, shaking her head. "You actually believe this, don't you? I have no idea what to say to you. And even if I could suspend belief for this discussion, I still don't see what any of that has to do with what's gone on between us today."

"It's everything to do with it. I dinna handle today at all well. I know that and I'm sorry for it. But when I thought you in danger this morning, when I came out of the shower and you were gone, it frightened me, Sarah. And I'm no a man who knows fear or how to deal with it."

"Oh, Ian." She did pull her foot away then, moving forward onto her knees and placing her palm on his cheek.

He wrapped his arms around her, pulling her close, burying his face in her hair.

Strawberries. She smelled of strawberries. His favorite.

The aroma lightened as she pulled back to look at him.

"I never meant to frighten you. But I'm not going to allow anyone to tell me what I can and can't do. And besides, I told you. There was nothing at Glaston House to fear."

His jaw dropped. "I canna believe you, of all people, could sit here and say that. What of the evil you touched for yerself just last night?"

She drew back, a frown wrinkling her brow. "I didn't feel any of it this morning. I mean, who knows? Maybe the whole thing was my imagination. Simply the product of everything that happened." Both feet were tucked under her this time. "Maybe . . . maybe the excitement, the alcohol, the stress of seeing Brad there. All that combined might have contributed to it. Like a migraine or something. I still find it almost impossible to believe something like that could have been real."

"Oh, it was real, Sarah. Verra real. I canna believe you still try to deny all that you've seen for yerself. Reynard Servans is evil personified. He's a Nuadian Faerie. And I want yer promise to stay away from him and his brother."

If that's even what he is.

"Ramos was a perfect gentleman. I didn't feel anything evil or bad about him."

"But you did with Reynard. You must trust those feelings. I'm telling you, yer in great danger from that man."

"Honestly, Ian. You can't seriously expect me to believe the man is a Faerie, for God's sake, just because I had some bizarre response to him."

"Verra well. Let me ask you a question. Do you remember where Reynard Servans told you he was from?" He'd already said more than he'd intended, and still she wasn't convinced. He might as well share with her what it was he'd remembered while at Glaston House.

"Switzerland. Why? What does that have to do with anything?"

"Going back to my earlier story for a bit, do you know what they call those of the legend in Switzerland?"

When she shook her head in response, he answered his own question.

"Servans. They're called Servans in Switzerland."

Sarah wasn't ready to accept the truth yet. He felt sure of it. She stubbornly clung to her myth of reality, refusing to acknowledge the truth of what he told her.

If she couldn't accept she was Fae, couldn't accept that he was, how could he expect her to believe she was his Soulmate? There was no point in discussing it. He'd have to wait.

For now, he should do the right thing. He just hated to let go of her.

After their talk, and her agreement not to see the Servans brothers again, Sarah and Ian had sat in silence, drinking their wine, each lost in their own thoughts. At one point, he'd pulled her close, wrapping his arm around her. She snuggled there still, in the protection of his body, her head on his chest. He could feel her shivers against him now. The gauzy dress he found so fascinating was no protection against the chill of a damp Scottish night.

The right thing would be to take her back to her cottage and let her go inside, but that would mean the loss of her body next to his. The loss of her essence surrounding him, lulling him into a sense of . . . what?

Completion. When he held Sarah, it felt like she belonged there, as if she were a part of him, an integral extension like his arm or his leg . . . or his heart. His own heart pounded in his chest at the thought.

Another shudder, this one more pronounced, and his common sense overruled his desire.

He'd do what was right. As he always did. It was his destiny. He was, after all, a Guardian.

"Come on, it's gone cold. Let's get you home." He lifted his arm but she wrapped both of hers around his chest, holding on.

"Not yet. I'm not cold." Her next shiver belied her brave words.

"Sarah, luv, yer shivering hard enough to rattle the damn bench." He kissed the top of her head, flooding his senses with the aroma of fresh strawberries. "Come on now. Get up, lass."

She shook her head against his chest and gripped him more tightly. "No. I'm not ready."

"Not ready for what?" He looked down at her quizzically.

"For tonight to be over. I don't want to let go yet."

As if that's what he wanted.

"Did I say anything about tonight being over? We just need to get you inside." He grinned as a thought occurred to him. "And if letting go is yer problem, I can fix that."

He turned in her grasp and slid his free arm under her legs, standing as he did so.

Her gasp was accompanied by her arms flying up to clutch around his neck. He didn't even try to prevent his chuckle at the little squeaky sound she made.

"Put me down. You can't carry me all the way to the cottage. I'm too heavy."

"You were the one who dinna want to let go." He grinned. "Besides, yer a mere feather, darlin'. I'm no putting you down till we get there, so put an end to yer wiggling and hang on."

She studied him for a moment as if to judge the depth of his sincerity before laying her head on his shoulder. With her every exhale, a little puff of air stirred the hair against his neck sending tingles throughout his body, awakening need deep within his core.

He paused at the door to the cottage, shifting her weight as he fumbled with the handle and her head popped up.

"My sandals. I left them in the gazebo."

"I'll bring yer shoes down tomorrow. Dinna fret yerself over it."

Inside, he kicked the door shut with his foot before leaning down to deposit her feet on the floor. Sarah's arms remained locked around his neck as he straightened, drawing her up next to him. His own arms closed around her reflexively.

Time stood still as he searched her eyes, open and accepting.

"Is there an 'us,' Ian?"

In response, his hands slid up to her cheeks, framing her face, his fingers moving, as if of their own accord, up into the silken curls. He rubbed the strands between his fingers, watching her mouth, the quick nervous move of her tongue to moisten her lips.

Just a taste. He could still do what was right, follow his destiny.

He lowered his head and nibbled her lips, the lips he'd hungered for all evening. They were every bit as satisfying as he'd remembered. At the lightest touch of his tongue they parted, allowing him full access. He tasted the wine they'd shared earlier, so much better now, shared this way. Beyond that, he tasted Sarah. Savored her.

It wasn't enough. He wanted more.

He trailed kisses down the creamy softness of her neck, stopping to nip at the tensed muscles there, following their path to her shoulder. His fingers drifted to the rounded neckline of her gauzy dress. He pushed out and the elastic willingly gave way, gliding down the sides of her shoulders, exposing more of the skin he wanted, needed.

He was nibbling his way down one of those shoulders when his breath caught in his throat.

Sarah was busy, too. He hadn't noticed when she'd let go of his neck or how she'd slipped those delicate hands under his shirt, but as her fingers moved up his chest, a shiver went through him and the hair on his body rose with chill bumps.

Hair wasn't the only thing on his body that had risen.

She groaned and he smiled against the soft skin of her shoulder. They'd been here before. He knew what she wanted, but he needed to hear her say it.

"What, Sarah? What do you want?"

"Would you do something for me?" Her fingers clenched against his skin as if she were soaking up the very texture of him.

"Ask it, luv. Anything you want."

"Take off your shirt for me, Ian. Just that one thing," she whispered.

"Aye." He tugged the shirt over his head and tossed it away, his hands returning immediately to her shoulders.

"But be warned, luv, as the saying goes, one thing leads to another." He gently pushed the elastic neckline a second time and said a quick prayer of thanks for the ingenious Mortals who'd invented the stretchy miracle as the material slipped easily down her arms.

She took her hands from his chest only long enough to pull them from the sleeves and then they were on his back, stroking, exploring.

One more push and the opening grew larger, slipped again, falling to her waist. His hands guided its progress, appreciating the soft bare skin he found there. One last push channeled it over the swell of her hips, and the gown fell to the floor, pooling at her feet.

"That must have been the 'another' you warned me about," she murmured.

A witty comeback formed in his mind, but it fled his conscious thought completely when her tongue brushed across his nipple. Once, twice before settling there, tiny little flicks lighting a fire in his body, in his very soul.

He'd suddenly forgotten how to breathe.

Back to her shoulder, he nibbled his way across. A bra strap impeded his journey and he grasped it with his teeth, his hands too fully occupied exploring the newly exposed terrain of her lower back. Soft, flawless territory, open to the lacy bit covering her perfect heart-shaped bottom.

He pulled the strap off her shoulder and traced with his tongue the spot where it had lain. His hands, moving up, hit the material stretched across her back, smooth and unbroken as his fingers trailed across it. He pulled her away from him.

Ah, as he'd thought. Front latch.

He lowered his head to her breast, sliding his hands down her back, cupping that perfect bottom and pulling her close. One suck through the material of her bra and her hands stilled on his back. A second and her breath caught in a small gasp. Moving his head, he popped the fastening open with his teeth, freeing the most beautiful breasts he'd ever seen. His mouth moved over one, his tongue lavishing it with the same care she had shown him. She moaned and slipped her fingers into the waistband of his pants, sliding down, down, her fingers trailing fire in their wake.

To hell with the right thing.

This was his destiny. Sarah was his destiny.

He slid his arm behind her legs and straightened, lifting her for the second time that evening. He headed for the bedroom, but stopped outside the door.

"*This* is the 'another' I warned you about." He searched her eyes, looking for any sign of hesitation. "We dinna have to do this if you dinna want to." He wasn't sure he'd survive it if she told him to stop, but he had to know after everything that had passed between them today. If she wasn't ready to accept her heritage, she might not be ready to accept him. He had to give her the opportunity to make that choice.

"No, I want this, too."

He carried her to the bed, lowering her gently. Sitting down next to her, he removed his shoes and socks, feeling his nerves spark to life before standing to fumble with his belt buckle. His hands stilled as he looked at her lying there, watching him, her tilted green eyes heavy with desire.

His Faerie goddess.

He wanted this to be better for her than any she had ever experienced, ever imagined, and here he was, suddenly as nervous as if it were his first time.

She moved to the edge of the bed on her knees. Reaching over, she grasped his belt and undid the buckle with trembling fingers, but stopped at the zipper.

"You want to do this part, right?"

He lowered the zipper and worked himself free, watching her eyes widen.

"Problem?"

She shook her head. Reaching out a finger toward him, she hesitated, then withdrew, putting her hand in her lap.

"Wow. That's pretty impressive when you take the time to look."

He laughed. As quickly as the nervousness had come, it was gone. He stepped free of his pants and climbed onto the bed, covering her with his body.

He ran his hand across her stomach, stopping at the lace barrier of her underwear. Once more he searched her eyes. The excitement he saw there mirrored his own.

"These are quite lovely," he said, running the tip of his index finger along the band of lace. He delighted in the chill bumps that sprang up under his fingers as she responded to his touch. He slid the lacy barrier down her legs and tossed it across the room.

"But no half so lovely as what you hide underneath the lace."

The heat of color bloomed in her cheeks and spread down her neck. He watched it for a moment before giving in to the desire to bury his face in that heat, tracing its progress with his tongue.

Lost in the softness of her, he left the color behind, making his way down her body, stopping for a time at each perfect breast, caressing and tasting until her breath came in quick little puffs.

Farther down, onto the pale, flat expanse of stomach, he rubbed his cheek against her smooth skin, savoring its texture and scent. The smell of her skin intoxicated him.

On he moved, nibbling and tasting his way to her soft, tender thigh. He left a wet trail on her delicate skin with his hot tongue before lifting his head and blowing a gentle puff of air, feeling her shiver under his hands as he did so.

She gasped when he turned his head, exhaling his warm breath over another part of her.

"No, wait," she panted. "You don't have to—"

"Oh, but I do." He needed this, needed to know every intimate detail her body had to share.

Her hands fisted in the covers as if she fought the sensations he gave her, but she pressed into him, her involuntary moan of pleasure sending a rush of arousal to every fiber of his being. He wanted more, wanted to send her over the edge of the precipice where she held herself.

Stroking the inside of her thigh, he slipped his finger into the warm depths of her as he tormented her sensitive nub with the tip of his tongue.

She yelled out his name, her body bucking against him as he felt the muscular spasms around his finger.

He slid up her body, covering her gasping breaths with his mouth, nipping at her lips, capturing her tongue with his own.

Centering himself, he entered her, pushing deeper and deeper as she wrapped her legs around his back, lifting her body to meet his, thrust for thrust.

Again and again, until once more she reached her

peak and broke around him like a wild ocean wave crashing against the shore.

Blond curls clung to her perspiration-dampened face and he brushed them back. Her eyes fluttered open and the passion he saw in them inflamed his desire for her.

He pushed into her again, slowly at first, then faster and harder as she urged him on, until at last he gave in to his own frenzy of sensation, taking her with him once more.

She laid in his arms, cuddled next to him as he kissed her face, her eyes, her mouth.

This was what he wanted. To see her satisfied. To claim her. To know she belonged to him.

No matter what it took, he would think of something, find some way to reconcile the two halves of his life.

Eighteen

*E*very muscle in Sarah's body ached. From all the minute stinging sensations, she was sure she would discover tiny little burns in all sorts of sensitive places, all caused by Ian's sexy five o'clock shadow.

She had never felt so good in her entire life. Ever. Period.

She lay very still, enjoying the rhythm of his slow, steady breathing.

His hand rested possessively across her stomach, her back snuggled up against his front. She felt each exhale against the top of her head. Surely this was heaven.

Stretching slowly, she wiggled out of Ian's grasp and slid off the bed. She turned for one last look at him before leaving the room. He was incredible, even in the dim moonlight sifting through her curtains. So what if he thought himself descended from Faeries. Weren't there plenty of people who thought they had lived prior lives as famous people? It was only an odd-ity, an off-the-wall belief. And while one day she might have to give it more thought, for now she didn't want to, didn't want to deal with it.

Instead she toyed with the idea of waking him, exploring what new delight he might have in store for her, but he looked so peaceful sleeping on her pillow. Besides, he'd worked hard tonight. He'd earned his rest.

She tiptoed across the room, doing her best not to wake him. A blush heated her face when her hand encountered her underwear hanging from the door handle, but practicality quickly beat out embarrassment and she grabbed the panties, slipping them on after quietly pulling the door closed behind her.

She padded into the central room, looking around for something to put on. Ian's shirt hung haphazardly from her laptop where his toss had deposited it. She retrieved the silky T-shirt and slipped it over her head. Smelling of aftershave and man, it felt sexy against her bare skin. Exactly like Ian.

She grinned.

Oh Lordy, do I ever have it bad. And she felt wonderful. She pulled the neck of the shirt up over her nose and breathed deeply, delighting in his scent. He made her feel . . . She stopped in the center of the room, frozen. She hadn't felt anything.

Well, that wasn't exactly true. She had felt amazing physical sensations, exhilarating fulfillment, unbelievable joy. She had felt cherished. But she hadn't felt anything coming from Ian.

Perhaps she'd been so wrapped up in what was happening she'd missed it? Although that had never happened before. Ever. Even at Glaston House she'd felt trickles of his emotions. Nothing overwhelming, simply a light undercurrent of what he'd felt. But this time, the only emotions she'd experienced had been her own.

She glanced at the clock on her desk. The digital clock blinked 2:12 in big red numbers. She couldn't have slept for more than thirty minutes. She should go back to bed.

Instead she leaned over the desk and, out of habit, pressed the ON button of her laptop. The screen jumped to life, wiggling through its various gyrations until it was ready. Waiting.

She clicked again and the blank page, the page that had haunted her day and night for months, appeared on the screen. The cursor, her enemy, suddenly looked much friendlier than she remembered, the blinking regularity inviting rather than mocking. Colors, snatches of dialogue, faces danced behind her eyes.

Without thought, she slid into her chair and placed her fingers on the keys. The characters flooded her mind. Their words, their thoughts, their feelings hit her in a jumble. She began to type, giving them life on the page before her. The page that was no longer blank.

Ian awoke with a start, forcing himself to remain perfectly still. He fought the urge to search the area, overcome with the feeling that something was missing.

Sarah.

He sat up in bed. The murky predawn light revealed his surroundings. Her room. Her smell. Her essence surrounded him. For the first time in his memory he felt complete.

A faint tapping noise attracted his attention and he crawled out of bed to investigate, stopping only to pull on his pants before opening the bedroom door.

He spotted her immediately, sitting at the desk, typing away at the little computer. So much for the tapping noise. She sat, one bare foot tucked under her, wearing only his T-shirt, her curls a golden riot around her head. The woman looked like she belonged in his clothes. Or maybe it was only that he felt more like she belonged to him when she dressed that way.

His first inclination was to cross the room, remove his shirt and lay claim to her again, proving she was his. But he resisted the urge.

He leaned against the door frame, rubbing a hand idly over his chest as he watched her work. He'd seen her sit and stare at the screen before. He'd watched her pace and search for what she couldn't find. He'd never seen her write. It was a fascinating scene, every emotion she put on paper working its way across her face.

He wandered into the kitchen and put coffee on to perk. Only when it was ready, and he had filled a cup for her, did he approach. Leaning over her, he kissed the spot behind her ear he found so irresistible.

"Ummm," she purred leaning into him. "When did you get up?"

"Just a bit ago, luv. What about you? Why did you no wake me?"

She rose from the chair, turning to snake her arms up his chest before answering. "You looked so perfect sleeping in my bed, I didn't want to disturb you. Be-

sides"—her cheeks took on the pink glow he enjoyed—
"I thought you might be tired."

He laughed. "Tired because I worked so hard, or because I worked so well?"

The pink color deepened. "Both." Her hand slid across his chest, reminding him exactly how satisfying that work had been.

"Take yer coffee, luv, before I spill it. With yer hands on me like that, I'm no to be trusted."

Her delighted smile at his words traveled directly to his heart.

"I've got to get back to the main house, Sarah. I'd like to be gone before daybreak."

"Why?"

He smiled at her innocence. "So pryin' eyes dinna get the wrong impression about my spending the night with you."

Prying Faerie eyes, belonging to one particularly nosy Faerie to whom he didn't particularly want to explain any of this.

"Wrong impression?" She laughed. "Are you afraid they might mistakenly think we were doing something like . . . well . . . like what we did?"

"Exactly."

He pulled her close and kissed her. Kissed her until he felt her body relax and mold into his. He held her away, looking down at her face. Her eyes were still closed.

He loved that she responded to him as she did. He had put that look on her face, that dreamy, faraway expression, and he felt powerful at having been the one to do it. And thankful. Thankful that she'd allowed him in.

"If daylight were no so close, I'd show you right now how I feel about being with you."

She smiled. "I don't care if people know."

"But I do. I'm no willing to risk yer reputation."

"Oh, Ian." She ran her hands up his chest again. "You are perfect, you know that? My perfect hero."

"I'm a long way from perfect, luv, but we'll discuss that tonight. I have to go now." He kissed the top of her head, breathing in the scent of her one more time. Enough to last him until he saw her again this evening.

His hand was on the door when her touch on his back stopped him.

"Wait, Ian. You can't leave dressed like that." She grasped the bottom of the shirt she still wore to pull it over her head.

He grabbed her hands, stopping her.

"Stop. I prefer to walk away with the picture of you wearing that in my mind to keep my thoughts busy all day." At her raised eyebrow he continued. "Besides. Are you wearing anything under that shirt?"

She shook her head. "Not much."

"I dinna think so. You pull that off, luv, and I'll never make it out of here by daylight."

He turned and walked out, closing the door behind him. Only outside, standing on the cold stones of the path, did he realize he hadn't even thought to put on his shoes. The woman rattled him something awful. He grinned and sprinted toward the manor house. There was no way he was going back in for them. He'd never be strong enough to walk away from her twice this morning.

The house was quiet as he stealthily crept up the

stairs and into his room. He thought about turning on the light, but decided against it, instead opting to lie down on his bed, using the dark as an ally.

In the stillness, with his eyes shut, the scent and feel of Sarah fresh in his mind, he could almost imagine she was here with him, just out of reach.

He would allow himself that pleasure for now. When he awoke again, he would deal with the mess he had made. He would face then the decisions he didn't want to face now. Later, after he had slept, he would need to figure out what to do next, how to keep Sarah without losing who he was, or, for that matter, whether he even cared who he was as long as he had her.

For now he would simply enjoy the memory of his night with Sarah and the knowledge of how much he needed her. For now he would enjoy the anticipation of being with her again.

Nineteen

The first thing Ian heard was the rain. Pattering softly, steadily down, it washed away all color, leaving behind a cold gray backdrop.

Anola sat huddled in the corner, her profile clearly visible to him, long dark curls cloaking her shoulders, reaching well below her waist. She had always been such a beautiful woman.

She turned, not seeing him yet, dabbing the end of her apron at her eyes. Dark, exotic gypsy eyes, exactly like his own.

It stabbed at his heart to realize she was crying. Before Larkin's death, he'd never seen her cry. Afterward, she had never stopped.

"Mother?"

The voice of a child. His voice, as it had been.

She turned slowly, trying as she always had, to conceal her tears.

"Ian? Is that you, lad? You've grown so. Yer a fine strong man to be proud of."

She reached out her hand to him and he started forward only to be blocked by an invisible wall.

"Mother? Are you really here?" How could it be Anola, dead over six hundred years?

Of course. One of his dreams.

Her hand dropped to her lap and she shrugged, a gesture he remembered well.

"Och, I forgot. You canna come to me. It's all right, me wee brave bairn. I've spoken to yer father. I've begged and pleaded, but he's ever the willful, stubborn Fae." She smiled, though her tears began to fall again.

"Dinna cry, Ma. What is it? What can I do?"

The rattle of armor was the only warning before a burst of light, brighter than the sun, filled the room. When it abated, Ian looked up to find Larkin standing over him, his face contorted with rage.

For a moment he thought to cringe, but he was a man now. His father's anger wouldn't frighten him anymore.

"I warned you. And you swore to me." Larkin dropped his head into his hands. "Swore to me. And now look what you've done."

"I've done nothing but what I promised you, Father. I've guarded the Fountain. I've protected the Mortals."

Larkin's head snapped up. "Nothing?" he shouted. "Nothing, you say? Protected the Mortals, have you? You bedded the woman. I warned you to use caution or you'd have to choose. Now it's come to that. You've tipped the scales of fate with your actions."

"Sarah? This is about Sarah?" Ian's stomach lurched, and for the second time in as many days the unfamiliar pain of fear lanced through his system. What did this warning have to do with Sarah?

"Larkin," Anola cautioned. She stood beside her husband, her hand on his chest. "Be gentle with the lad."

"It's not my doing it's come to this. His own actions have set him on this path. I'm doing everything I can. More than I should." He trailed his hand down her dark hair before turning back to his son. Calmed by the touch of his beloved wife, sorrow replaced the anger. "You will see for yourself, my son, and you will have to choose. I can say no more."

"I dinna understand, Father." Ian reached toward Larkin, but the light faded, gray closing in all around him, wrapping him in an impenetrable blanket of mist.

The rain still fell softly, chilling his exposed skin. He was in the forest now, within sight of the Portal at Thistle Down. His parents had disappeared, but there were others ahead on the path. He couldn't see who they were, all their faces and words indistinct. All except her.

Sarah's golden curls shone like a beacon. The others, those whose visage blurred when he tried to identify them, faded away. Only Sarah remained.

His stomach clenched as he recognized her fright. He felt it, and anger, twining together, curling around him like a tangible thing. He needed to protect her, tried to run to her, but it was as if something physically held him back, pushed him to the ground and barred his path to her. He could only watch as a pulsating red sphere formed around her, the glow emanating from within her, surrounding her.

He felt danger growing, yet he couldn't move, couldn't call out to warn her.

The crack of a shot rang out and he watched helplessly as the red glow instantly evaporated and she crumpled to the ground, blood flowing freely around her where she lay.

Whatever force held him disappeared as suddenly as it had come and he ran to her side, scooping her into his arms, cradling her to him.

"Sarah, luv, open yer eyes. Speak to me."

Dark lashes fluttered against pale cheeks.

"I'm sorry I didn't believe you, Ian," she whispered. "But it's all right. I couldn't allow him to harm you. It was my choice to take the risk."

"No," he roared, clutching her body to him as the soul within drifted away. He couldn't lose her. Not this way.

"Yes," a quiet voice responded. His father's voice.

The forest gone, his arms empty, he was back in the gray room, his father standing before him.

"Now you've seen what her choice will be. You, too, must choose. If you love the woman enough, you will make the right choice."

The rain stopped. The clouds lifted and the gray mist evaporated, burned away in the radiant sunlight that shone off Larkin's silver armor. The light grew brighter and more intense until the room itself disappeared in a brilliant flash of white light.

"Choose wisely, my son."

The words echoed in his mind.

"No." Ian's own bellow brought him awake, his body damp with perspiration. He lay on the bed breathing heavily, as if he'd just completed a long run.

The dream again. Another warning of danger. But this time, finally, he knew what it meant. Sarah was the one in danger and he was responsible for her predicament. Somehow his being with her would bring about her death. He should have known he couldn't have her. Now he had a choice to make to save her life.

He sat up on the side of the bed and scrubbed at his face with his hands, praying to the Earth Mother that it wasn't too late.

Sarah completed him. He needed her more than he needed his next breath, but he would do what he had to do, what he should have done to begin with.

In the final analysis, what did his need for her matter when balanced against her life? He wouldn't risk that. He wouldn't risk her. Better he should spend eternity alone, in his own private hell, than risk harm to Sarah.

His choice was made.

"You're sure this is what you want to do?"

As he watched Dallyn stand and cross to the opening of the gazebo, Ian briefly considered that Sarah's ability to read another's feelings would be useful now. The Fae was a master at hiding his true thoughts and feelings.

"Want?" Ian shook his head. "Hardly. It's what I must do. My choices are limited."

"Then you believe this to be the choice you must make?"

Ian nodded, not trusting his voice at the moment. He'd related the entire dream to Dallyn, the warning, everything. Well, not everything. He hadn't told him about last night. There were some things the Fae didn't need to know.

"And how do you suppose Sarah will respond when she learns? Are you sure this would be her choice as well?"

"This is no her choice to make. It's mine."

"We each of us choose turns along the path to our destiny. She must make choices as well as you. Have you thought to discuss it with her?"

Ian shook his head. "I told you what will happen, what I saw happen, if I stay. You know my dreams always come true. If I stay, if I'm here with Sarah, she will make her choice and she will die. I'll no be responsible for that."

"Your dreams do indeed give you accurate visions of bits of the future, Ian. But as such they're open to interpretation. What if it's your absence that triggers the events you saw?"

"That's ridiculous. I was there. I held her dying in my arms. It canna happen if I'm no here. My father warned I'd have to make a difficult choice to prevent what I saw. I've made that choice. She's safe here at Thistle Down. They canna cross the waters without being invited over, and they'll never be invited here. She's promised she'll no see them again."

"So. You'll give her up. Just like that. Turn your back and walk away." Dallyn turned to pluck a rose from the vine entwined about the gazebo. Lifting it to his nose, he inhaled deeply before turning back to Ian, pinning him with a stare. "Is she the one, do you suppose? Your Soulmate?"

"No," Ian denied. "That soul was torn from the

body it occupied centuries ago, cast into the chaos. Lost to the Fountain forever."

Dallyn shrugged. "They're never lost, Ian. Only out of order." He smiled sadly. "You've lived a long time since then. It could have happened, you know, the next cycle."

Ian glanced down. Spotting Sarah's sandals on the floor, he stooped to pick one up. He wouldn't consider it. Couldn't. It would only make it harder to do what he must. If he stayed, she would die. He had seen it. And those dreams, those visions, were never false.

"It makes no difference. Even if yer right, I canna stay. I'd only lose her again, and this time it would be my own fault. I canna live with that." Clutching the sandal tightly, he turned and walked away.

He wouldn't look down the path toward the cottage. He feared catching sight of her. He'd rather hold the memory of her as he'd seen her last, her face soft and distracted from his kiss.

His father's words rang in his mind. "If you love her enough, you will make the right choice."

Reaching the car he'd already packed, he got in and closed the door. He laid the sandal he carried on the seat next to him. Pulling out of the drive, he didn't look back.

He was making the right choice, the only choice he could.

Sarah's stomach growled, drawing her attention from the glowing laptop screen and the world growing there at her fingertips. She glanced out the window and was surprised to find it was dark. How long had she been sitting here? She glanced at the clock, shocked to see the whole day gone by.

She stood and stretched, her back stiff and sore from leaning over the desk all day. The rest of her sore from last night. She smiled at the memory.

Rolling her neck, she shuffled to the bathroom and turned on the water. She hadn't even changed today, was still dressed in Ian's shirt. She pulled it off and, from the doorway, tossed it onto her bed before returning to the bathroom and her shower.

The warm water poured over her head and down her body, washing away the haze that cocooned her when she wrote. She moved farther from the world of her own creation and firmly back into the real world.

All those months without having written a single word worth keeping and now, suddenly, as if someone had flipped a switch or unlocked a door, it was back.

She felt good; for the first time she could remember, everything in her world was right. And everything, she quickly acknowledged, included much more than her writing. It included Ian.

Ian. Where was he?

Rinsing her hair, she wondered if he'd come to the cottage and she'd been so involved in her writing she'd simply not heard him. Surely he would have come inside. It didn't matter. She was certain he'd be here shortly. He'd told her he was coming back this evening.

She climbed from the shower, wrapped herself in a warm, fuzzy robe, and considered for the first time that exhaustion might be a stronger force on her body at the moment than even hunger. Padding barefoot to the kitchen, she poured a glass of milk. The sofa beckoned her, but before settling in, she opened the front door, straining to see if Ian approached in the darkness. Satisfied he wasn't on the path, she gave in to the lure of the comfortable sofa and curled up to wait for his arrival.

She took a couple of sips from the glass before setting it on the end table. Her eyes burned from long hours at the computer and lack of sleep. If she closed her eyes for a bit while she waited, it would help.

Any minute now.

He would be there soon, flooding her with the warmth of his emotions. She reached out with her feelings, concentrating on Ian.

She closed her eyes and leaned back against the soft cushions of the sofa.

Sarah awoke with a start, her heart beating out a rapid tattoo in her chest.

Had it been a dream that woke her? No, more like the opposite of a dream, as if in her sleep she'd experienced a complete absence of everything.

A total void.

The last thing she remembered from the night before was trying to reach out and connect with Ian. Obviously the higher powers that controlled her feelings—Faeries, if she were silly enough to believe Ian and Will—didn't intend for her to do that. As she thought on it now, she hadn't felt him earlier when he'd kissed her good-bye. So lost in the wonder of her own feelings, she hadn't realized at the time that she'd felt none of his.

She shivered and sat up stiffly from where she'd

been slumped in the corner of the sofa. Sunlight danced in the windows and through the open door. She glanced to the clock. Noon. She'd slept for hours.

As she rose and walked through the cottage, checking for signs of Ian's presence, a tiny seed of doubt took root in the back of her mind.

No indication of his having been there through the night.

She stopped at the door of the bedroom, her eyes and thoughts settling on the bed, still rumpled and unmade from the last time she'd slept there. With him.

A small nervous giggle bubbled to her lips as the seed of doubt sent up fresh shoots. What if he wasn't coming back?

Shake it off. Save that imagination for the book.

"Damn!"

Two steps from the bed, she stubbed her toe on something hard. Ian's shoes, the one she'd just found and the other peeking out from under the edge of the bed. She remembered he'd left barefoot. Of course he'd come back for those.

She picked up the shoes and placed them on the dresser, avoiding the eyes of the woman reflected in the mirror. The woman in the mirror looked frightened and unhappy. Sarah didn't want to deal with those emotions right now. No, better to avoid that woman. Normalcy, routine—that would soothe her.

She straightened the bed and carefully folded the shirt she had tossed there last evening. Ian's shirt. She lifted it to her nose and inhaled deeply before tucking it under her pillow and walking to her closet.

The doubt was still there, eating away at her. No

amount of mundane house chores was going to end it. What she needed was to end the wondering, silly as it was. There was a perfectly good reason he hadn't come to her last night as he'd said he would. She'd get dressed and walk up to the manor house to return his shoes. In the process, she would see what was keeping him. He'd simply been busy, no doubt.

With a plan and a purpose, she set about getting ready.

"What do you mean, he's gone?"

Sarah sat stiffly on the edge of the sofa, clutching the heavy shoes to her chest. She had known something was wrong, felt it the minute Martha answered the door and insisted she come into the library for tea with Mr. McCullough.

Especially when it was Henry, not Ian, who joined her there. The little seed of doubt had blossomed into a full-grown tree, branches arcing all through her stomach, leaves blowing about, making her feel ill.

"Gone where?"

"To . . . um . . . to London." Henry fidgeted with the handle of his teacup, not quite making eye contact. "Some business he needed to deal with right away, I believe. Quite important. Verra important." His voice trailed off.

"When will he be back?"

She tried to keep her voice light, detached. But when she glanced up and caught Henry watching her, she didn't need to touch the older gentleman to pick up his emotions. His discomfort and pity flowed freely through the air washing over her in waves.

"Well, you see . . . that is, I'm . . . um . . . not quite

sure of that exactly. It depends on how long the . . .
uh . . . important business takes him to . . ."

She rose to her feet, interrupting his stammering
attempt at an explanation. She wouldn't put either
one of them through this.

"Thank you, Henry."

She headed for the door, but stopped and walked
back to her host, holding out the shoes. "When—if—
Ian returns, you should give these to him. They're
his."

She didn't look at the man, couldn't bear to see the
pity she knew would be reflected in his gaze. She
simply turned and started for the door. The few sips
of tea she'd managed to swallow before she'd heard
the news soured in her stomach, threatening to reap-
pear. She had to get out of here.

"Sarah," Henry called after her. "Wait." Then a
muffled "Where is that bloody cane? Martha, hurry!"

By then she was out the door, pulling it shut behind her.

She needed to get to the cottage. To be alone. She
had to get away. She couldn't stand the thought of
anyone seeing her raw emotion on display, yet she
knew she had no way to control it right now. Her swift
strides quickly accelerated until she was running.

She should have expected this.

After all, hadn't she been the one who said it
wouldn't work?

Sarah curled up on the bed in the little cottage she'd
come to think of as home in the short time she'd been
here. It was late evening; she had no tears left.
Clutching Ian's shirt to her like a substitute teddy

bear, she sought some sort of comfort. There was none to be found in either the shirt or the cottage. Or her thoughts.

Her grandmother always told her not to take herself too seriously—that there was nothing special about her. If men were after her, it was either for her money or a quick roll in the sack. And once she gave them whichever they wanted, they'd be gone. Grandmother may have been right after all. She should have known better. Did know better. But, given the chance, would she change what had happened?

No, she wouldn't regret what she'd done. Couldn't regret Ian. Everyone deserved one great love in their lives, even if they didn't get to keep it. At least she'd known him and what real love was. That was enough.

Or so she would tell herself every time it started to hurt. Once it quit hurting all the time. If it ever quit hurting all the time.

"It will stop. Eventually."

She crawled from the bed and stumbled to the bathroom, turning the faucet on full blast. She splashed the warm water over her face and dried off on a soft yellow towel while she breathed in the mist steaming up from the basin.

She'd survived and gone on before.

Glancing up, she wiped the steam from the mirror and stared at the puffy face that returned her gaze. She acknowledged the loss and sorrow she saw reflected there. She had freely chosen to allow Ian into her heart, in spite of the risk. Even though she had known he was perhaps the one person in the world who would have the power to do this to her, she'd still chosen to hand over her heart to him.

"Never again," she promised as fresh tears rolled down the cheeks of the woman she watched. The face in the mirror disappeared behind the curtain of steam gathering again on the mirror until the droplets of water forming there began to roll down, making it look as if the mirror itself joined her in shedding tears, trying to wash the pain away.

Yes, she would survive this. She would go on. But she would never again choose to open herself up to the kind of pain that accompanied love.

She promised herself that she had taken her one and only risk on love.

Twenty

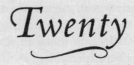

The persistent pounding finally caught Sarah's attention, pulling her back to the real world, out of the story in which she had immersed herself for almost two weeks. She wanted to stay there, where life didn't hurt with every memory. But the knocking wouldn't stop.

"Just a minute," she called irritably, straightening from the chair she had occupied for hours. Ruthlessly tamping down any hope it might be Ian waiting on her steps, she unbolted the latch and threw open the door.

"Oh my." Martha stepped back, running her hands down her crisp white apron as if smoothing imaginary wrinkles. "Are you feeling all right, dearie?"

Disappointment welled in Sarah's chest, even though she had known it wouldn't be Ian knocking at her door.

"I'm fine, Martha. Is there something I can do for you?" She didn't want to visit or discuss how she felt.

She didn't have the energy for it. It was much better to work and let her mind fill with the story and the characters. In their world, she felt no pain.

"Oh, yes . . . there's a telephone call for you. Up at the manor house. I came down to fetch you." The woman looked at her expectantly.

"Who is it?" Sarah could barely force the words out past the building emotion. Would he call her? Explain what had happened, why he'd just up and left with no word?

"I've no idea, dear. She'd no give her name." A look of irritation passed across her face. "She asked that I run get you while she waited."

A second wave of disappointment rolled over her. "Oh, well, hold on a second."

She looked around the room. Her shoes had to be somewhere. There, under the chair. She slipped them on and hurried to follow Martha back, concern building as they neared the house.

Only her agent knew she was here, but it didn't sound like Laine to refuse to give her name. Still, perhaps there was a problem with the deadline for the book. She almost smiled. For the first time in months, she felt certain the book would not only be on time, it would be finished long before it was due.

They entered the kitchen through the back door and Martha handed her the telephone, walking a discreet distance away and turning her back to wait while Sarah took her call.

"Hello?"

"Is this Sarah Douglas?"

She didn't recognize the woman's crisp voice. "It is. Who's this?"

"Hold please."

In the space of a heartbeat, another voice sounded on the line.

"Sarah?"

A deep, cultured voice that she recognized immediately.

"Ramos. What a surprise."

"Surprise? But I told you I'd see you again." He chuckled. "Have you so little faith in all men or is it just me?"

If he only knew.

"I'm surprised you found me." Or that he'd even tried.

The chuckle again. "Not such a task, my sweet. I knew you were a guest at McCullough's estate and it took very little effort to track that down."

"Where are you?"

"Edinburgh. Have you had an opportunity to see the sights here yet? It's a lovely old city."

"No. I'm afraid I haven't seen much of anything. I've been totally involved in my work."

"Do you mean to tell me you haven't seen anything of the countryside since you've been here?"

"Well, I drove here from Glasgow when I first arrived. And then from here down to Glaston House and back."

"Those don't count. Have you gone out and met the people, seen the sights, looked at what the country has to offer since you've been here?"

"No. I haven't really had the time."

"Then you're overdue. Please. Allow me to show it to you. Tomorrow. I'll come get you early and we'll play tourist, take in some local color, enjoy ourselves."

"I'm not sure."

She'd promised Ian she wouldn't see Ramos or his brother again. But Ian was gone with no word. And somehow that seemed to indicate that any promises made between them were no longer binding.

"What's wrong? McCullough standing there glaring at you?"

No. That certainly wasn't the case.

"Edinburgh is rather far away for you to run over and pick me up, don't you think?"

"Not at all. Barely a couple of hours. And we can enjoy the sights on the way back to the city or find something else entirely to do. We'll make a day of it."

"Well . . ." She knew for a fact Ramos was no threat to her, in spite of what Ian had said. She'd felt the sincerity and the good in him when she'd touched him.

"Come on, Sarah. We'll have a great time. All work and no play makes Sarah a dull writer."

Why not? She'd done nothing but sit at her computer for the past week, trying not to wonder what had gone wrong. Why not enjoy herself having a day out with a handsome, attentive man?

"Fine. Do you know how to get here?"

"I'll manage it."

"What time should I expect you?"

"How's eight? That will give us plenty of time."

"Eight it is. See you then, Ramos."

"Until then."

She held the receiver in her hand for a moment after his end went dead. What was she getting herself into?

Hanging up the phone, she looked back at the

housekeeper who was industriously straightening the contents of a drawer. "Thanks, Martha."

"You're sure yer all right, dearie? I could whip up a quick lunch for you if you'd like. No a problem."

"That's really sweet of you, but no thanks. I have to get back to work."

She smiled at the woman as she let herself out the back door and headed down the path toward the cottage, thinking about the telephone call and the man who'd made it.

Ramos was a good person. She'd have known if he weren't. But his going to all the trouble to seek her out was confusing. Still, it didn't really matter. She needed a change. A distraction. If nothing else, playing tourist for a day might get her mind off the things she didn't want to think about. Besides, seeing him again *felt* like the thing she was supposed to do.

Entering her living room, she started to close the front door, but stopped herself. No more hiding. She'd done that for the past week. She left the door wide open, then moved to the windows, opening each in turn.

Continuing on into the bedroom, she stopped as she caught sight of her reflection in the large mirror.

"Good Lord. No wonder Martha was worried. I look awful."

The woman staring back at her from the mirror needed serious help. Her face was pale, sporting great dark circles under her eyes. The eyes themselves red rimmed from exhaustion and the occasional crying bout. Her hair was a mass of tangles, looking as though it hadn't felt the touch of a comb for days, which, in fact, it hadn't.

Sarah shook her head in disgust. When had she let herself turn into this?

Well, nothing a hot shower and a quick nap wouldn't fix. Oh, and maybe some teabags on those eyes. And a good meal. When was the last time she'd eaten? If she had to ask, it had been too long.

"Pity party's lasted long enough. Time to rejoin the world of the living."

Perhaps Ramos's call had been exactly what she'd needed.

Her heart might be broken, but she wasn't.

"You're sure that's the name she said? Ramos?" Dallyn walked to the edge of the small terrace, hands clasped behind his back. "Your housekeeper was close enough to hear her clearly?"

"Please. Martha misses verra little that goes on around here. It's exactly as I told you." Henry sipped his tea before casting a quick glance at the pacing Fae. "He's one of the men they met at Daniel's, is he no? The ones that had Ian so worried when he returned."

"I'm afraid he is."

"What have you been able to learn about him?"

"Ramos? I haven't been able to dig up a single piece of sod on the man."

"*Dirt*," Henry automatically corrected. "Not *sod*." The Fae was forever trying out new sayings so that he might blend in, yet he never seemed to get them right.

"Ah, yes. Dirt." Dallyn returned to the table, pulled the chair out as if to sit, but stopped, looking down the path toward the cottage. "Not a single thing. It's as if the man's existence had been intentionally hidden from us."

"And the other one, the brother? Have you discovered anything about him?"

"There's nothing to discover about Reynard. I know him well. Knew him well," the Fae amended as he began to pace the length of the terrace again. "Though he had no brother. He was one of the instigators of the original troubles. I expected one of the Nuadian High Council to be behind this. I just hadn't anticipated it would be Reynard. Although I suppose it could be worse. And I don't like it that this Ramos character, whoever he is, is calling on Sarah."

"That would mean Ian was correct? That Sarah could be in danger?"

"Oh, yes. I would say it's a safe bet they have designs on our little American guest."

Henry lowered his gaze to the cup before him. "Ian isna going to be happy with this. He verra specifically told her she was no to see either one of those men again."

Henry's head snapped up at Dallyn's derisive snort.

"Well, he did," Henry defended.

"And what of it? Did any of us actually expect her to listen to anything he'd said after the way he left? I think not." Dallyn shook his head as he paced. "No, I think not."

"She did seem a bit disturbed by his leaving."

Another snort drew Henry's attention back to his guest.

"Really? Do you think so? Was it her refusing to leave the cottage for a week that convinced you? Or perhaps her sitting at that confounded machine tapping away around the clock? Maybe the sound of her sobbing at all hours of the day and night?" He stopped pacing and glared at Henry.

Dallyn was obviously agitated, something quite unusual in itself. That alone made Henry nervous.

"I dinna know about all of that. She's kept to herself."

"Yes, well, I've gone to check on her several times since Ian left."

"There was nothing else he could do."

"He could have stayed. Seen it through."

"You know verra well why he dinna. Why he felt he couldn't." Ian had given him only the barest details, but Henry knew that Dallyn had been told the full story.

"I know why he *thinks* he couldn't stay. I happen to believe he was rash in his interpretation, his logic colored by emotion. A fairly common Mortal failing." He shrugged.

"Then perhaps we should call Ian. Tell him what's going on. You could order him back."

Dallyn paused once again at the table, arms folded, tapping one finger against his chin in thought. "Not yet, my young friend. All in due time."

Henry felt the power of Dallyn's next words in the man's piercing gaze.

"Fate has a hand to play out here. Both Ian and Sarah have choices yet to make. All in due time."

Twenty-one

" . . . On the bonny, bonny banks of Loch Lomond."

Sarah stopped and looked around guiltily. Thank goodness, Ramos had crossed over to the gift shop to get a soda for her. The little snatch of song had slipped out as she stood looking over the splendor of that same lake. Scotland was perhaps the most beautiful place she had ever been. To think she might have missed seeing all this if Ramos hadn't called and practically insisted on showing it to her!

As if on cue, he stepped out of the shop. Two young women sitting on a bench outside the little store stopped their conversation to watch him walk toward her. She had to admit, he was a compelling sight, striding across the road in the dark pants and fitted polo shirt that exactly matched the color of his eyes. The girls, of course wouldn't know that. Dark sunglasses covered the pale green eyes that always gave the impression of missing nothing. His long black hair was pulled back in a low ponytail, exposing

a small diamond stud in his ear that sparkled with reflected sunlight when he turned his head to check for
oncoming traffic.

For the second time since her arrival in Scotland,
she found herself on a road trip with a handsome man
who was basically a stranger. This time, however, she
felt no pressure. Amazing how freeing it was to spend
time with someone to whom you weren't attracted.
Someone who was truly just a friend.

She looked back at the girls still staring after
Ramos. They'd probably think she was crazy for not
being attracted to a man like him. Perhaps they were
right. He was good-looking in a dangerous sort of
way. Dangerous. That was the perfect description.
Ian's warning raced through her mind.

No. Ian was gone, and she would not think about
him or about anything he had ever said. *Gone. Done.
Never happened.*

"Here you go." Ramos approached her carrying
two orange and blue cans. "The shopgirl assured me
this is, by far, the most popular native soft drink.
IRN-BRU."

He popped her drink open before handing it to
her, then did the same with his own. As she tipped
the can up, she noticed his wrinkled expression in
response to his own taste of the orange, fizzy drink.

"Hmm. . . . Perhaps they're popular with a younger
set. What is that flavor? Bubblegum?" His face was
still wrinkled in distaste.

She giggled. The smooth, sophisticated Ramos
making faces was not at all what she'd expected. It
totally blew the dangerous label she had just decided
on for him. "No. I'd say it's more like Halloween

candy. Those spongy, peanut-shaped candies, you know?"

His eyebrow lifted and she giggled again, certain he had no idea what she was trying to describe.

"Yes, well, if we come across any of those particular candies, you will point them out, won't you? I think I'd like to avoid them."

He took her elbow to direct her back to the silver Bentley Continental GT he'd left pulled off to the side of the road.

Once they were on their way, Sarah's curiosity took center stage, forcing her to begin the so-far fruitless quizzing all over again.

"So. If you won't tell me where yet, have you at least decided *when* you're going to tell me where we're headed?"

When he had picked her up that morning, he told her he had located an opportunity to interact with the native population at its best, but that their destination was a secret. Her only clue was that they were headed west, and that only because of the electronic compass on the dash of the car.

Ramos arched an eyebrow and glanced at her over the top of his designer sunglasses. "You're really not a very patient woman, are you?"

"No. Patience is not one of my virtues." She drummed her fingers on the arm rest. "At least give me a hint."

"Very well. A hint." He paused as if thinking of something suitably vague to tell her. "All right, how's this? It starts at one o'clock and we should be there by then."

"And what is it that starts at one?" She pulled her

own sunglasses down on the bridge of her nose and batted her eyelashes at him expectantly.

"That's all you get, my sweet. You'll have to wait and see."

Neither her continued wheedling nor her long, dramatic sighs were successful in getting anything more from him other than laughter. Finally she gave up trying to discover their destination and simply concentrated on enjoying the scenery.

They settled into a comfortable silence, breaking it occasionally to point out some new sight they passed. It was after one of these longer silences that Ramos cleared his throat, garnering Sarah's attention. He stared straight ahead, casting one quick glance her direction.

"Though I don't particularly like to admit it, I believe it's just possible that your bad habits are rubbing off on me."

"Which of my bad habits would you be referring to?" She wished she could see his eyes behind those dark lenses.

"Your unrelenting curiosity and lack of patience. I find myself similarly struck."

"Not much fun, is it?" She smiled in his direction. "So what is it you're dying to know? Unlike you, I'm open to answering anything." Almost anything, she silently corrected herself.

"What convinced McCullough to let you come with me today?"

Anything but a discussion about Ian, that is.

"There was no need to convince anyone of anything. I'm not a child to be given or refused permission to do something I want to do. You asked, I said yes. It's as simple as that."

"Really?"

"Really."

She looked out her window, refusing to make eye contact with him. The disbelief in his voice, and in him, hung heavy in the car, as if it had a life of its own.

"Very well. Then what did he say when you told him you were coming with me?"

"Where are you taking me?"

"What?"

"You heard me. I answered one of your questions, now you have to answer one of mine."

He arched a look over the top of his sunglasses. "I don't recall making any such bargain."

She shrugged. She would not discuss Ian. The day had been so pleasant, she would not allow that pain back to the surface.

"This is a pretty little village. What did the sign back there say it's called?"

After a slight pause, Ramos answered. "Invergarry. It's where we've been headed. Down this way," he added as he turned onto a smaller road, passing through the town.

Cars pulled off to either side of the road to park where they could, and a crowd of people gathered in a ball field to their left. A banner flew above the field announcing a welcome to the Glengarry Highland Games.

"Here we are. Shinty Park. Their Highland games are a local festival. I thought this would give us a good flavor of the real people."

They climbed from the car and wandered down into the crowds.

Food booths sat along the outer perimeter, and areas of competition were set up within the field. Young girls in Highland dress milled about a small stage, giggling and waving to one another. At the far end of the field, several men in kilts appeared to be taking practice throws with a heavy metal ball. The sound of bagpipes drifted across the field as a small pipe band marched in their direction, stepping in time to the wailing notes.

Sarah looked around in awe. "This is wonderful. How did you know about it?"

"I didn't. I wanted to attend an authentic Highland games while I was here and the concierge at my hotel found this one taking place this weekend. So, here we are."

They wandered from competition to competition, watching the locals and visitors alike enjoy food, drink and one another's company. Everyone they met was friendly and welcoming. It was a perfect summer day for such an outing, the sun shining brightly with only a few wispy clouds floating overhead. Sarah had already learned how quickly that could change, so she was enjoying the warmth.

"Come now," a tiny old lady called from a booth they passed. "Yer a fine, strong lad. Pay us a pound to toss the boot. See if you canna impress yer lovely lassie with the strength of those great, fine muscles. All the money goes to the Fireman's Fund."

Several men gathered in rows on the field, hefting large firemen's boots, testing their weight. The field itself had markers down the side showing the distance.

"Go on." Sarah pointed at the field. "It's all for charity. Show me what you've got."

Ramos removed his sunglasses and handed them to her, grinning like a little boy as he took to the field for the event.

The growing crowd of men and boys lined up on the field, all carrying on a loud, good-natured banter about who would be throwing their boot the farthest down the field. Sarah smiled as one small boy struggled with his practice throw, trying to heft a boot almost as large as he was.

She moved to the edge of the field and lifted her hand to shade her eyes, wishing she wore a hat. Of course, if she'd only known where she was going, she would have brought one. Lost in that train of thought, she was surprised to feel a tug on her skirt. Looking down, she was even more surprised by what was doing the tugging.

"H'lo, Auntie."

A happy little face beamed up at her. The small girl holding on to her skirt had huge green eyes framed by long dark lashes and a riot of blond curls pinned back from her face on either side with big bows. She wore a sundress made from a tartan that matched the bows.

"Hi, honey. Are you lost?" She didn't see any adults who appeared to be searching for the child.

"Nope."

"Are your mommy and daddy around?"

The little girl giggled, daintily placing her free hand over her mouth. "Yes, Auntie. My da's out there." She pointed to the field where Ramos and the others were beginning the first round of boot tossing.

Obviously the child had her confused with some relative. She looked around again but still saw no one rushing their direction.

"Who's supposed to be watching you while your daddy's on the field?"

"Doogie. But he went for a cake, over there." She pointed toward the lines of people at the food booths. "I'm hot. Let's go sit under them trees." The little girl began walking away, still holding the hem of Sarah's dress.

Quite naturally, Sarah followed. Although the child might not consider herself lost, Sarah was a little concerned.

"What's your name?"

"Rose."

"That's a pretty name. I'm Sarah. How old are you?"

"Five." Rose stopped and looked at the ground where she dug her toe into the grass. When she looked back up, her cheeks were pink. "Well, almost five. I *will* be five. My next birthday."

"Oh. I guess that would count, then." Sarah smiled down at the little girl and winked. "Lots of ladies don't tell the whole truth about their ages. It's a woman thing."

The child nodded and plopped down on the ground in the shade of a large tree, the hem of Sarah's skirt tightly clutched in her little hand.

Sarah sat down, her back against the trunk of the tree. Rose immediately crawled up into her lap, her emerald eyes sparkling.

"I gots roses in *my* Faerie kiss on my back. Wanna see?"

She turned her back and Sarah immediately spied the dark red birthmark just below Rose's shoulder blade, clearly exposed by the crisscross straps of her little sundress.

Faeries again. Was there no escaping them in this country? Everyone she met seemed obsessed with them.

Sarah tilted her head, studying the child's back. On closer inspection, the mark really did look like a bouquet of roses.

"Where's your Faerie kiss?" Big emerald eyes studied her.

"I don't have one."

"Oh. You sure?" Rose clearly doubted her word on this.

"I'm sure. No Faerie kisses."

The little girl's response was halted by a shout coming toward them.

"Rosie!" A boy, only a couple of years older than Rose, his hands filled with sweets, ran across the edge of the field to where they sat. "I told you to stay right where I left you, over by the boot guys."

Rose shrugged. "I got hot, so I'm sitting here with Auntie Sarah."

The brown curly head turned in Sarah's direction, doubt aimed at her from a second source.

"She's not our aunt, Rosie." His little brow wrinkled. "Sorry, lady."

"Not a problem."

He held out one of the cakes to his little sister, but she ignored it.

Rose let go of Sarah's dress and wiggled around in her lap until they were face to face. She rolled her little eyes in an expression of exasperation that belonged on the face of a much older female, especially accompanied as it was by her one-line response.

"Men."

She shook her head and made a *tsk*ing noise before she placed both her little palms flat against Sarah's cheeks.

Sarah's breath froze in her lungs. Feelings equally as strong as the ones she'd received from Will coursed through her system. Wave after wave of curiosity, recognition and happiness crashed over her. The flood of emotion that swamped her was so intense, her eyes closed, and for a moment she thought she might lose consciousness.

"I knew it," the little girl whispered as she placed a kiss on Sarah's cheek. The deluge of emotions stopped as quickly as they had begun, although the child still held Sarah's face in her chubby little hands.

"Rosalyn Maura MacKiernan! What do you think you're doing?"

Sarah opened her eyes to search for the clearly American, clearly breathless, voice. It came from a woman standing in front of them, hands on her hips. Or, more accurately, where her hips would be if she weren't so very pregnant.

"Look, Mommy. I found an auntie." Rose beamed at the woman. "But she doesn't gots a Faerie kiss like ours." The child jumped off Sarah's lap and ran to the woman, giggling and hugging as much of her as she could throw her arms around. She took her mother's hand and tugged her forward. "Auntie Sarah? This is my mommy."

"No, stay where you are." Rose's mommy held up a

hand when Sarah tried to get up. "Give me a moment and I'll join you down there." She laughed as she maneuvered herself onto the ground. "I feel like the proverbial beached whale." She wiped a hand across her face. "It looks like you've found the only shade around the field. Oh, I'm Cate, by the way. Cate MacKiernan."

"Cate." Sarah nodded. She wanted to say more, but still felt weak from the bizarre encounter with Rose.

"Are you feeling okay? Dougal," she called to the little boy standing quietly to the side. "Run get a bottle of water out of our cooler for Sarah. She looks a little pale."

"I'm fine." Exhausted was more like it.

"Yeah, well, too much sun maybe." Cate frowned at her daughter. "I'm sorry if she was bothering you. Sometimes Rosie can be a bit, um, impetuous."

"No. Not bothering." Completely drained. Bled dry of every bit of energy in her system.

"Rosie?" Cate spoke quietly, nodding toward Sarah.

"Oh. I forgot." The child returned to Sarah's lap, once again placing her palms on Sarah's cheeks. "Sorry, Auntie. I got excited that I found you."

Warmth spread across Sarah's face, moving out to her whole body. Within seconds, she felt as though nothing had happened. Physically, at least. Mentally was a whole different matter.

Rose dropped her hands to her lap and snuggled her head against Sarah's shoulder, the smell of baby shampoo wafting up from her curls.

"I'm hearing an American accent. Are you here on vacation?" Cate's question was followed by a dazzling smile, evidence of where Rose had gotten her sparkling green eyes and friendly attitude.

"Working vacation. I'm a writer." Confusion reigned as she stumbled over her answer. *What just happened with that child?*

"How lovely. Are you here for long?"

"Only a couple more months." Here she'd just gone through an extraordinary experience, yet this woman continued to visit and ask questions as if nothing had happened.

"It's beautiful here, isn't it? My husband was born here so we try to spend part of our year in each place. Where are you from in the States?"

Dougal returned and quietly handed a cold bottle of water to Sarah. She twisted off the cap and took a drink before answering.

"Denver."

"No way," Cate laughed. "We live outside Granby. What a coincidence."

"What's a coincidence?"

At the sound of the deep male voice, Sarah looked up. One of the men from the field had joined them and Ramos stood directly behind him. Any questions she had for the woman would have to wait.

"Sarah, this is my husband, Connor. Connor, this is Sarah . . . I'm sorry, I don't know your last name." Cate attempted to rise, but settled for a laugh and allowed her husband to haul her to her feet and tuck her under his arm.

"Sarah Douglas. It's a pleasure to meet you." Sarah kept her hands on the child in her lap. Considering the way her day had gone so far, she didn't want to risk shaking hands with another stranger.

"My pleasure, Sarah." Connor turned to Ramos. "So this is yer woman?"

Ramos shrugged and smiled.

Sarah narrowed her eyes, but any reply she might have intended was cut short by Cate's excited chatter.

"Sarah's from Denver. Imagine that. Come all this way and meet someone from home." Cate pointed down at the child who had dozed off in Sarah's lap. "Rosie's adopted her. Sarah's an auntie now."

Connor smiled down at the sleeping child and motioned behind him with his thumb. "This is Ramos. We met on the field. More of yer coincidence, I guess. I'm meeting him while Rosie's adopting his Sarah."

Cate leaned around her husband, extending her hand and a smile to Ramos.

Connor squatted down and lovingly ran a hand over the tousled curls of the sleeping girl. In one fluid movement, he scooped the child into his arms and stood.

"It's past time to have this wee lassie indoors, and her mother, too. You ken we agreed to stay only long enough for you to help cousin Elspeth get the lassies in their dancing frocks for the competition. I dinna want you tiring yerself out, Caty." He nodded to Sarah before he turned to go.

Ramos reached down, offering Sarah his assistance to stand. She allowed him to pull her to her feet, even though she was still smarting a bit from the 'yer woman' remark. She needed to speak to Cate before they left.

"Do you know what happened back there?" She kept her voice low, speaking directly to Cate, her back turned to the others.

Cate nodded and then rummaged around in her pocket, pulling out a card, which she extended to Sarah.

"Here's my card. My family has an office in Denver and you can reach me through that number, whether I'm still here or back home. We'll have time to chat then. It's been such a pleasure to meet you, I hope you'll give me a call when you get home." Cate leaned as close as her bulk would allow, giving Sarah a hug. Just before letting go, she whispered, "We'll have a long talk and I can answer some of the questions I'm sure you'll have."

Sarah watched as the friendly family walked to their car, loaded up and pulled away. Her stay in Scotland, and the people she met, continued to get stranger and stranger. She clutched the card in her hand before tucking it into her pocket. That was one number she didn't want to lose. She had every intention of making that call.

"Are you okay?" Ramos interrupted her thoughts.

"I'm fine. Why?" She turned to find him peering at her intently.

"I don't know. You seemed a little out of it for a bit there."

No kidding.

They'd stayed until early evening, enjoying the music and competitions.

Ramos glanced over at Sarah in the passenger seat. Her sunglasses were pushed up on her head, leaving white rings around her eyes, surrounded by pink. Too much sun for her fair skin. He should have thought of that.

"Have fun today?"

"Oh, yes. I wouldn't have missed it for the world." She scooted in her seat, turning to favor him with a huge smile. "Thank you so much for pushing me into coming with you."

"I knew you'd like it."

"I had a wonderful time. It was a great day."

"You say that like it's over."

"Isn't it?"

"Well, it is getting late. You hungry?"

"Famished. That chocolate-covered shortbread wore off quite a while ago."

He grinned. "I don't know that I've ever seen anyone enjoy chocolate as much as you do. You made eating that look almost sinful."

"Guilty as charged. You found my weakness. So, do we get to have chocolate somewhere on our way back?" She gave him a big fake smile, showing her teeth and batting her eyes.

He laughed. "Even better. I've made dinner reservations at a lovely spot in Glen Coe. Of course, there is always the chance they'll have something chocolate for dessert."

"Ummmm. I love dessert." She leaned back in her seat, closing her eyes, but then popped back up. "Hey, it's going to be getting dark by the time we get there and have dinner, isn't it?

"I should imagine so."

"Driving these roads in the dark isn't particularly safe." She turned her head and looked out the window. "Or so someone once told me," she added in a murmur.

"Well, whoever that someone was, they were absolutely correct. That's why I made the other reservation." He smiled at the suspicious look she turned on him.

"What *other* reservation?"

"I've reserved a room for the night in Glen Coe as well." He arched an eyebrow and flashed a smile that had worked miracles on more than one woman in his lifetime.

"*A* room?" He had her full attention as she swiveled in her seat again, facing her body toward him as far as her seatbelt allowed. "As in one single room to be shared by the two of us?"

He turned up the intensity of his smile.

She didn't appear to be fazed. "Oh, I don't think so. One room is *not* going to work. Not unless . . ." She turned to face straight ahead, a smile playing around her mouth.

"Unless what?"

"Unless you're planning to sleep out in this cute little car tonight."

He laughed before responding. She had a hell of a wit once she loosened up. "I reserved two rooms."

It was her turn to arch an eyebrow.

"Hey, can't blame a chap for trying. I thought I'd see what you'd say." He grinned at her again.

After a few moments of silence, she pinned him with an appraising look. "You like playing the role of bad boy, don't you?"

"Is that what you think I do?"

She nodded and looked out her window into the gathering dusk. "I bet you fool a lot of people with that act. For the record, though, I'm not one of them. You might play the bad boy, but you're really a good guy. Trust me when I say I know that for a fact."

An act? Perhaps she was right. Being the bad boy suited his needs. Growing up as he had, trained from birth to fight against the life and death struggle his people faced every day, it was easy to lose sight of who he really was, what he really believed. Sometimes, remembering he was in reality the good guy was the only thing that kept him going.

He just never expected it to feel so good to have someone else acknowledge it.

"It's so beautiful here." Sarah's voice sounded as wistful as she'd looked holding that little girl this afternoon, her blond curls almost blending with the child's as they sat together on the ground.

Ramos watched her now, sitting next to him on a picnic table behind their hotel, her elbows on her knees, her hands supporting her chin as she stared out at the lake. After dinner she'd wanted to wander out for a walk and they'd ended up here, watching the moon dance over the water in silver ripples.

"See the little island out there in the loch?" She pointed off to their left. "The desk clerk told me that centuries ago feuding clansmen were rowed out to that island and left there until they settled their differences."

"Sounds remarkably civilized." It should be that way today, he thought, saving innocents like Sarah from getting caught in the middle of battle.

He casually placed his arm around her shoulders, pulling her closer to his side.

She turned to look at him, arched an eyebrow and

pointedly removed his arm, scooting back to where she'd been. "I thought we covered this ground in the car today. Didn't I make myself clear?"

"No clearer than my response."

"Which was?"

"Can't blame a chap for trying." He grinned and moved his arm again, but she caught hold and pushed him back.

"Okay, let me make it crystal clear for you then. I like you. I like you a lot. As a friend. That's it. Friendship is all I have left in me to give right now. If that's not enough for you, then so be it."

"All you have right now?" He watched her closely. He didn't like the air of sadness that clung to her this evening.

She nodded her response.

"Then that's all I ask." He grinned again. "For now." He allowed the silence to stretch out before he broke it once again. "It's because of McCullough, isn't it?"

"What?"

"That you don't have anything else left to give. It's because of him, isn't it?" He wanted to hear it from her. Needed to know how she really felt. How deeply involved she was. How much she knew. About many things.

She turned away, looking out over the lake. "I suppose we should get an early start tomorrow. I hadn't really planned to be away overnight."

Again she avoided his questions. But this time he didn't plan to let it go.

"Have you called him yet to tell him you're staying

the night with me?" He intentionally kept his tone light.

She shook her head. "I'm not staying *with* you. We're merely staying at the same place. There's a huge difference."

"You didn't answer my question."

Silence.

"In fact, you haven't answered any of my questions about McCullough today."

Silence.

"Why is that?" Her continued evasion puzzled him.

"I'm not discussing Ian with you. That's an off-limits subject."

"But isn't he going to be worried when you don't come back tonight?"

"No." Her voice was little more than a whisper.

"Let me be honest here. At Glaston House it was obvious that the two of you were involved in a relationship. You can't blame me for wanting to know what I'll be walking into when I deliver you back home."

"You don't have anything to worry about, Ramos. There won't be any angry boyfriends waiting to wreak havoc on you when we get back."

"So you're telling me he won't be waiting with swords drawn when we drive up?"

"No."

"And you're not going to call him and tell him where you are?"

"No."

"And in spite of how possessive he seemed, you're

saying he isn't going to be the least bit worried when you don't show up there tonight?" None of what she was saying meshed with what he'd seen for himself.

"No."

"Well, then, I'm hopelessly confused. If I were in McCullough's place right now, I'd be sick with worry. At least tell me why you won't call." He grinned, hoping to coax a smile from her, until he caught sight of the glistening drop rolling down her cheek. Moonlight glinted off the tear, giving the appearance of a diamond rolling down her face.

"I'm not calling because he's not there. He's gone."

"When's he due back?" A sick feeling started to grow in his stomach.

"I don't think he's coming back. At least not as long as I'm there," she whispered, ending in a little hiccup of a sob.

He pulled her to him, running his hand across her hair and down her back. He should have done something earlier, should have anticipated this, reacted sooner. But his instincts had failed him. Watching McCullough with her in England, he'd been so sure the Guardian would never willingly leave her side.

Anger rolled over him. As his father had always told him, Guardians were without feeling, mere attack dogs for the evil Fae who controlled them. The same Fae who had abused his people, stealing their homes and thrusting them out into the Mortal world. They had no concern for the innocents they trod upon.

Thinking of those innocents, his conscience stung only a little at his avoiding the red flag he'd wanted to pursue on this night. Now wasn't the time to trouble

Sarah with questions about the startling reaction she'd had to Reynard. It was obvious the woman was a Sensor. He needed to know what she could possibly have sensed in his father that affected her so violently.

He looked down at Sarah weeping silently in his arms. She was a nice lady with a good heart. He had liked her from the moment he met her. He'd hoped to avoid this. To intervene before McCullough had the opportunity to hurt her. But he'd been too late. Taken too long to press his case, too long in moving forward with the plan.

It was for the best that the Guardian was gone. In all honesty, he was relieved.

Because now that Ramos had come to know Sarah, come to respect and understand her, to care for her, how could he possibly eliminate the man she loved without being as bad as the Guardian himself?

Damn the Guardian to hell.

Twenty-two

*I*an was living in hell.

Had been for the past two weeks. Fully expected to spend the rest of his life there. A hell so severe, he couldn't imagine a way for it to get any worse.

You'd think at the very least everyone could leave him alone and let him suffer in peace.

"Look, I don't know what happened, and I know you don't want to talk about it. I promised I wouldn't ask again. But for God's sake, Ian, you can't keep on like this." Danny paced back and forth across the shiny wooden floor of the London flat, tunneling his hand through his hair. "Come back to Glaston House with me. Spend some time there. Wind down."

"No." Ian didn't think he could ever go there again without holding his breath, expecting at any moment to see Sarah walk around every corner. Without being haunted by the smell of her, the memory of her. "No. I'm staying here. I'm fine."

"Like hell you are. You've barely eaten anything

and you look like death warmed over." Danny stopped his pacing in front of the chair where Ian slumped. "Will you at least consider driving out on Friday, spend the weekend with us?"

"I'll consider it." He'd say anything to shut his friend up, to get him out of here. He stood and put a hand at Danny's back. "Now go home to yer wife and son. Go. I'll be fine."

Danny shook his head as he allowed Ian to push him toward the door. "You'll go out and get something to eat? I'm calling to check on you tomorrow, I mean it."

"Yeah, I'll take care of it. You worry like an old woman. Go."

With one last fretful look back, Danny shoved his hands deep in the pockets of his raincoat and hurried through the drizzle toward his parked car.

At last. The solitude he craved.

His friend meant well, was only trying to comfort him, but Ian didn't want comfort. Didn't deserve it. All he wanted as he stretched out on the dark leather sofa was to escape into the black void of sleep. Only there was he without any thought at all. Thought was his enemy now, because every conscious moment, with every breath he took, his every thought was of Sarah.

He lay back, slowed his breathing and began to drift, reaching for that place where he could be nothing, know nothing, feel nothing.

The harsh jangle of the telephone jerked him back to the hell he'd been working to escape. With his eyes still closed, he briefly considered ignoring it, but the noise would continue and then they—whoever they were—would just call back, starting the whole process over again.

"What," he snarled into the receiver as he grabbed it.

"Ian?" Henry's quiet voice faltered for a moment. "Is this a bad time?"

Ian calmed himself. None of this was Henry's fault. "No, Henry. Sorry. What can I do for you?" He sat forward on the sofa, rolling his neck from side to side to relieve the tension curled there.

"I'm afraid we may have a wee problem. I was no sure who else to speak to."

"What is it?" The roof again, the plumbing, the electric—none of it really mattered.

"It would appear Sarah's gone missing."

That mattered. He sat up straight, his full attention on the conversation.

"What do you mean, gone missing? Gone as in took a walk, lost in the woods—what?"

"Gone as in dinna return last night from her, um, outing with that man."

How could he possibly feel like he was going to throw up when he hadn't any food in his stomach?

"What man?"

"That Ramos man. The one who picked her up yesterday to take her sightseeing."

"Ramos Servans? You let her leave the grounds with Servans?" He was on his feet, pacing as far as the telephone cord would allow. "I dinna understand. She promised she'd no see either of them again," he murmured, half to himself.

"That's exactly what I told the General."

"Dallyn knew she was going?"

"Oh, aye. He said she had her own choices to make."

Bloody cryptic Fae. "Does he know that she dinna return? That she's gone missing?"

"Well, no. When we realized she'd no come home, I dinna know for sure what to do. Finally I decided I'd call you, as I'd wanted to when we first learned she was going off with that man. I figured you'd know what was best." Henry sounded rattled.

"Verra well. You did fine, Henry. Here's what I want you to do now. First of all, go find the General. Tell him what's happened. Tell him I want her found. Immediately." *If anything's happened to her . . .*

"Right. I'll find him."

"And I want to talk to him. You have him call me as soon as she's located."

"Aye, I'll try. Anything else?"

"Keep me updated. I'll be waiting."

"Right."

Ian held the phone long after the line had gone dead, as if in some way it connected him to the place he really wanted to be. He reined in his first inclination to drive up there and find her himself. He couldn't give in to that even though he felt helpless here, so far away from her, unable to do anything to protect her.

But being away from her was the only way he could protect her.

If I'm there, she dies.

Unless Dallyn was right and he'd interpreted the dream incorrectly.

In spite of his earlier lack of imagination, the severity of his hell had suddenly ratcheted up a notch.

* * *

The car pulled to a stop in the driveway, Ramos hopping out almost before the motor died to come round and open her door. No doubt he was anxious to get rid of her.

"Thanks again for the trip. I had a great time." Sarah smiled at him, expecting a hasty departure to follow.

He pushed his sunglasses to the back of his head, staring at her for a moment before answering. "So did I. What say I pick you up tomorrow and we go see the sights in Edinburgh together?"

"I'm surprised you'd want to."

"What makes you say that?" Now he looked surprised.

"After the spectacle I made last night, you have to ask?" She could feel her face color with embarrassment. The last thing she'd planned to do was cry all over his shoulder. But she'd done it anyway.

"That?" He made a scoffing noise. "That was nothing. That is, after all, what friends are for. To be there when you need them. So, we on for tomorrow?"

"I'm afraid not. I'm behind in my writing and I've taken the last two days off to play."

"Very well. I'll give you that. Saturday, then. Everyone takes the weekend off. Even big, famous authors like you, I'd imagine. I'll come up with something special, I promise."

She had enjoyed her time with Ramos. And he did make her laugh. Why shouldn't she see him again?

"Okay, but what about this? We come back early Saturday and I'll fix dinner here. That way, I can do something for you."

He paused as if considering her offer, then grinned. "I have a better idea. I'll come out Friday afternoon. You fix us an early dinner. Then we'll drive back to the city, spend the night—two rooms, of course"—he waggled his eyebrows up and down causing her to chuckle—"and we'll have a full Saturday for whatever we want to do."

"Deal." She stuck her hand out to shake on the agreement.

He took the hand she offered, using it to pull her to him. Wrapping his other arm behind her, he dipped her over backward for a long kiss.

Another surprise. "What was that for? Just a chap still trying?"

"Not at all. That was entirely for the benefit of the audience." He shot a quick glance toward the front of the house before covering his eyes with the sunglasses he'd pulled off his head.

But not before she saw the laughter there. *Yeah, he likes to play the bad boy.*

"See you Friday afternoon, my sweet," he called loudly as got back in the car.

More loudly than he'd needed to, obviously still playing to the audience.

After waving to the retreating car, she turned to find both Henry and Martha standing at the foot of the stairs. She had to stifle the giggle that threatened to bubble out as she looked at them. They were like matching statues, both with their arms crossed and both with irritated little frowns on their faces.

"Good afternoon," she called, waving as she started down the path toward the cottage, a quick escape in mind.

"One moment, young lady. Hold it right there." Henry broke his pose and limped toward her. "Where have you been? We've been worried sick about you."

Martha kept her post by the stairs, but nodded vigorously to show her agreement.

"Why on earth would you be worried about me?"

"We expected you back last night. When you'd no returned this morning, I was beside meself."

"Near gave him a stroke, you did, missie." Martha kept her distance, but clearly wanted her say.

"I even had Dallyn out hunting for you."

Her first instinct was to be irritated, but looking closely, she could see that Henry was, in fact, very upset. His cheeks were a mottled pink and his hands shook. She suddenly felt very guilty. She hadn't given a second thought to her host's reaction to her being gone last night.

"Oh, Henry. I am sorry. I didn't mean to put you out." She reached the older man and gave him a hug. She considered it a good sign that he allowed her to do so. "We spent the day at the Glengarry Highland Games. It got dark and we decided it was safer to stay there than try to drive back. I never thought to give you a call. It didn't occur to me that anyone here would even notice I was gone."

"Well, we did notice."

"Yes, we did," Martha added.

"I should expect in the future you'll take care no to get caught out like that." He seemed somewhat mollified.

"Or, if I do, I'll make sure to call. Okay?"

"Verra well." He turned and limped back toward the stairs.

"Verra well," Martha echoed, getting the last word in, before following Henry into the house.

Sarah headed to the cottage. She could use some time to herself. After the events of yesterday, she was emotionally drained.

It had been a while since she'd had to account for her whereabouts to anyone and she found it left her with myriad emotions. She was irritated with herself for not having been a more thoughtful guest. She felt guilty for Henry McCullough's obvious upset.

But, worst of all, she was disappointed that it was the wrong McCullough who had been worried about her.

Twenty-three

"*H*ello. May I come in?"

Sarah jumped, startled, turning toward the voice.

"Hello, Dallyn. It looks like you're already in."

Her odd neighbor stood in the center of her living room, hands behind his back, looking around, taking in everything. "Your door was open. I took that as my invitation."

He smiled and she was once again struck by what an extraordinarily handsome man he was.

"What can I do for you?"

"Ah, lovely lady, first it's what I can do for you." He pulled a package from behind his back, extending it to her.

"You brought a gift for me?"

"I did."

She rose from her desk to take the package. "What is it?"

"I have no idea. I'm not a snoop."

"But you said . . ." She stopped herself and shook

her head. She should know by now not to expect a logical conversation with Dallyn.

The postmark on the package was Edinburgh. *R.S.* in the upper left-hand corner. Ramos.

"I said I brought it and I did. Not that it was from me. How would I know what the package contains?" He spoke as if to himself. "No need to get your nostrils out of joint."

"I'm sorry, Dallyn. My misunderstanding." She set the package on the table and tugged at the brown paper wrapping.

"Yes, I suppose it is. Henry picked it up at the post today. Asked me to drop it by when I came."

"Well, thank you. Let's see what it is . . . oh my."

The last of the mailing paper pulled away, exposing a square brown box, much like jewelry would come in. But it wasn't jewelry. Sarah had ogled a box like this before.

"DeLafée," she breathed.

Oh Lord, edible decadence in a box.

With a feeling nearing reverence she lifted the lid and admired the eight small tapered chocolate cylinders, each hand coated in edible gold leaf.

"Faeries?" Dallyn looked at her quizzically.

"Way better. Chocolate." She held it close to her face and sniffed. "Ummmm. Swiss chocolate pralines."

"Faerie chocolate? I never heard of such a thing before." Dallyn still watched her, a small confused scowl wrinkling his brow.

"Faerie chocolate?" She frowned at him. What was he rambling on about now?

"DeLafée." He pointed to the wording on the lid. "From the Fée. Faeries."

Surrounded. Everywhere she turned.

"I give up." *To hell with what he thinks of me. I can't possibly be any crazier than he is.* "Apparently, Dallyn, I'm a descendant of Faeries. And since I've been in Scotland, they've gone out of their way at every possible turn to make sure I know it." She took one of the little chocolates in her fingers, then offered the box to her guest. "Want one?"

"How delightful. You could say I descend from them myself, fair lady. Welcome to the family. And, yes, I think I would like to sample this Faerie chocolate of yours."

She started to giggle, but the chocolate she'd bitten off melted in her mouth, oozing over her taste buds, and she moaned instead.

"I'm going to have to agree with you on that. This is quite delicious." Dallyn took another tiny bite from the end of his piece. "Unique texture and flavor."

"The taste of self-indulgence, Dallyn. These are pure decadence. Sit down and close your eyes while you finish it." She followed her own advice. "I'll have to give Ramos his due on this one. He sure knows how to pick an impressive gift. A tad ostentatious, maybe, but impressive nevertheless." She smiled and licked a bit of the chocolate from her fingers.

"Ostentatious?" Dallyn still took tiny bites from his piece.

"He's a man who likes to make a show of things. Spare no expense."

"He spared no expense on this gift?"

"No, he didn't. These are mighty pricey. About ninety-five bucks a box last time I saw them." At his blank look she tried again. "Roughly forty-five or fifty pounds?" His look didn't change. "Forget it." Maybe the man really was one of the elusive Fae. That would certainly explain a lot. "You don't shop much, do you?"

"I do not." He was down to the last bite of his chocolate.

"Are you married?" At his look of alarm, she laughed. "Okay. I guess I have my answer to that one." She held out the box again. "Want another?"

His hand wavered over the candy. "I probably should not." But he took one anyway, again starting at the tip with a tiny bite.

Sarah took another piece as well. It was so rich she might regret taking a second one, but, you only live once.

"What are you doing here, anyway? Did you just come down to deliver the candy?"

"No, as I said, I was on my way here so Henry asked me to bring the package."

"So . . ." She dragged out the word, waiting for him to fill in the blank for her.

He didn't respond.

"Did you have a reason for coming by or was this intended to be a social visit?"

"Oh." His eyes popped open like a man who'd forgotten where he was.

No doubt about it, she'd turned him into a certified chocoholic. You'd think he'd never had the stuff before.

"I had a reason." He took another tiny bite, and his eyes fluttered shut again.

Patience at an end, Sarah leaned forward in her seat and placed a hand on his knee. His eyes fluttered open.

"What reason?"

"Oh. These are wonderful, you know? Yes, the reason. Well"—he smiled sheepishly—"to tell you that you can't see the young man again who sent these to you." He took another bite.

"What? You're here to tell me I can't see Ramos again? You're joking. Right?"

She watched him for a moment. When his lack of response indicated he was serious, she felt herself getting angry.

"In the first place, what on earth makes you think you can waltz in here and tell me what to do? I think you need to explain yourself and pretty darn fast."

Dallyn licked the last of the chocolate from his fingertips, and placed his hand over hers. "I haven't waltzed in centuries, my dear."

The smile he favored her with was pure seduction. She felt its impact down to her toes. Perhaps she'd underestimated the man. But, no, as before, there was nothing to fear in his touch. Still, she had an undeniable urge to fan herself.

"And as to why I think I can tell you what to do, that's simple. It's because it's important to Ian that you not see this man again."

At the mention of his name, Sarah jerked her hand back, using it to capture another chocolate. If Dallyn thought they were going to discuss Ian and what *he* wanted, she'd need more chocolate than she had in the entire cottage. A veritable swimming pool full of the stuff.

"What Ian McCullough wants or doesn't want is of absolutely no consequence to me. And, since it would seem he still talks to you, you can tell him I said so."

"You did promise him you wouldn't see either of the Servans men again."

"Yeah, well, obviously things changed."

"You're breaking your promise?"

She snorted her disbelief. "Yes, I am. I happen to believe that, based on his not sticking around, all bets—and promises—are off. Feel free to pass that little tidbit along as well."

He had the gall to look offended. "How can you say that? After everything he's done for you?"

"I beg your pardon? Everything he's done for me? Look, I don't know what he told you"—she paused, feeling her face color as it occurred to her what kind of a conversation the men could have had about her—"but he didn't do anything for me."

"Young woman, Ian McCullough gave you the greatest gift someone can possibly give. Is it too much to ask that you give him something in return? Something as simple as peace of mind, freedom from worry?"

"You aren't making any sense at all. For the record, Ian gave me nothing. And I owe him nothing." Sarah popped the remainder of the chocolate piece she held into her mouth and closed the lid of the box. At this rate, all that lovely chocolate would be coming right back up if she weren't careful.

"Then allow me to explain so it does make sense to you. Ian's gift of love saved your soul. Aren't you willing to do the same for him?"

"Gift of . . ." She sputtered for a moment, unable to form a coherent thought, let alone speak. "Love? That's not my idea of love. It's pretty clear-cut. He got what he wanted and he left. No good-bye, no discussion, not even a note. Just gone. That speaks volumes to me about his so-called love."

"But he did free your soul. He made you whole again, didn't he?"

"Once again, Dallyn, you've lost me. I haven't the foggiest notion of what you're talking about." As usual, he spoke in riddles—about what, she had no idea.

"It's quite simple. You're whole again."

She threw her hands up and flopped back against the sofa, crossing her arms defiantly. This was getting worse and worse.

He tried again. "Think, Sarah. What do you want? What's important to you? What do you care for most in life?"

Ian.

No, she'd never admit that to him. She grasped for something else. Something she could admit to.

"My writing."

A large smile blossomed on Dallyn's face. "I suspected you'd say that. It was Ian's love that gave back to you the ability to write again. The ability that you'd lost when you first arrived. Creation comes from the soul. Your soul was bound and suffering when you came here, withering away waiting for you to accept what you are, waiting for you to find your other half. Ian is that other half."

"Well, apparently you forgot to give Ian this pretty little speech. He doesn't think he's my other half. In case you missed the news bulletin, he's gone, without so much as giving me the common courtesy of an explanation. As I said, no discussion, no good-bye, not even a 'kiss my ass.' So my soul's just going to have to suck it up and get over it." *Just like I have to.*

"You must understand, Sarah. He had a good reason for leaving."

"Oh yeah. I'm sure he did. 'Really important business,' I believe was the excuse Henry stuttered over."

"In a way. He left to protect you."

"Protect me? Hardly. He left to get away from me."

"You're wrong. Just as your soul cried out for him, his is crying out for you even now. You must be willing to risk everything for him when the time is right, as he will risk everything for you. And for now you must be willing to do as he asks."

"That is such a load of bull—" She stopped herself. Dallyn didn't deserve her wrath. This wasn't his fault. He was only trying to help his friend. "My risk-taking days are over. Understand this, and feel free to share it with Ian. I'll see who I want, when I want, as often as I want, and there is nothing you, or Ian, or anyone else has to say about it."

"So you're going to see this young man again?"

"I am."

"Sarah, do you have any idea of the chance you take? How you tip the scales of fate with your actions? Can't you—"

"No," she interrupted, and stood, walking to the door. "I think it's time you left, Dallyn. I appreciate what you're trying to do, but it really isn't any of your business. Please, just go."

At the door he stopped, placing a hand on her shoulder. "When the time comes, I hope you'll remember what I've said to you."

"Whatever. Good-bye, Dallyn."

Giving her shoulder a squeeze, he left.

She stood in the doorway, watching him walk away until he reached the curve in the path and she could see him no more. She walked to the desk and opened the drawer, pulling out her travel paperwork. Perhaps she should call the airline. It didn't matter how high the charge to change her tickets, she didn't think she could stay here much longer. Between the constant Faerie garbage and the painful memories of Ian, life was getting out of hand. She stuffed the envelope in her pocket.

A girl could only take so much.

Dallyn hated surprises.

Unless they were ones of his own making. Unlike this one. He especially disliked the ones he should have anticipated and prepared for. The ones that shouldn't have surprised him at all.

It would appear things were a tad more involved than he'd thought. Obviously young Ian hadn't been completely forthcoming about the extent of his relationship with Sarah. No matter. While it did complicate the situation somewhat, it also served to further confirm his initial suspicions.

Not that he'd needed confirmation after he learned that Ian had seen the woman's soul. Anyone who was old enough to remember the before times knew that the only soul you could ever see was that of your Soulmate. Those two were meant to be with one another. How many lifetimes had passed with those two souls missing an opportunity to be together?

After the Nuadians disrupted the flow of the Fountain, this had been the fate of so many. That, along with the years of war, had directly contributed to the decline in the number of his people. It was exceedingly difficult to put the broken pieces back together, to right the flow, to reconnect the proper pairings of souls.

True, that wasn't his job. His was only to protect. Others would have the responsibility to repair. And, yes, the High Council frowned upon any of the Fae meddling in the affairs of Mortals, but, on occasion, a little judicious meddling was necessary.

At least in his opinion it was.

He sat on the lowest branch of a tree outside the Portal door, twirling a fresh green leaf between his fingers. A storm was coming. He could sense the energies gathering in the air. He'd need to stay alert. Wait and watch for the opportunity he sought. It would only come once, and if he missed it, there was no telling how many more lifetimes would pass before another presented itself.

He smiled as he hopped lightly off the branch and disappeared through the Portal. What the High Council didn't know wouldn't hurt anyone.

Or so he hoped.

Sarah let the book she'd been reading fan shut. She leaned back on the cushioned bench and closed her eyes, shaken by the things she'd learned. The fragile old texts she'd so carefully stacked on the wooden table in front of her seemed to mock her now, as if the long-dead authors scorned her for how little she knew of her world.

After her conversation with Dallyn she'd been too rattled to concentrate on her writing. Tired of everyone explaining things to her as if she were a backward child, she'd gone to the manor house to ask if the nearby town had a library. It was time for some serious research.

Instead Henry had ushered her into his library and given her free rein. What she'd discovered was amazing. The McCullough library housed an impressive collection of works covering sacred texts, legends, religions and, what she'd actually sought, Faeries.

Wanting privacy, she'd brought the texts out here to the gazebo, where she could read without concern for being interrupted. And read she had.

As she sat forward, placing this last text on top of the others, her eye lit on a bulge under the far cushion and she stretched over to investigate.

Her sandal. The sight of it jarred her as the memories of the night she'd left them flooded back, washing over her. She'd completely forgotten about leaving them here. She stood and looked around, lifting all the cushions to peek underneath.

Only the one shoe in sight, the other nowhere to be found. Another mystery, as unsolvable for her at this moment as the one that had led her to this spot earlier today.

She'd spent hours out here perusing the Faerie lore collection, ending up as confused as she'd been before she started. Everything Ian had told her was documented in these texts, up to and including the Swiss name Servans. Everything except what she wanted most.

Everything except proof that it was real.

At the first tentative knock, Sarah considered ignoring the visitor, pretending to be gone. She wondered if Dallyn might have returned for another round of what he was dishing out today.

Hiding wouldn't work. She might have shut her door, but the windows were wide open. Whoever was knocking had only to move a little to either side and they'd see her sitting there.

She'd never get her book finished at this rate.

Sighing in resignation, she rose and went to answer the door.

"Hello, dearie. Is everything all right out here?

"Yes, Martha. Everything's fine. Why?"

"Well, yer door's closed. You dinna ever keep it closed, except for after . . ." Her voice trailed off and she cleared her throat, keeping her eyes trained on her suddenly interesting feet. "You've a phone call up at the house."

"Thanks." *For the call and for not finishing that earlier comment.* She didn't need to be reminded that everyone here knew how upset she'd been by Ian's leaving.

Once again she followed Martha to the manor house and answered the telephone in the kitchen. Once again, an efficient female voice confirmed it was her on the line before handing the call off.

"Good afternoon, my sweet."

"Hi, Ramos. Why do you do that? Have someone else call for you?"

A low chuckle preceded his answer. "I'm guessing some of the people there might prefer you not speak to me. If they knew it was me, I'm not sure I'd ever get to talk to you."

"Ah. Good answer." Before her conversation with Dallyn, she might have denied Ramos's assertion. Now she suspected he could be right.

"Have you been thinking pleasant thoughts of me today? Like what a wonderful, generous bad boy I am?"

"I may have. But I'm sure you knew I would when you sent that little gift."

He laughed. "Little? You wound me to the quick. Sweets for my sweet. Clever of me, wasn't it?"

"A regular old box of candy wouldn't do?"

"Not for you. It had to be a rich, sinful chocolate so I could imagine you with your eyes closed, making that little face of sublime satisfaction. Besides, sending a regular old anything wouldn't fit my image."

The tease she heard in his voice made her smile. "Yeah, I almost forgot. Bad boys like to spend big."

"Everything about us bad boys is big."

"Well, I guess I'll be taking your word for that."

"You don't have to. I'd be happy to demonstrate." He paused. "No?"

"No."

His laughter filled the phone line.

"Not funny, Ramos."

"But it is from my end of the conversation. I can picture you standing there, blushing bright red, with your attentive audience hanging on every word."

She glanced behind her. Martha had her back turned, busily straightening the contents of a drawer. The same drawer she'd straightened the last time Sarah had taken a phone call from Ramos.

"Are you still coming tomorrow, or were the chocolates an apology?"

"I'm counting the hours, my sweet. So we're still invited to come across your drawbridge and whisk you away?"

"We?"

Another laugh. "Of course. My traveling companions and I. I'm bringing a lovely bottle of wine in a particularly delightful vintage, and perhaps another, even more decadent form of chocolate to sweeten you up."

"I like your choice of traveling companions. Yes, you and all your friends are invited to cross my drawbridge, your arrival highly anticipated."

"Exactly what I wanted to hear."

A clatter from the counter behind her where Martha stood distracted her, nearly drowning out his response. The housekeeper had knocked over a box of pasta, scattering little uncooked tubes all over the floor.

"I need to get back to work. When do you think you'll be here?"

"Is four acceptable? Or better yet, three. No, I don't want to wait that long, two. Or . . ."

Chuckling, Sarah interrupted him. "Four. I'll plan on your being here at four."

"Until then." His end of the line went dead.

After hanging up the receiver, she bent down and began picking up little pasta tubes, unsure whether the sudden feeling of dread that swept over her came from the woman who'd been eavesdropping on her conversation or the man with whom she'd spoken.

Twenty-four

"You canna allow this to happen. You have to do something to stop it."

Ian balanced the receiver between his ear and his shoulder as he hopped from one foot to the other, pulling on his pants.

"I did all I could." Dallyn's voice floated to him over the line.

"I canna believe that. Yer without a doubt the most powerful man I know and yer telling me you canna make one small woman bend to yer will?"

"She may be small, but she's a mind of her own, that one."

"Did you no remind her of her promise? She said she'd no have anything to do with that man."

"I did remind her."

Ian huffed an irritated breath as he hunted for his shirt in the pile of clothing he'd dumped out of his suitcase.

"And? Did she have a response?" Sometimes it felt

like pulling teeth to get a straight answer from the Fae.

"I believe her exact words were something along the lines of all bets being off because you'd left. Oh, and promises. She included promises as being off as well. Said I should feel free to tell you that."

"Bloody, stubborn woman. Well, you simply have to keep them out until I can get there. That's all there is to it." He tucked the receiver under his chin while he pulled on his socks.

"How do you expect me to do that? She's invited them. It's out of my hands."

He had felt so safe. So sure there was no way they could get to her. Never once had he considered she would invite them across the water. Unless they could be stopped, unless he could get there and stop them, the last six centuries of his life would have been wasted.

"You must do something."

"What would you have of me? Should I try to *talk* them off the estate?" An unusual trace of irritation sounded in Dallyn's voice, fueling Ian's concern.

"I dinna care what you do. Or how you do it. Stop them however you like. You canna let them cross onto the property."

"If I had the power to do anything violent on the Mortal Plain, we never would have needed Guardians, now would we? My job is to meet them on the other side of the Portal with whatever amount of force is required. *If* you fail in your job. Stopping them before they enter the Portal is your job, Ian. It's why you're supposed to be here."

He felt the rebuke in Dallyn's words. Deserved it

and much more. Of course he was supposed to be there. His being there was all that stood between life as it is now and a return to utter chaos.

His being there would also mean Sarah's death.

How could Dallyn sound so sure of himself? Ian wanted to rage, to throw the phone through the wall, to pound someone's face. It was a testament to his sheer force of will that he managed to speak at all.

"What time did you say she's expecting him?"

"According to Martha, they should arrive at four."

He glanced at the clock. Half past one.

"Dinna let her out of yer sight, not for an instant. Swear it to me."

"I will do my best."

"No. I'll have yer oath on it. No double talk, no Faerie riddles. This is too important."

"I so swear."

"Good enough." Ian slammed down the phone without waiting to hear more. Sliding into his shoes, he grabbed his keys and cell phone off the coffee table and ran for the door.

He flipped the phone open, hitting the speed dial as he sprinted toward his car.

"Danny? No. I'm no coming. Shut up and listen. I'm on my way to the airport. I need a plane ready to take off in the next twenty-five minutes. And I'll expect a car waiting when I land. Oh, and make sure it's a fast one." He flipped the phone closed and unlocked the door of his own automobile. Too bad it wouldn't be waiting when the plane landed.

There was no possible way he could get to Thistle Down Manor before Ramos and whoever would be with him. The best he could hope for at this point was arriving in time to prevent total destruction.

The best he could pray for was accomplishing that without sacrificing Sarah.

Three forty-five. Fifteen minutes and counting. Sarah's hand shook as she applied her mascara.

Soft music filled the cottage along with the aroma of lasagna bubbling in the oven. The table was set, the kitchen cleaned, and still she couldn't quite rid herself of the feeling of impending doom that had settled over her at the end of yesterday's telephone call.

"Stupid."

What was the absolute worst that could happen? She could burn dinner. No, the absolute worst-case scenario would be a renegade asteroid impacting the earth and destroying all life.

She smiled at herself in the mirror as she picked up her lipstick pencil. *Way too much Science Channel television.* The asteroid option was one she could quickly discard.

But she couldn't rid herself of the unnamed dread so easily, or the nerves that accompanied it, so she gave up on the lipstick, opting for a little clear gloss. Better no color at all than looking like she'd had her makeup done by a deranged preschooler.

One last quick inspection in the mirror before she flipped off the light, closed the door and headed to the kitchen to check her lasagna. After all, she hadn't ruled out the burning-dinner scenario.

Everything looked fine. She turned off the stove, leaving the casserole inside to finish and stay warm.

She rolled down her sleeves and buttoned the cuffs at her wrists. She was as ready as she was going to get.

Anything else? Another glance at the table and she thought of the beautiful etched crystal pieces she'd seen in the top cabinet above the refrigerator. She dragged a chair over, climbed up and retrieved two delicate wineglasses.

Ramos said he was bringing a bottle of wine.

She had just finished drying the freshly washed goblets when a light knock sounded at her door.

"Come in," she called as she started toward the sound, both wineglasses still in her hands. "Look what I found in . . ." The words froze in her mouth as she looked up.

An unsmiling Ramos stood in her doorway, but it was the sight of the people who accompanied him that brought her to a halt, silencing whatever thought of small talk she'd had.

Reynard Servans and Nicole Tanner flanked him.

The delicate crystal slipped from Sarah's hands unheeded, shattering on the floor at her feet.

Three forty-five. Ian glanced at the clock on the dashboard and silently cursed. He had been driving for twenty minutes, battling traffic as he raced toward home. At this speed, it would be at least another forty-five minutes and that was assuming optimal conditions. He flipped open his cell phone and dialed Henry again, apprehension as high as his impatience.

Four rings. Five. Where could they be? Six. No one had answered the last two times he'd dialed.

"McCullough residence."

"Martha. Thank the Fates." Relief flooded through him, leaving a vague weakness in its wake. "What's kept you from answering the bloody telephone?"

"I'm sorry, sir, but I canna get either of them for you right now. His Lordship is in London for a time and Mr. Henry is unavailable."

"It's me, Martha. Ian." Had the woman gone daft?

"Yes, yes I know. But you'll have to figure it out on yer own. Everyone's tied up here. Good day."

The click that followed vibrated with an ominous air of finality.

Silence pressed at him from the telephone he gripped in his hand as fear clawed at his gut. Something was wrong. Very wrong.

He pressed the accelerator toward the floor, fearing he was already too late.

"Mon petit cadeau de la fée." Reynard smiled as he reached her side. "What a shame. Your lovely crystal is ruined."

"What are you doing here?" Sarah's reaction added to the doubt growing in Ramos's mind.

"You invited me. Aren't you pleased to see me again?" Reynard's hand closed around her upper arm and he pulled her toward him.

Watching the reflection of dread grow on Sarah's face as his father's grip tightened on her arm, Ramos regretted not having pursued the subject of what she'd sensed in the man when he'd had the opportunity. Suddenly it seemed of utmost importance to him to know why she had reacted so violently to his father's touch.

"Father." Ramos hadn't intended the rebuke to

sound so sharp, but his concern was building. Things were not going at all as he had hoped.

Reynard's head snapped up, irritation filling his eyes, as his hand dropped to his side. "Very well. As you wish. For now."

"What's going on here, Ramos? Why are these people with you?" She backed away from Reynard, her hand rubbing the spot where he had held her.

Ramos crossed to her, placing his hand on her shoulder and, in the process, discreetly inserting his body between her and his father. "Let me explain."

Reynard interrupted. "We've some unfinished business, you and I, *ma petite*. That's what's going on."

She ignored Reynard, perhaps the first time Ramos had seen anyone disregard his father so completely.

"You can begin your explanation with what *she's* doing here." Sarah tilted her head toward Nicole, her voice faltering just a little. "And by telling me what's wrong with her."

Reynard had insisted on keeping the Mortals who'd traveled with them under a compulsion. Ramos had argued against the practice to no avail on their way here.

"A simple compulsion, Ramos. It doesn't harm them in the least and it makes everything progress so much more smoothly," Reynard had claimed. But it concerned Ramos that his father gave no thought to free will or the value Mortals placed on it.

Ramos glanced at Nicole now. As much as her emotionless stare unnerved him, it was obviously more upsetting for Sarah.

"She's all right, don't be frightened," he started.

His father interrupted again. "I'm attempting to

allow you to do this your way. Sit her down and explain our needs now or I will be forced to do it myself." The promise sparking in Reynard's gaze was disquieting.

"I don't understand any of this, Ramos." Sarah's gaze remained focused on him.

"I know." He led her to a chair, kneeling down in front of her after she sat. "We need your help, Sarah."

Hurt shone in her eyes. None of this was what he'd wanted. He'd known it should be handled differently. If only his father had given him more time. In time, his friendship with Sarah would have allowed him to explain all this to her, to ask for her help. But once Reynard had learned of the Guardian's departure, he'd insisted on moving forward immediately.

"Then why not just ask me for it the first time we spoke? Why all this charade of flirting and being my friend?"

An inelegant snort issued from his father. "Friends. Don't be ridiculous. You can't be friends with females. Especially not her kind. They respond only to total domination."

Sarah's eyes narrowed as she slowly looked up at Reynard. "My kind? What *kind* would that be?"

His father glanced at her dismissively. "Mortal, of course."

Any number of emotions skittered across Sarah's face, ending with a carefully blanked mask settling there.

"As opposed to whatever *you* are, I assume. And that would be what exactly?"

In spite of what Ramos had feared, she remained calm, her voice actually growing stronger.

"A true Fae, of course." Reynard arched an eyebrow. "A full-blood."

"Ho-ly shit."

She surged up from her chair, the mask gone, replaced with pure anger. Ramos rose in unison with her, holding her where she stood.

"I am sick to death of all this Faerie garbage. Has everyone in this whole freakin' country gone totally insane?"

"It's not garbage, Sarah. It's real. Surely you know that by now." He had to calm her down. An angry Sarah would result in an angry Reynard. And that was something to be avoided at all costs.

"Father, will you now give me a moment alone? As I'd asked?" He bit off each of the words sharply.

Some unspoken emotion passed between the two men in that moment, communicated in the force of their locked gazes. Sarah couldn't name what it was, but she could feel the friction of it crackling in the air around her, dancing across her skin.

"Very well. You may have your moment, Ramos. But make it quick. I've grown weary with all the waiting." Reynard flicked his wrist and Nicole, clutching her handbag, obediently followed him out the door.

"Please. Sit." Ramos motioned to the chair behind Sarah.

Sincerity flowed from him, so, in spite of her confusion and anger, Sarah decided to give him a chance to explain. She sank back down and he knelt in front of her just as he had before, his hand on the arm of the chair.

"Many centuries ago my people lived under the

tyranny of their despotic rulers. They finally revolted, fighting for their freedom, their very lives, but they were overcome by treachery. The victors showed no mercy. My people were banished from their homes, thrown out into the wilderness, left to fend on their own. All these years they've suffered, struggling to survive in a harsh, alien environment. Now, at last, with your assistance, they have the chance to return to their homeland. Won't you help them, Sarah? Help us?"

"Us?" She waited for his nod before proceeding. "First I need answers, Ramos. Will you give them to me?"

"If I can."

"You called him 'Father.' You're telling me your people are"—she paused, hating to say it, to give it credence by speaking the word out loud—"Faeries?"

As Ian had claimed.

"In spite of how it may look, Reynard is my father." He shrugged. "Those from the Faerie don't age in the same way as Mortals."

From the Faerie. The phrase was everywhere. De la fée. In the books she'd read. The candy he'd sent. Reynard's comment.

"Your father said something to me when he came in. Something about the Faeries. What was that?"

Ramos looked perplexed for a moment. "Ah, yes. *Mon petit cadeau de la fée.* My little gift from the Faeries."

"Because he thinks I'm descended from Faeries as well. And that's why you think I can help you?"

"We *know* you're descended from our people, my sweet. And that *is* why you can help us. You have the ability to see the doorway to the Realm of Faerie. With your assistance we can enter and take back what is rightfully ours. We can reclaim our homes from the evil tyrants who tried to destroy my people."

Every word she had read about the Fae passed through her mind. Everything she had been told. She had written off Will's stories as imagination and fancy, but she knew in her heart the child had not lied to her. She would have felt a lie. Especially from someone whose emotions had been so closely tied to her own. When Ian had tried to explain more to her, she hadn't wanted to believe him either, but, again, she had known he wasn't lying. And she had the information from what she'd read.

Time to put all that knowledge to the test. Time to make a decision. Could she accept the knowledge as fact? And if she did, what then?

"The battle between your people and the others, it was fought here in this world at one time?"

Ramos laid his hand on top of hers. "Yes. Until the evil ones found a way to steal the powers of my people, leaving them stranded and defenseless in this world."

She looked down at his hand clasping hers. He believed what he told her.

"Were you there? Did you see this happen, experience it?"

He shook his head, a sad little smile on his face. "No. Like you, my sweet, I'm half Mortal, and only recently born into this world."

"Recently?"

"You must understand, in comparison to a true Faerie's life span, my twenty-eight years is nothing."

"So you know of these things from . . . ?"

"My father."

Reynard. The most concentrated evil being she had ever experienced.

"It's all a lie, Ramos." Her decision was made. "What he's told you is not what happened at all."

He blinked rapidly, the only outward sign of his inner turmoil. "No. My father wouldn't lie to me."

"Of course I wouldn't lie to you, boy."

Ramos jumped to his feet at the sound of his father's voice.

"Has she agreed to help yet?"

"No. I won't help you." Her decision was made. She would not be talked about as if she weren't present. And she would not help the ones Will had so aptly termed the "really bad guys."

In the blink of an eye Reynard crossed the room, grabbing her hand and dragging her close to him, his breath fanning over her face. "Enough. You *will* do as I say."

Sarah felt a tingle, something like every hair on her body standing on end, but she'd been prepared for his touch this time. She already knew the feel of evil. She'd banished it from her being once before and didn't plan to allow it another foothold.

"You know, for such a superior being, you don't hear so well. I said I *won't* be helping you."

Ramos's quick intake of breath only momentarily distracted her attention, and not for long enough to prevent her seeing shock pass over Reynard's face.

He quickly schooled his features, hiding whatever he might feel. But he hadn't removed his hand from hers. He was disturbed by something that had just happened. Disturbed and surprised.

Just as she was disturbed by the smile slowly growing on his face and the satisfaction she felt replace his surprise.

"Oh, but I think you will, *ma petite*. The old man who lives up in the big house? You like him, yes?"

What she didn't like was the gleam in Reynard's eye or the excitement she felt building in him. "Henry? What have you done to him?"

"I haven't done anything to the man. But should you continue to refuse us the assistance we need, I can't speak for what might happen to him. Or his hired help."

Martha and Peter, too. Sarah felt ill. "You wouldn't hurt those poor people." She jerked her hand from his grasp as a new thought occurred to her. "You *can't* hurt them. You don't have any power to battle in this world."

Reynard studied his fingernails as he walked toward the door, stopping there to smile at her again, a slick, oily expression that made her stomach knot.

"No, you're quite correct about that. *I* can't do anything to your friends. But someone else might." He looked at his son. "Tell her, Ramos."

"Not you! You wouldn't do something like that." She couldn't believe it of him.

Ramos lowered his head, but not before she'd seen the sorrow evident in his eyes. "Bradley Tanner holds them in the house now."

"God knows Brad's a complete jerk, with no consideration for anyone. But he wouldn't do anything to hurt those people." The relief she felt was short-lived.

"Perhaps not if he were himself," Ramos conceded.

"Why is he not himself?" Doubt crept through her

and she stole a glance at Nicole. The woman stood quietly, too quietly, at the door, a completely blank look in her eyes.

"At last you begin to understand." Reynard laughed as he snapped his fingers and Nicole came to his side. "You see? Mortals are so easy to control. Aren't you, my pet?" He ran the back of his fingers lightly down Nicole's cheek. "Bring her, Ramos." Reynard left the room, Nicole trailing behind.

"It's a compulsion, Sarah. My father holds one on Brad as well. He'll do anything he's told to do. If it's something abhorrent to his nature, he may fight against it, but ultimately he will do whatever my father bids. He can't help it."

Ramos took her hand, and she pulled away from him. But not before she felt his confusion.

"I can't believe you're a part of this, that you would have anything to do with something so horrible."

"We have to go now." Ramos put his hand at her back, urging her forward, without meeting her eyes.

With the threat to Henry and the others, she had no choice. She'd have to do what they wanted, whatever it was. Fear curdled low in her stomach.

If only she'd listened to Ian. If only she'd opened herself to all she'd been told. If only he were here to save her one more time.

Ian honked impatiently at the cows milling around his car. He let off the brake again, inching forward, his bumper coming to rest against the leg of a brown-eyed beauty who had no interest in moving. He rolled down his window and pitched a half empty paper cup of coffee at the offending bovine. The top popped off on impact and the lukewarm brown liquid splashed on her side, quickly washing away in the soft rain that fell. The whites of her eyes gone large, she lowered her head, and, with a mournful bellow, she ambled out of his way.

"About bloody time," he fumed.

His hands cramped from gripping the wheel so hard. He dropped one away, flexing his fingers. With the herd of cows behind him, he hit the gas and his car lurched forward, spraying water from the standing puddles he slammed through. He was close now.

He switched his hold on the steering wheel, flexing the fingers of his other hand. His nerves were so on edge he couldn't concentrate on forming a coherent plan of attack. What was wrong with him? He never let an impending battle get to him like this. Never.

Of course he'd never had this much personally at stake before either.

Up ahead he caught sight of the entrance to Thistle Down Manor. Even before he made the turn into the drive, the nerves that had been plaguing him since the call he'd received earlier this afternoon were supplanted by anger. Pure and simple.

Dallyn stood just inside the gate.

Ian pulled to a stop, flinging open his door before the gravel of the drive had settled.

"Yer supposed to be watching over her. You gave me yer word you'd no let her out of yer sight."

"And I was until moments ago. She's fine for now. You, on the other hand, need to know what's happening here before you go barging in and cause more problems than you can solve."

The rebuke reflected on the Fae's face only irritated Ian more. Perhaps because he knew Dallyn was right. He fought back the fear and fury warring for control of his being, clenching and unclenching his hands until he could trust himself to speak.

"What's the situation?" He had to think and behave like the warrior he was or all was lost. He concentrated on the cold rain pelting his face, focused on the calm he needed to recapture.

"That's better." Dallyn reached out his hand, bringing it to rest on Ian's shoulder. "I have faith in your abilities to do what needs to be done."

Ian needed to reclaim that same faith.

"They're here." It wasn't a question. He already knew. Martha's end of their telephone conversation had all but told him that.

"They've a man in the manor house. I suspect you'll want to deal with him first. He has Henry at gunpoint, along with Peter and Martha."

In his house. They had invaded the sanctity of his home. Threatened his nephew. The growl that started low in his throat was beyond his control.

"The one in the house is a Mortal, Ian. He's under a compulsion. You'll need to take care not to harm him."

"The *one* in the house? Where are the others?" The sick roiling in his stomach hit him before the words were out of his mouth. "Sarah?"

The flicker in Dallyn's eyes should have been answer enough. "They've taken her. She's on the path to the Portal, though progress is slowed by her having no idea what it is she searches for."

"Does she lead them . . . willingly?"

"No."

Ian released the breath he hadn't realized he'd held. One fear down. Sarah wasn't a part of this. He looked up to find the Fae's reproachful gaze fastened on him.

"You knew she wasn't in league with them." Dallyn shook his head, holding up a hand. "No, I didn't read your thoughts. I didn't have to. It was clearly written on your face. Best you not let her see that doubt. She's already more than a little irritated with you."

That had to be a huge understatement. Ian just hoped this day would end with her still able to vent that irritation. He'd willingly receive it.

Leaving the car, he started for the manor. He'd have to approach quietly.

"I'll wait for you as long as I can."

Dallyn didn't need to add any clarification. Ian understood. The Fae would wait until the others approached the Portal. Then he would need to do his job. Stop them on the other side.

"How much farther?"

Reynard's voice grated on her nerves. The fact that he continued to ask the same question at every twist and turn didn't help. Nor did the rain. The gray afternoon felt as if it were closing in on her.

"I don't know." Sarah gritted her teeth, trying not to scream her response.

"You must feel something by now. We've been walking for quite some time. Are you stupid?"

Sarah came to an abrupt halt, wrenching her arm from Ramos's grasp as she turned to face the man— no, the Fae—several paces behind her. The sight of

Nicole sickened her, the woman's face expressionless as she hurried to keep up with the others.

"Look. I have no idea where this place is or even what I'm looking for, so how the hell do you expect me to be able to tell you when we get there?"

"You should feel the pull toward it." Reynard stopped as well, glaring at her. "Do you?"

"No. Maybe."

They were on the path Ian had warned her to avoid. It was the only place she felt any sort of pull at all. The farther she went, the stronger it got. She'd brought them this way wondering what she would do if she actually found this Portal they sought.

When she found it. Not if. She accepted that now. Believed all of it. Too late.

If only I'd listened to Ian. The thought pounded at the back of her mind, over and over, to the point she almost thought she could feel him. Feel his presence moving toward her.

I'm sorry. Sorry I doubted you. She closed her eyes and let her shoulders sag, feeling the weight of being alone in this. Of knowing she had no one but herself to depend on now. No one but herself to blame. She tried to fight the overwhelming despair, refusing to let the tears that threatened fall.

Ramos's touch brought her back from the edge, a second before Reynard's condescending voice struck at her again.

"You'd best get moving, girl. The longer you delay, the more likely it is one of your friends at the manor house will suffer some sort of accident. Some sort of *fatal* accident."

The chuckle that followed his threat pushed her

over the edge. Thankful for the rain that camouflaged her tears, she wiped them both from her face and started toward him. Only Ramos's newly established grasp on her elbow held her back.

But it didn't silence her. Nothing could have done that.

"You disgust me. You are, without a doubt, the most vile, evil creature I have ever experienced."

"So I've been told. Now get moving."

She turned her back on him at Ramos's urging, stumbling forward again.

"Don't fight him, Sarah." Ramos spoke so quietly she was forced to lean in closer to hear his words. "His mind is made up."

"If he's so determined that I do what he wants, why doesn't he just use that compulsion thing on me? Turn me into a zombie, like her." She tilted her head back in Nicole's direction.

He looked at her oddly before answering. "I believe he tried. At the cottage."

The tingling and Reynard's surprise.

Ramos shrugged. "I've never seen it not work before. Obviously you're too powerful for him to control."

Powerful? Hardly.

"Then there's nothing he can do to me."

"Don't antagonize him. He can be a very dangerous man to have as an enemy. He's only trying to save our people."

"You have no idea, do you?" She glanced up at him. "You say you know what I am. Do you know that I feel the truth about people? That I feel the truth about you? About him?"

His fingers tightened on her elbow. "Yes. We figured out that you're a Sensor."

"When we spent the day together, I told you the truth I felt in you. You're a good person. Too good to be a part of this." She had to make him understand. "Back there on the trail, I told the truth about your father. He's nothing like you. Your father is pure evil. Everything he's ever told you about your people was a lie. I've seen the blackness in him. I will not help him. I can't let myself be consumed by that evil. Please don't try to make me do this. Please don't let him do this. To either of us."

Though doubt flickered behind his eyes, the years of conditioning were too strong. He dropped his gaze and pulled at her arm, urging her forward.

Her head bowed, she stared at the ground as she made her way farther into the forest along the overgrown path. The wet leaves slipped under her feet, making small squishing noises.

She would just have to figure out what to do on her own. If ever she'd needed the guidance of the Fates—or Faeries, as it were—it was now. If she was indeed one of their own, now was the time for them to come to her aid. She concentrated, opening herself to everything that was around her, praying for their help.

All she could feel was Ian. His essence surrounded her, filling her with a confidence she was sorely lacking.

Looking up, she realized how much she needed that confidence boost at this moment. And wished she had even more. There, tucked into the bushes and rocks, surrounded by ancient gnarled trees, stood a carved stone archway.

None of the others seemed to notice. Her stomach lurched and for a moment she thought she might be sick.

Obviously she'd found the Portal.

Ian slid to a halt, reaching out to the nearest tree to steady himself. Despair rolled over him in waves. Sarah's despair, forcing him to take great gulps of air just to remain standing.

She needed him. Called out to him.

He tilted his head, listening. No sound but the patter of rain.

"Have faith, luv," he whispered in answer to the silent plea. "Yer a stronger woman than you know. You've powers beyond yer own dreams." He closed his eyes, willing her to feel him. "Take courage. I'm coming for you. I *will* save you. I swear it."

Squatting down, he ran his hand over the sodden earth. Evidence of their earlier passage was easy to find. They'd taken no care to hide their movement.

He was very close.

Bradley Tanner had been the man in his home, threatening his family and those he held dear. It hadn't taken much for Ian to subdue him. Compulsion or no, Tanner was no match for him. He'd used care, as Dallyn had warned. Tanner would recover, with very little memory of the incident, as was typical of Mortals held under a compulsion. Ian was almost embarrassed at the pleasure he'd received from taking the man down. Almost.

But the pleasure had been short-lived when he'd stepped outside and found the Fae gone. That surely meant the others were nearing the Portal.

Now, as he rose, he looked around, suddenly struck by a jolt of familiarity. The gray mist closed in on him, feeding his own anxiety.

He hurried forward, no longer needing the signs the others had left behind in order to follow them. In spite of everything he'd done, all the pain and sacrifice, it was still coming down to this.

His dread grew as he neared the spot where he knew he would find them. The spot he had already seen.

In his dream.

Sarah gasped and covered her ears with her hands. She turned in a complete circle, peering into the surrounding forest. She barely noticed as Ramos moved away from her, off the path and into the woods.

"What game do you play with us now, *ma petite*? I tire of your attempts to delay." Reynard's hard glare was the least of her problems.

Her hands moved as if of their own accord from her ears to her mouth, to cover the bubble of hysterical laughter she felt coming.

I'm losing my mind.

She had heard Ian's voice, as clearly as if he'd stood next to her, whispering encouragement, promising to save her.

Reynard stood in front of her, only inches away. "Get moving."

"No." Perhaps it had only been her own conscience she'd heard. Whatever the source, it was what she'd needed. "It's over. This ends now."

The time had come for her to make her stand. She would not be the means for evil to wreak havoc on the world On any world.

Reynard's hands closed on her shoulders, squeezing, but she felt no pain.

"You'll move or I'll—"

"There's nothing you can do to me," she interrupted, hearing the wonder in her voice that she felt. "You have no control over me, no way to force your will."

It was all true. He was one of the Fae and he had no power over her.

She was so close. He could feel her confusion, her distress. His need to soothe her consumed him.

"I'm coming for you. Hold on, luv. I'll save you." Over and over he sent the message to her, concentrating on her emotions as they connected with his own.

He was so absorbed in his effort to console her he missed the first sign, the slight current of tension in the air. But he'd been a warrior for too much of his life to miss the second, the almost imperceptible flash of movement.

By the time Ramos emerged from the cover of underbrush, Ian was instinctively ready for combat. His mind shifted automatically into battle mode, fully engaged in the tactical back-and-forth, anticipating his opponent's moves rather than reacting to them.

He absorbed the impact of the other man's body against his own, using his adversary's momentum to propel him into position, rolling to his feet only an instant before Ramos did the same.

They circled, assessing one another, seeking any opportunity for an advantage. Ian didn't plan to give him one.

Seizing the initiative, he attacked, drawing Ramos

in as he'd expected. Grabbing the man's arm and neck in one smooth motion, Ian turned a sharp circle, pushing Ramos's face to the ground. What he had not expected, however, was the quick recovery by Ramos, pulling up and to Ian's side, using his leg to lock Ian in place.

The younger man was good, but experience had its benefits. Ian rolled behind Ramos, blocked his turn and, wrapping his arm around Ramos's neck, cut off his air.

The battle was at an end as far as Ian was concerned. He could taste victory. There was no way for Ramos to break free of the hold Ian had on the man.

It was in this position he felt it again, the small wave of tension preceding violence. Scanning the area quickly, looking for another attacker, he caught sight through the trees of the clearing on their left.

What he saw chilled him to his core.

An involuntary noise, more animal than human crawled its way up and out his throat. The younger man, startled, strained to look in that direction as well.

"Oh, Christ," Ramos breathed. "What's he thinking to do now?"

The horror in his voice reflected the horror Ian felt.

It was the exact scene from his dream.

Whatever the cost to him, he had to find a way to stop what he knew was about to happen. He needed to be closer. There was only one way he could think of to get there quickly.

Ian loosened his hold. Instantly the younger man produced a knife and held it to Ian's throat.

"Look to the clearing, McCullough. End your struggles and come with me before things there spiral completely out of hand."

Ramos nudged him forward, but Ian needed no encouragement. The clearing was exactly where he wanted to be.

Rage distorted the beauty of Reynard's features, revealing the monstrous nature Sarah had felt in him before.

"You think to defy me? We'll see about that," he snarled, his features righting themselves. "Ramos, bring him."

Sarah felt the wind knocked from her as surely as if she'd been struck. Behind her on the path, Ramos stepped from the forest, his arm around Ian's throat, a knife held there.

"Let him go." She spoke quietly, the words intended for Reynard only, though her gaze was fixed on Ian. His absolute stillness baffled her, yet she was grateful he didn't struggle. She tried to rein in the fear that threatened to engulf her at the sight of that knife. Ramos wouldn't use it, would he? Then again, she wouldn't have thought him capable of any of this.

"Please," she added.

Reynard's hand slid from her shoulder to her chin, turning her face to meet his eyes.

One look and the fear momentarily overwhelmed her, swamping her senses. There was nothing there to give her hope. With his touch she could see to the depths of his soul, yet all she could find was an empty black pit of malevolent inhumanity.

"It's very simple, *ma petite*. Take me to the Portal now, or Ramos kills him. You can watch the mighty Guardian, sworn Protector of the pitiful Mortals, die, his lifeblood spilled out on the ground. Here. In front of your very eyes. Is that what you want?"

"Sworn Protector of the Mortals?" Ramos's voice sounded confused to her ears, but she couldn't turn to look at him. Couldn't break eye contact with Reynard. "Is that true? You never told me that."

"There are many things I've not told you. Many things you've no need to know."

"Is it the truth?" Ramos demanded.

"Aye, it's true." Ian's voice. "I've spent the last six centuries protecting them from the ravages caused by yer people. Those who murder Mortals at random for nothing more than the energy released when their soul is forced from its host before its time. Thousands upon thousands of lives lost to those monsters. Those same monsters who would capture the Fountain of Souls for their own purpose, throwing the cycle of life out of balance again, risking what's left of humanity in both worlds."

"Father?"

"You doubt me, son? You'd listen to the words of a Guardian? A creature who's no more than a lap dog to the enemies of our people?" Reynard's displeasure flowed through his physical link to Sarah as his fingers tightened their grip.

"Ian doesn't lie to you, Ramos. What he tells you is the truth. I attest to that. It's as I told you before." She had to convince him, had to get him to drop the knife from Ian's throat.

"Father? Is what the Guardian says true?"

A cruel smile curled Reynard's lip. "In a manner of speaking."

"*We're* responsible for all those deaths?" The horror in Ramos's voice washed over Sarah, his acceptance of the truth bringing him physical pain, which she could feel.

She couldn't let that distract her. There was much more at stake here than one man's pain.

"Deaths that were of no consequence. Mortal deaths. Once we retake the Faerie Realm, once you taste the power of the Fountain, then you'll understand why all of this has been necessary. You will take me to the Portal, Sarah. Now." Reynard's eyes sparkled, and once again the tingling started, this time in her face, where he touched her.

"Of no consequence? Father, have you forgotten that I am as much Mortal as I am Fae? That those Mortals whose lives you so easily dismiss are my people, too?"

Reynard's eyes narrowed and the tingling in Sarah's face grew more intense, as if tiny needles poked her skin. His jaw clenched and his hand on her face trembled.

"Try as you will. You have no power over me," she whispered.

Surprise, disappointment, disgust and, finally, resignation—each in turn flowed through the connection before his hand dropped from her face. Their gazes remained locked as he responded to his son.

"No. I haven't forgotten what you are. Nicole." He glanced away, toward the woman Sarah had all but dismissed from her mind. "Kill one of the men. I don't care which. Perhaps that will help our little Sarah to understand how serious we are."

Sarah looked at the other woman. Her handbag lay on the ground, and a large gun in her hand was pointed directly at Sarah. No wonder Ian hadn't struggled. She watched as the gun slowly turned toward Ian and Ramos.

"You can't mean that. He's your son."

Reynard shrugged carelessly. "He's also a Mortal."

The gun now pointed directly at the two men, though Nicole looked as if she fought her own body to stop what she was doing, an expression of desperation replacing the blankness that had been there only moments before.

"No." A mere whisper of protest was all that Sarah could manage as she turned back to see the smile of pleasure on Reynard's face.

She placed her hand on his chest. He had to stop this. Though she didn't touch bare skin, a connection formed immediately, opening her to his emotions. Satisfaction at his complete control of the situation, anticipation of the imminent death of one of the men. No remorse, no compassion, not even for his son.

One glance toward the two men and her decision was made. Ian risked his life for her. He may have left her, but now, when she needed him most, he had come back. To save her. Just as Dallyn had said he would.

"No," she screamed, bringing her other hand up to Reynard's chest.

She felt her face grow warm. A rage born of desperation filled Sarah's mind. A red haze of fury such as she had never known washed over her. Determination to succeed at any cost consumed her.

Not Reynard's.

All her own.

She would not allow the man she loved to die. She would risk everything for Ian.

Ian watched in horror as his dream replayed itself before him in real life, each vague detail brought into sharp, clear focus.

Now he knew the invisible force that had held him in his dream was in reality fear. Not for himself, but for Sarah. When his attention had been drawn to the clearing, the scene unfolding there had forced him into submission. It was the only way he could think of to get near the action, to be in a position to act to change what he knew was going to happen.

It wasn't Reynard, rage distorting his face as he held Sarah that struck fear to his soul, or even that they stood only meters away from the Portal. It was the gun Nicole Tanner clearly aimed at Sarah that stole Ian's ability to fight, binding his hands as surely as the finest steel could have. That and the knowledge that Sarah *would* be shot.

Nicole raised the gun and he stared directly down the barrel, thankful it pointed in his direction. It didn't matter if the woman pulled the trigger as long as she didn't fire at Sarah.

Sarah had looked in his direction, a strange little smile on her beautiful face before she turned and screamed at Reynard, her hands to his chest as if to push him away. But she didn't push.

If he lived for a thousand years, he would still be able to describe every horrific detail, playing out in slow motion, burned into the fabric of his psyche.

Reynard's screams of agony drew his attention

away from the gun an instant before he heard the discharge. Ramos's shoulder hit his chest broadside, knocking him to the ground, Ramos landing on top of him with a loud grunt.

Ian scrambled to push the man off of him, desperate to get to Sarah, knowing she was in danger.

Reynard's screams continued. By the time Ian freed himself and was on his knees, the red glow surrounded both Sarah and Reynard, flames engulfing her hands on his chest. The Fae pushed at her, unable to move her hands away from him, unable to escape the glowing sphere.

Nicole lifted the gun, aiming once again at Sarah. Ian sprang to his feet, sprinting for the woman.

Another shot rang out in the clearing as Ian's body slammed into Nicole's, knocking her to the ground.

The red haze evaporated as Sarah crumpled.

"No," he roared as he tore the gun from the limp hand of the woman he'd tackled and raced to Sarah's side.

Such a tiny hole in her chest, but the blood pooled beneath her as he cradled her body to him. Just like the dream.

"Sarah, luv, can you hear me?" This couldn't happen.

Dark lashes fluttered against pale cheeks. Just like the dream.

"I'm sorry I didn't believe you, Ian," she whispered. "But it's all right. I couldn't allow him to harm you. It was my choice to take the risk." Her words echoed from the dream.

"No, Sarah, you canna do this to me." He clutched her body to him, rocking back and forth. Minutes. He only had minutes left to do something, anything. He wouldn't lose her. Not this way. He had to change it all somehow.

"What about the Fountain?"

Ian looked up with a start. He'd forgotten completely about Ramos.

The man held his shoulder, blood running down his arm. "Snap out of it, McCullough. Are you going to let her die?"

The Fountain. If he could get her there in time, bathing her wound in the Fountain of Souls just might save her life. But there would be a cost. Once he made the decision to do this, there would be no chance of redemption for him. The Fae would never allow him to remain a Guardian once he'd violated the Fountain for purely selfish purposes.

There was no choice. He knew what he needed to do.

Rising, he scooped up her limp body and started for the Portal.

"I'll take care of things here." Ramos pointed toward Nicole, still unconscious on the ground.

Reynard was gone.

"Thanks." Ian hesitated at the Portal. That didn't seem enough to say to the man he'd thought his enemy, the man who'd taken a bullet for him.

"Go."

Without a backward glance, Ian carried Sarah through the doorway.

"You've chosen wisely, my son."

The words drifted to Sarah as she fought to open her eyes, the struggle almost too much for her. But the lilting tenor and the strength of the voice enticed her, whetting her curiosity, compelling her to see the man who spoke.

"Now you understand the importance of your Soulmate, of preserving her life at any cost. You made the right choice, Ian. I'm proud of you. Your mother and I both are."

"Thank you, Father." Ian's voice.

Blinking took so much effort, but what she saw infused her with the energy she needed to stay awake.

She lay on the ground held fast in Ian's arms, cradled against his chest. Turning her head slightly brought him into focus, a view of his neck and chin as he looked up, away from her. Whiskers dark against his skin drew her attention, and she lifted her hand, trailing a finger over the rough chin she'd never expected to touch again.

"Sarah."

Only one word, but his tone conveyed a wealth of meaning to her. His hand covered hers, clasping it to his chest, where his heart pounded under her touch. His attention focused solely on her. She gazed into his eyes, the mysterious black pools that fascinated her so, and thought for a moment she saw a man there, beckoning to her. Lifting her free hand, she brushed her fingers first against the damp curls at his neck and then down the trail of moisture on his face.

"I thought I'd lost you." His voice broke.

"No. You found me. You came back and saved me."

He gathered her to him, hugging her tightly. "I'll never leave you again. I swear it."

She looked past his shoulder at a magnificent stone fountain, flowing with iridescent colors and movement, as if it were alive with energy. The forms of two people hovered there, shimmering as the color swirled around and through them. She had to concentrate to be sure she really saw them, but they were there, a tall man with long blond hair and a dark woman with Ian's eyes, tucked protectively under his arm. They turned toward one another and embraced. Light glinted off the man's armor, causing Sarah to blink, and they were gone.

Ian stood, lifting her easily. He kissed her lips and smiled. "Let's go home, luv. Picture it in yer mind."

She did, only a little surprised when the picture that formed wasn't of her house in Denver at all, but was instead that of Heather Cottage.

Twenty-five

The kiss lingered on her lips. She could taste it, feel it there. Sarah lightly ran her finger over the spot, half expecting to find a physical manifestation of the kiss. It had been that powerful.

Of the hundreds, perhaps thousands, of kisses Ian had showered on her in the weeks since their return from the Faerie Realm, Sarah held this one as the best.

The one Ian had shared with her just after the minister said the words "I now pronounce you man and wife."

She watched him across the garden, his head thrown back in laughter at something Daniel had said. He looked so carefree, so young. Laughter threatened at the memory of his trying to explain his real age. To think she'd worried about being too old for him. He had been absolutely correct. Age was just a number.

Ian caught her watching and winked, his sparkling

black eyes telegraphing feelings of love strong enough to make her toes tingle with the promise they held. The feelings of desire he layered on top made the rest of her tingle, and the laughter she'd held back bubbled out.

They could do that now, since the Fountain, communicate feelings wordlessly to one another. She didn't need to touch him or even be in sight of him for it to work. In fact, she no longer needed to touch anyone to discern their feelings. She had only to open herself up, to want to know. The most pleasant side effect was that she now had the ability to close herself off as well. Touch no longer triggered feeling overload. It was very freeing.

"A pennant for your thoughts, my dear."

Sarah smiled at the striking Fae couple who approached her.

"Penny, Dallyn, not pennant," Darnee corrected. "If you're going to attempt their slang, you must pay more attention."

He shrugged and grinned at the woman, flipping his hair back over his shoulder before favoring her with a look hot enough to melt concrete.

Darnee seemed completely unaffected. Then again, Sarah hadn't seen the woman affected by much of anything in the short time she'd known her.

"Thank you again, Dallyn." Sarah reached for his hand, giving it a squeeze. "For everything."

Ian had explained to her how he had expected to run into resistance when he had taken her to the Fountain, and how odd it was that they encountered no Fae, not even the omnipresent Fountain guards, during their time in the Realm of Faerie. He could think of only one explanation for the ease of their visit. Dallyn.

"No need to thank me. It was my great honor." The Fae lifted her hand, lightly brushing it to his lips.

Dallyn had given her away in the wedding ceremony. He'd said it only seemed right, as the eldest Fae present, that he should be the one to do so, given her heritage. Sarah had agreed.

Darnee placed a graceful hand on Sarah's stomach and looked up. "You're wrong, Dallyn. I'm sure this is a boy."

The Fae laughed, placing his hand on top of hers. "Must you always contradict whatever I say, woman, regardless of what you truly believe?"

"Merely keeping you on your toes, General."

"How did you know?" Sarah sputtered. She'd only told Ian last night, only confirmed it yesterday afternoon. Apparently another side effect of her dousing in the Fountain.

Another careless shrug, accompanied by a knowing grin. "There are many things I know, child. Speaking of which, didn't you tell me you would have some of that wonderful Faerie chocolate here today?"

Sarah laughed at the waggle of his brow as she directed him to the table with the goodies he sought. He took Darnee's hand, pulling her along, promising her a taste treat fit for the Earth Mother herself.

The laugh settled into a contented smile as Sarah looked around at all the people who had joined them to celebrate this special day. Now that her Great Adventure, as she thought of it, was over, these people who had been a part of the experience had all come to mean so much to her.

The smile died on Sarah's lips as she caught sight of Ramos. He kept himself apart from the merriment of the wedding reception, leaning against a tree at the far edge of the garden.

Ramos had made the "problem" of the Tanners disappear, taking them away from Thistle Down before they'd recovered, convincing them they'd been the victims of a horrible auto accident. They had no memory of anything else. It had all been handled so smoothly, Sarah suspected that Ramos might have been able to explain how a compulsion worked from firsthand knowledge. Knowledge of placing one that is, not being under one.

He nodded when he caught her looking in his direction, and smiled. She didn't need to see through the dark glasses covering his eyes to know the smile never made it that far. Still handsome with that air of danger clinging to him, he seemed almost unapproachable now. His sorrow and guilt were so strong she couldn't bear to do more than lightly touch at the edges of his emotions. It didn't take a Sensor to feel the pain radiating off that man.

"No frowning allowed on yer wedding day, Mrs. McCullough."

Ian was behind her, his arms around her, pulling her up against him, where she fit like the last piece of a puzzle. She felt warm and safe as she snuggled back against him. Fulfilled, complete. Whole.

His gaze followed the path hers had taken. "He's got to work through this on his own, luv. You canna fix it for him."

"I know."

She did know. Intellectually. But that didn't mean

she would give up on trying to help the man. Because emotion was a different animal all together. He'd been the one to try to help her when she'd needed it.

She smiled to herself as she hit upon an idea. Tomorrow she'd give her new friend, Cate MacKiernan, a call. The woman was a wealth of information. Perhaps together they could think of something.

"Do I sense a plot forming behind that lovely smile?" Ian bent near her ear, lingering to place a kiss in the spot that drove her wild.

She was saved having to answer by Will's approach. Her ring bearer, tuxedo jacket missing, little tie askew, raced in her direction, calling her name. He skidded to a stop, throwing his arms around her, his head resting against her middle.

"There you are. I wondered when I'd find you." He patted her stomach and then grinned up at her. "Hi, Sarah. Ian."

"We've been right here."

"Not you. Her. In there." He tapped on Sarah's stomach.

"How do you know about . . . it?" Ian stuttered over the last, as if he couldn't quite commit himself to the fact that Will knew about the baby.

"Duh." Will rolled his eyes. "I *feel* her. Besides, I've been waiting for her for a long time. Her name is . . ." He paused and grinned. "Nah, I'll let you wait and find out when they get here. See ya." He called the last over his shoulder as he ran back across the yard.

"They?" Sarah squeaked.

"They. Probably means nothing. He's only six. Slip of the tongue." Ian tightened his hug for a moment, his eyes following the retreating form of the little boy. "Still. We'd best have the doctor check closely when we go see him." He kissed her again.

They.

She turned in Ian's arms to properly kiss him back.

She'd been wrong. Her Great Adventure wasn't over.

It was just beginning.

Epilogue

$\mathcal{D}$allyn rolled the small golden fruit between his fingers before tossing it into the air. He caught it between his teeth, a look of sublime satisfaction on his face. Leaning back in the oversized chair, he propped his feet on the heavy wooden table, reaching for another fruit.

"You spend too much time playing with your food." Darnee leaned against the wall, watching his performance.

"I don't play with it. I enjoy it. Savor it." He tossed and caught the fruit as he had before, popping it between his teeth, allowing the juices to spread through his mouth. "I learned that from the Mortals." He grinned.

"How can you be so cavalier after what we just sat through?" Darnee paced along the opposite side of the table.

"I beg your pardon. I am rarely cavalier. And never without good reason. There is no point to be made in allowing the Council meeting to distress you. We have no control over them. Lest you forget, *we* report to *them*." As always, she needed to relax. Telling her so, however, was likely to get his ears boxed.

"I feel certain there are those on the Council who could aid us if only they were not all so busy jockeying for their own position. We face a crisis, yet none of them will come forward to help. They tie our hands and then sit and look to us to find their salvation. Everything we have worked for is coming to an end." She flopped into the chair across from him, propping her boot-clad legs on the table, the mirror image of his own position.

He took a moment to admire those long legs while deciding how to answer. Darnee really was a beautiful woman. She was also much too impatient. Much too bound by the rules. And quite lethal. Not a good combination. Unfortunately she was also too much like a sister to him to evoke feelings other than platonic, a fact he sometimes regretted.

"We will continue to seek the descendants. The only difference is that now we will have to shift our focus from searching out new Guardians to protection and defense of the females."

Darnee pulled her feet from the table, and leaned toward him, "Why did you not tell the Council what happened in that clearing?"

"I did. They fought, Ramos risked his life to save Ian, and Reynard escaped after the Mortal woman shot Sarah."

He reached for another fruit and she brought her hand down on top of his, trapping it against the bowl.

"You did not tell them anything about what hap-

pened to Reynard. What Ramos and Ian both saw
Sarah do to him. Why not?"

He patted her hand, lifting it from his own. He'd
lost the desire for fruit anyway.

"They would not have believed. A true Fae should
not be able to be wounded on the Mortal Plain. It
cannot happen."

"But it did. Her hands burned into his chest. They
both saw it. They both heard his screams." She shook
her head slowly. "Where do you think he is now?"

"He is off licking his wounds, I would guess." He
paused, wondering how much to say to her. Wondering that she hadn't figured it out for herself. "Assuming he survived."

Her eyes grew wide, understanding coloring them
the deepest green. "You do not think he did, do you?
That is why you did not tell the Council, is it not? It
is against everything we have known for centuries
that something like that could happen."

Dallyn shrugged. It had happened. He didn't doubt
the story of either man. Which left him with only one
possible conclusion. The gifts were returning to the
world of man. The powers all Fae possessed at one
time but could no longer access on the Mortal Plain
were, after all these generations, reappearing in the
hands of mixed-race Fae. Half-Mortal descendants.
The potential for catastrophe was beyond frightening,
especially to ones such as he and Darnee who had witnessed the original destruction firsthand.

"For now, it is enough that we know. That we be
prepared. That our Guardians be prepared."

"But should we not try to warn the Council? What
if . . ."

"No," he interrupted. "You saw them when we told them the Nuadians were actively seeking the females. You saw their resistance to accepting Ramos, to understanding that his father had a vastly more devious plan for that young man. Only his own innate goodness kept him from becoming a deadly weapon turned against us. How long did it take to convince them of something as simple as that? Something with the facts clearly in front of them?" He stopped, breathing deeply, reaching for the calm. He was too old to lose control. Was it his fault the Council chose not to pursue healing, deciding there were none qualified to carry on that work?

"So we wait." Something eerily close to fear shone in her eyes.

"We wait. But while we wait, we make sure our Guardians are prepared for the worst. And we stay vigilant, aggressively searching—"

A knock cut short the discussion. Before either of them could rise to answer, the door opened and their visitor entered. Both jumped to their feet, bowing their heads respectfully.

Pol held up a hand, shaking his head. "No, there is no need for that. May I speak with you?"

"Certainly, Your Highness." Darnee extended her arm in welcome. "Please be seated."

"I was much moved by your impassioned presentation before the Council today. I have decided to help you. If . . ." He paused, steepling his fingers in front of him, concentrating his hard, unreadable stare on each one in turn.

Suspicion curled in Dallyn's gut. This Prince of the Fae had long avoided the responsibilities of his seat on the Council, sitting back and allowing others to take the lead. Why now?

"If?" Dallyn encouraged.

"If we can keep this just between us. Knowledge of my involvement goes no farther than this room. I rather prefer the reputation I have worked hard to get. I find I can accomplish much more if everyone one is busy looking the other way."

"And what do you want of us?" Dallyn was taken aback by that revelation, but waited to hear more.

"Unlike the others, I have maintained a connection to my descendants." He paused and bowed his head while they absorbed this information. "They are, quite naturally, gifted. And their gifts are growing, as I suspect could be the case with other descendants. A tidbit of information I assume the two of you might also suspect, based on the urgency of your pleas today."

Dallyn could do no more than nod his agreement.

"It has been many centuries since our people were ruled by Royalty. Few of the Royals are left. As a result, most have forgotten."

"Forgotten what?" Darneé leaned toward the tall, elegant Prince.

"Our line was Royal for a reason, my dear. Our powers were stronger than those of other Fae. Therefore, it stands to reason that as powers grow in the descendants of the Fae, they will grow stronger in the descendants of Royals, does it not?"

"I had forgotten," Dallyn murmured. It was so long ago, like a tiny detail from a bygone childhood story.

"Yes. Most have. And I must admit I have seen no

reason to remind anyone. Nevertheless, based on your report"—he narrowed his eyes as he gazed at Dallyn—"or more specifically, what *was not* in your report, I believe the time has come for me to act, to press forward with my plan."

"And that would be?" The suspicion flooded back. If this Prince thought to overthrow the Council, he had seriously misjudged the Captains of the Guard.

"I plan to set my descendants on the course of Healing. To give them the task of reuniting the Soulmates torn apart in the Siege of the Fountain."

"How is that possible?"

"I have children who are strong enough at last. One has even demonstrated the ability to control time."

Dallyn sat back, stalling while he tried to accept the significance of Pol's claim. If it were true, it would go far to explain why the Prince didn't want anyone to know. Talk about rule bending.

"And how do you see us fitting into your plans?"

Pol stood and paced, much as Darnee had earlier. "I propose we combine our efforts. I organize my Healing army, for lack of a better name, and the two of you continue to locate and protect. I believe you were correct in your assessment of the danger. Now that the Nuadians have come so close to successfully reentering our world, they will aggressively pursue other female descendants to try again. Working together, attacking both ends of our problem, I believe we have the opportunity to rebuild what was lost. Before it is too late."

Dallyn stood, glancing over at Darnee before replying. "I think I speak for both of us when I say, you can count on our assistance, Your Highness."

Darnee nodded her agreement.

"Then it is done. We are bound by oath to the survival and security of both worlds." Pol strode to the door, turning at the last minute. "I knew I had judged you well. I will be in touch."

After his departure, Dallyn and Darnee quietly sat back down.

"I hardly know what to say. That was completely unexpected. And yet exactly what we needed. The Prince is an answer to our prayers." She rose and walked over to the large window at the end of the room. Gazing out, she was clearly lost in thought.

"Yes, he certainly is." Dallyn narrowed his eyes as thoughts of his own raced through his mind.

The ground rules for their new association were quite clear, the responsibilities well defined. Still. There could very well be those among the descendants of the Prince who were better suited to be Guardians than Healers.

Dallyn smiled as he reached into the bowl in front of him. Tossing the golden oval into the air, he caught it with his teeth and rolled the sweet fruit in his mouth.

The last time he'd bent the rules things had worked out quite well. Perhaps he had as much talent for Healing as for Protecting. Perhaps the lines weren't so clearly drawn after all.

Perhaps he just needed to find a way to meet some of Prince Pol's descendants.

He pierced the fruit in his mouth, and laughed.

"What?" Darnee turned to stare at him questioningly.

"Nothing really. I was just thinking how things are looking up." He stood and reached his hand toward her. "Come on, we've much to do."

She joined him and they left the Hall. They each needed to contact their Guardians to set the wheels in motion.

Dallyn paused to give her a light kiss before parting company. He rubbed his hands together as he left the building, enjoying the feeling of anticipation.

Darnee had been wrong earlier. Everything wasn't coming to an end.

It was just beginning.

DISCOVER DESIRE AFTER DARK

WITH THESE BESTSELLING PARANORMAL ROMANCES FROM POCKET BOOKS!

PRIMAL DESIRES SUSAN SIZEMORE

Only one woman can satisfy this Vampire Prime's
every hunger…

THIRTY NIGHTS WITH A HIGHLAND HUSBAND MELISSA MAYHUE

Transported back in time, a modern-day woman falls in love
with a Highlander descended from the faerie folk—who can
only be hers for thirty nights.

IN DARKNESS REBORN ALEXIS MORGAN

Will an immortal warrior stay true to his people—or
risk everything for the woman he loves?

SOMETHING WICKED CATHERINE MULVANY

Wicked desires lead to insatiable passions—passions
no vampire can deny.

THE LURE OF THE WOLF JENNIFER ST. GILES

Be lured by a seductive shape-shifter whose dark allure
is impossible to resist…

DESIRE LURKS AFTER DARK...

BESTSELLING PARANORMAL ROMANCES FROM POCKET BOOKS!

NO REST FOR THE WICKED KRESLEY COLE

He s a vampire weary of eternal life. She s a Valkyrie sworn to destroy him. Now they must compete in a legendary contest— and their passion is the ultimate prize.

DARK DEFENDER ALEXIS MORGAN

He is an immortal warrior born to protect mankind from ultimate evil. But who defends the defenders?

DARK ANGEL LUCY BLUE

Brought together by an ancient power, a vampire princess and a mortal knight discover desire is stronger than destiny...

A BABE IN GHOSTLAND LISA CACH

SINGLE MALE SEEKS FEMALE FOR GHOSTBUSTING.... and maybe more.

Available wherever books are sold or at www.simonsayslove.com.

 POCKET BOOKS
A Division of Simon & Schuster
A CBS COMPANY

 POCKET STAR BOOKS
A Division of Simon & Schuster
A CBS COMPANY

15606